MOTHER

JACK STAINTON

ALSO BY JACK STAINTON

This novel is entirely a work of fiction and any resemblance to actual persons, living or dead, is purely coincidental.

An imprint of Windmill Streams *Publishers*

Mother

For Mum & Dad

AUTHOR'S NOTE

Thank you for reading 'Mother'

This is part two of 'The Family' Trilogy - three novels based around the central character, Matthew Walker.

They can either be read as individual stand-alone books, or in chronological order.

Either way, I hope you enjoy!

1

THE SIGHT of his motionless body offered me little satisfaction. The man, who I would have willingly killed myself, lay forlornly before me. Graham Meadows. My brother-in-law. My enemy.

"Matt."

The sound of my name being called sounded so faint, as if attempting to stir me from a dream; a deep sleep I wasn't yet ready to wake. I fought it. Pushed it to the back of my mind. My eyes flickered from Graham to Katrina. She held onto her makeshift cross. Two small pieces of wood, crudely woven together with dark green wool. Her lips moved, but no words escaped.

Is she praying?

"Matt!"

The tap on my shoulder made me jump from my skin. My head spun, my irritation obvious, ready to snap at whoever for daring to touch me.

We were in the woods, the woods adjacent to the family home. I'd escaped from the house, only to find myself trapped once more. After finding Lisa, we had faced Graham head on, and I know he would have killed us both if Katrina hadn't struck him first. He'd already seen to Lee Blackmore, but now he lay motionless, his head twisted at an acute angle.

"What the hell is it, Lisa?"

My voice felt detached, as if somebody had spoken on my behalf. But at least talking snapped me out of my trance. I took in my surroundings. The undergrowth. The trees. The shimmer of late afternoon sunlight penetrating through the dense foliage like a hundred mini-projectors, strategically positioned, ready and waiting for the reel of film to begin.

"Look."

My eyes followed Lisa's vacant stare. She glared at Graham. Without understanding what I was supposed to be looking at, I sighed aloud, and focused my attention on Katrina instead. She remained on her knees, propped upright. Her sobbing had abated, replaced by an undecipherable tune, which she hummed to herself. It sounded jolly; upbeat. Remarkably inappropriate, given the current situation.

More prodding, this time to my upper arm.

"I said, will you look?"

"What am I looking at, exactly?"

Lisa hadn't moved since I'd rushed over and helped her to sit upright. A few minutes earlier, Graham had knocked her flying, a body blow sending her crashing over. Upon landing, her head had snapped backwards; momentarily knocking her unconscious. She still appeared groggy, but at least some colour had returned to her cheeks.

"The blood, stupid."

Considering she may still be dazed, in shock, or both, I placated her by admiring the blood seeping from

Graham's head wound. A small amount trickled across the freshly dug grave beneath him. The very grave he'd dug himself earlier that day. A final resting place for Lee Blackmore, or possibly even me? How ironic that was where he had met his demise.

"I know. Katrina hit him pretty hard with that shovel."

I'd attempted to lift my tone, and hopefully Lisa's spirits. However, she didn't share my feigned enthusiasm. Instead, she pushed herself backwards, her hands and feet trying to gain purchase with the loose soil and pine needles below.

"Lisa?"

Suddenly, her pupils widened, and the remaining colour in her cheeks drained away. My eyes flicked from hers to Graham, to the blood and back again. Her behaviour freaked me out.

"Lisa!"

"The blood is still flowing," she claimed, pushing herself away from me; from the grave. "It's fresh blood."

"And?"

"And blood stops flowing as soon as the heart stops pumping. A little more may seep out, but not the amount coming out of his head."

Subconsciously, I pushed myself backwards too, attempting to catch her up. I couldn't take my eyes off Graham, either. Lisa was right. The blood appeared to be flowing freely from his head wound. But was she correct? Is that what *really* happens?

Katrina's squeal of excitement made my arms give way from beneath me. I hadn't seen her move or indeed stand up. She looked directly at me and grinned broadly; her yellowing teeth prominent in the early evening mist. A mist which had descended around us; swirling in the slightest of breeze. How could she switch from one mood to another with such ease?

A groan came from behind her. My eyes flicked back to Graham. Lisa grabbed my shoulder, her shaking arm reverberated throughout my body.

Did one of his fingers just twitch?

Holy shit!

A further squeal from Katrina. Her head twisted effortlessly from me to Graham, like a ventriloquist's dummy. Then she giggled and ran.

"Katrina, wait!"

She stopped dead in her tracks, as if somebody had applied an emergency brake, before turning slowly to face us.

"Did you really see the police officers at your house? Did they take your mother?"

I tried to recall what she'd originally told me. Graham had instructed her to run along; get home safely to her mother.

'The police have taken mother,' she'd said. 'And Amelia. I watched from the woods.'

But Katrina had a reputation for skewing the truth. Her own warped mind enabled her to say exactly what she wanted.

Katrina grinned, teasing, playing me at her own game. I'd been the victim of her antics many times before.

"Did the police officers take them, Katrina?" I repeated impatiently. "We *have* to know."

Finally, after further deliberating, she replied. "Of course not, silly. But I did just watch you kill him."

Katrina pointed at Graham. And then she ran. Quickly, back towards the footpath, disappearing out of sight. A faint cry of 'Mother' filled the dense woods; followed by that hideous cackle.

"We need to make sure."

Lisa stood beside me. As with Katrina, I hadn't heard her move. She held the shovel in outstretched arms. How had she retrieved it without me realising?

"Matt?"

Finally, I read her mind.

"No, Lisa, no," I said, shaking my head. "I can't do it."

Scrambling to my feet, I hastily joined her. Still, she held the shovel aloft.

"We have to, Matt," she repeated, shaking violently. "We have to finish him."

Scrupulously, I studied Graham, searching for any sign of movement. I continued to back away from the scene. Lisa echoed my every footstep.

"He's dead. He must be dead," I said. "Katrina hit him so bloody hard. Nobody could survive that."

"But what if…"

"If he isn't, he soon will be. He's lost a lot of blood. And if we don't touch him, then we can never be framed for it."

Instantaneously, we both looked at the shovel. She dropped it where she stood.

"Shit. Fingerprints. Matt, help…"

Lisa trailed off, the shock of what was unfolding finally rising to the surface. Grabbing her, I clutched her tight, feeling her silent sobs convulse through my body. Realising time was against us, I held her at arm's length.

"Listen. We've done nothing wrong. Graham killed Lee. He killed my aunt. And now Katrina killed Graham."

"So, what do we do?" I knew Lisa was doing her

utmost to remain brave and hold it together. "Didn't you say the police were coming up from the village? They'll be here soon."

I'd forgotten about the police. WPC Nina Murrow had left a message on Lisa's burner phone. They were going to make their way to the woods from the village below. It would detract from coming past the house, catching the family off guard. And the first thing they would stumble across would be Graham's body, conveniently laid out over the makeshift grave of the person he'd earlier killed.

"We need to get back to the footpath. Wait for the police."

I could feel Lisa nodding her head against my chest. Holding her tight, we awkwardly stepped backwards. My eyes didn't leave Graham.

True to her word, WPC Nina Murrow arrived via the village; accompanied by three other officers. It must have been around forty-five minutes after she'd left the message on Lisa's phone.

We led them silently back towards the scene. One officer spoke, checking on our condition, but neither of us replied. We just held each other, desperately seeking comfort.

Once back in the clearing, one of the police officers ran to Graham's aid. Another, the one who had been speaking to us, held out his arm, instructing us not to go any further.

"Wait here," he said.

Still holding Lisa in my arms, I led her to a nearby tree stump, where we gingerly sat down. Her whole body appeared to have gone into spasms. Hugging her tighter still, I recalled the two nights we had spent together in Cheshire, only three weeks previously, at the conference. My wife, Amelia, hadn't been able to attend because of her mother's illness, so Lisa and I represented the company instead.

There had been a spark between us ever since my first day at Opacy Property Management. Although my attention had been focused on Amelia Reid, I hadn't been able to resist Lisa's charm and flirtatious mannerisms. She may not have had the same stunning looks as Amelia – frankly, nobody could have compared to Amelia and the way she had dressed for my interview and subsequent first days in the office – but I found Lisa attractive, not for looks alone. She was good fun, the upbeat member of the team. And that cute little smile. I knew I had a reputation of finding many women attractive, but if it hadn't been for Amelia, I'd often wondered if I'd have ended up with Lisa instead.

Following the infamous night at the Cheshire hotel, Graham had turned up the next morning, nonchalantly waiting for us in the dining room at breakfast. Fortunately, I'd arrived first and made excuses on our behalf. Moments later, Lisa appeared. The sight of Graham sitting at the table drained the little colour remaining in her cheeks. I'd not been convinced whether Graham had known we'd spent the night together. After all, he had no proof, and could only have presumed the trip had gone ahead purely professionally. One thing was for certain, though: he'd have reported every single detail back to the family.

The sound of one officer talking snapped me from my trance.

"Miss!" he shouted. Everybody turned in unison. He leant over Graham, his hand on his neck.

"He's still alive!"

2

An hour later, I found myself in a small, soulless interview room at Epsom police station. The walls were painted a miserable grey and, perched high on one wall, were two tiny oblong windows. They let in a minimal amount of natural daylight. A single lightbulb hung over the brown Formica table, strategically placed in the centre of the room. The sensation of Graham being alive taunted me, and an oppressive feeling of claustrophobia threatened to overwhelm me. I'd never felt so grateful as when the door finally swung open.

Two gentlemen entered, neither in uniform. I didn't recognise them. Joining me at the table, they pulled out two plastic moulded chairs; one grey, the other a badly faded orange. One of them annoyingly scraped his chair backwards, along the tiled floor. He repeated his actions, dragging himself back underneath until his legs disappeared from sight. His colleague appeared as pissed off as me at the unnecessary screech.

"Matthew Walker?"

The annoying chair scraper addressed me first. His sombre tone matched the surroundings.

"We know you've been through a lot, so thank you for agreeing to give a statement. Hopefully, we won't keep you much longer."

Unsure whether I could speak, I instead offered a brief nod in return.

"This is my colleague, Detective Sergeant Tom Paine."

Glancing across the table, a wave of anxiety washed over me. I suddenly craved the familiar face of WPC Nina Murrow. She had been the friendly voice in the woods; the reassurance. The one person in authority who both I and Lisa had immediately entrusted. But from that moment on, I knew she was no longer in charge. Instead, I studied DS Tom Paine, hoping he would offer some kind of comfort.

Standing around five foot nine, I found it strange that an officer's physique could be so diminutive and wiry. My preconceived vision of anybody working in the police force was one of a powerful build, somebody whom you would never mess with. But DS Paine appeared more like someone you'd stumble across at a supermarket till or driving a delivery van.

"And I'm Detective Chief Inspector Clive Small." He paused, his eyes not leaving mine. "But just call me Clive. I think that's easier than any of this formal nonsense. Don't you?"

At a little over six feet tall, he fitted my conception of the quintessential police officer. Well built, broad-shouldered, and oozing an air of authority. He wore a dark blue, crew-neck jumper, complete with pristine white collared shirt beneath. His left sleeve had ridden above his wrist, showing off an expensive-looking watch. It soon became apparent why he allowed it to be on display, as he consistently glanced down whilst talking, a little too often for comfort. Maybe it was his method of applying pressure. A 'Get to the point' kind of duress. I didn't require any further intimidation. My palms were already damp. Strategically, I placed them on my thighs, underneath the table, out of sight.

Once again, I studied the DS. He remained stony-faced but not without a glimpse of compassion. Maybe that's why I had been drawn to him. However, it soon became obvious he wasn't conducting the interview. I offered a further solitary nod towards the DCI in reply to his question. Despite the invitation to address him by his first name, he would always remain DCI Small to me.

The receding hairline from his forehead exaggerated his cropped hair, greying at the temples. A day's stubble ruined the clean-cut exterior but somehow added to the tough-guy stance. Guessing his age as somewhere in the mid-forties, I noticed a large gold band on his wedding finger. Thick skin on either side wedged it into position. I doubted it had left his hand since the day he'd got married. DCI Small could never fit into the category of the most handsome men on the planet, but I still imagined a decent-looking wife at home, alongside the obligatory two children; one boy and one girl. The idyllic British family life.

"So, Matthew, or can I call you, Matt...?"

Opening my mouth to reply, the DCI had already decided.

".... so, Matt, in your own time. Can you tell us exactly what happened in the woods today, and how you happened to be there?"

"Well—"

Again, I attempted to answer, but he interrupted me further.

"In fact, Matt. Why don't you start from the very beginning?"

Finally, he sat back. Shuffling himself into a more comfortable position, he again dragged his chair back along the floor. Crossing his legs at his ankles, he rotated his thumbs, each encircling the other. The epitome of relaxation. It had the opposite effect on me. Fortunately, DS Paine sensed my discomfort.

"Here, Matthew. Have a drink of water. Just take your time."

Filling my white plastic beaker, he then replenished his own. The DCI held out his hand when he hovered the glass jug over his cup. Taking several small sips, I bought myself some time to relax.

You've done nothing wrong, Matt. You've done nothing wrong.

"Is Graham really alive?"

As soon the words escaped my mouth, I regretted it.

"Why? Were you hoping he's dead?"

DCI Small didn't move an inch. His facial expression never faltered. Taking a further gulp of water, I noticed my hand shaking. Finally, the detective showed some compassion.

"Let's just deal with your events first, Matt. We can address other issues later."

Once I began, and much to my surprise, the story began to flow. I spoke slowly and coherently, determined to stay in control.

"It all started around eighteen months ago. The day I had an interview at Opacy Property Management."

That hadn't been the entire truth. It had all started around twenty months ago, the day I met Julia at a hotel bar in London. It had been at the end of the opening day of a property trade show. At the time, I'd been working for an insignificant company in North London. They were a small-time operation, both in status and ambition alike. Julia had told me of an opportunity at Opacy; a potential big player in the commercial property field. However, I'd purposefully omitted her from my story. One, because she was the wife of Graham, and I knew she'd had a rough time being married to him. And two, I'd slept with her that night in the hotel. I didn't want to plant any seed of doubt into the minds of the two detectives sitting opposite me, or give them reason to believe there may have been any kind of personal vendetta against Graham. Besides, I liked Julia. She had even handed me proof of how the family had pieced together my ancestry. The Reids knew I would inherit a huge amount of money from my aunt Edith Weeks. Without the help of Julia, I doubt I would ever have been able to piece the two together.

However, following my *arranged* meeting at the hotel, everything else had begun eighteen months ago, stemming from that job interview. I'd been greeted by Amelia Reid, and I'd fallen for her as soon as I set eyes upon her. Her long, immaculate, straight black hair, and the deepest brown eyes I'd ever seen. The way she looked at me, I'd soon realised she thought the same way too. We had chemistry; the indiscernible sparks flying in both directions.

Amelia conducted the interview alongside the manager, Mike Whelan. Although he didn't carry the slickness of a forward-thinking city company, Mike knew the business like the back of his hand. They offered me the job without hesitation. It would be over a year later when I discovered I'd secured the job *before* the interview.

So, after many years of messing around and not

taking anything seriously, my life had fallen into place. Great job, gorgeous future wife, and an altogether prosperous outlook ahead.

Amelia introduced me to her family. Tracy Reid, her older sister, who — alongside Lisa who was elsewhere in the police station — also worked at Opacy. Their mother, Melissa, and Graham, their brother-in-law. Oh, and Tracy had a daughter. Katrina. Fourteen years old and mentally unstable – that was the best description I could think of, anyway. Katrina was homeschooled and generally left to her own devices. She would play on a squeaking swing in the garden or take herself off into the woods, which lay adjacent to the family home. Often, she wore a long white dress. I shuddered at the image.

One thing I didn't know at the time was that Graham was married to Julia. He'd admitted to having a spouse, but made excuses she travelled the world, working for a charity and looking after orphaned children.

"So, what went wrong with this idyllic lifestyle?"

DCI Small air-quoted the word *idyllic*, his sarcasm momentarily putting me off my stride.

"I guess, soon after we got married, it went downhill, shall we say?"

Amelia and the family began to act differently, even on our wedding day. During the reception, they asked me not to drink. Amelia briefly re-assumed her role as the perfect wife on our honeymoon, but once we returned, things slowly spiralled.

We couldn't afford our own place, not until we saved the required deposit, so Amelia suggested we lived at the family home; only for a few months. But I soon realised that a few months could easily escalate into many, many more.

And following moving in with them, the family acted

strange. Graham would play with Katrina's hair and touch her inappropriately. Melissa would make passes at me, even attempting to kiss me, as if they could construe such behaviour as normal. Amelia showed traits of jealousy whenever I spoke to Lisa in the office, or any other female.

"And you mentioned a family tree to my colleague, WPC Murrow?" DCI Small interrupted, glancing at his watch.

Ignoring any prompt to rush me, I continued to explain at my pace. Melissa and Tracy were forever organising piles of paper, scribbling on them, shuffling them into some kind of order. Eventually, I'd discovered what they were doing. They were family trees, and they all belonged to prospective employees of Opacy Property Management.

"How do you know that?"

"Because they attached every one to a curriculum vitae of somebody who had applied for a job with the company, or via the agency. And each one contained notes; 'rich uncle', 'father', 'grandmother'. And they marked out of ten. The higher the number, the better the opportunity to land themselves money."

"And you were special, because…?"

"Because, somehow or other, they had traced me back to Edith Weeks. An aunt I didn't even know existed. And she was due to leave her entire estate to me."

DS Paine handed his superior a piece of paper. He studied it before focusing his attention back on me.

"Hmm, they weren't wrong, were they? Seven hundred and twenty thousand pounds."

"Yes, and genuinely, a total surprise to me. But not to the Reid family."

Continuing, I explained how Lisa and I had tracked

down a friend of Tracy's ex-husband, Lee Blackmore. Tracy had been married to Ryan Palmer, Katrina's father, who worked with, and was best friends with, Lee Blackmore. Lee told me that Ryan had come into a lot of money after his parents had died. An only child, and all that. The Reid family knew and Tracy approached him at work. Allegedly, she was all over him, never leaving him alone. In return, Ryan fell for her. The same had happened to me and Amelia. The only difference is I didn't know I had an aunt worth a fortune, whereas Ryan already had his fortune.

The two detectives exchanged more papers. I allowed the DCI time to read, not wanting to interrupt his thought process. They spoke briefly, mumbling to one another.

"And you believe that this Ryan Palmer's body was already in the woods, and now Lee Blackmore has been killed and subsequently buried there as well?"

The detective gave nothing away, his facial expression not once offering any kind of emotion.

"Yes, I do. And Graham killed them. He killed my aunt. Katrina said she watched him kill her father years ago. It must be why she acts the way she does. Traumatised ever since and kept at home alone, not once speaking to anybody in the outside world."

"And why would Graham have killed them, Matt?"

The only explanation I could offer was the one I genuinely believed. Ryan had tried to escape, to get away from the family. But Graham had caught up with him in the woods.

"And Lee Blackmore?"

"Earlier today, Lee had found Ryan's grave. Fortunately, Lisa and I got away, but Graham caught him."

The DCI finally altered his position. Pulling himself

forward, he propped himself onto the table by his elbows. His hands met, and he intertwined his fingers, leaving his thumbs protruding upwards. Lowering his voice, he stared deep into my eyes.

"Caught him where exactly, Matt?"

I did my utmost to remain resolute.

"In the woods. He'd caught Lee Blackmore trying to dig his friend's grave with his bare hands. And he killed him and now he's buried him. I can show you precisely where."

3

LATER, that same evening, we returned to Lisa's home. Earlier, we had taken the train from Epsom into the city followed by a tube ride to North Ealing. I'd been to her house once before. The day she had faked a migraine at work to give us the opportunity to be alone. Mike suggested I gave her a lift home, much to the annoyance of Amelia. I'd only stayed around an hour. It had allowed us time to discuss our next plan of action. However, as we approached her front door, it wasn't so much our plotting that I remembered; it had been the kiss as I'd left that was etched across my mind. Lisa turned and offered me the briefest of smiles before placing her key in the lock. Did she sense it too?

Her property was a modest terrace. A 'two-up, two-down' in the middle of a street with identical properties flanking both sides of the road. Nonetheless, it still had a London postcode, and house prices had risen to a ridiculous level. Lisa had recently divorced, so I assumed her keeping the family home had been part of the agreement.

Could she afford to keep it on now that she had lost her job?

Following her inside, the first thing I noticed was how steeply the staircase rose to the right. Lisa took the narrow hallway which led straight ahead. Spotting a small living room to our left, I accompanied Lisa to the kitchen. Even though I'd been there before, I hadn't remembered how immaculate that particular room was. Ivory white cupboards stretched along one wall, with matching units below, interspersed with an impressive range cooker and a modern fridge freezer; one of those American-style fridges, double doors with a cold drink dispenser. Although state-of-the-art, I thought it a little presump-tuous for such a small property.

As if reading my mind, Lisa stepped to the appliance and opened both doors. Inside lay an impressive array of food, although it was the wine rack that caught my atten-tion. There must have been half a dozen bottles of white wine plus a further six or more bottles of beer chilling away. It would be the envy of many a bachelor; myself included. She removed two bottles of lager, retrieved an opener from a nearby drawer, popped them open and passed one to me.

"What are you smiling at?" she asked, before taking a huge gulp of hers.

"Oh, just you living my dream. That's all."

Lisa's story at the police station had corroborated mine, almost to the word. DCI Small had offered us a wry smile — did he think we were in cahoots? — as he explained what would happen next. He said we were both okay to return home. They had checked Lisa out for any lingering after-effects from her earlier blow to the head, although he instructed us not to leave the area for the foreseeable future. Lisa had given her address for both of us. Again, the DCI couldn't resist a glance and a knowing look towards his colleague. If I'd had the energy, I would have intervened and told him it wasn't as he imagined. But I didn't have the strength, physically or mentally. Over the past few days, I'd been drugged by Tracy, locked in a spare room and somehow escaped through a broken window, before eventually finding myself in the woods with crazed Graham.

"Lisa. Why am I here? You don't have to do this."

She placed her half-empty beer onto the table.

"It's the least I could do. Besides, where else would you have gone tonight?"

Another thing I had given no consideration to. As far as I knew, my car was still outside the Reids' house. My clothes and scant belongings were there too; my family home until forty-eight hours before.

"I need to go home. Everything I have is——"

"Shh, Matt. You can't go back there tonight. You heard what DCI Small said. The police are with them. Both detectives were heading straight over to talk to them. Undoubtedly, they'll be taken in for further questioning. You need to stay away, for a few days at least. Even then, surely you won't actually go back and *live* there?"

She glared at me, surprised I hadn't instantly replied.

Why aren't you replying?

"Matt. You won't. Will you?"

All I could offer was a shake of my head. Without thinking, I followed Lisa's lead and pulled out a chair to sit down opposite her. My body ached and my head throbbed.

"But what about my job?" I finally asked.

Lisa glared at me.

"You don't have a job. They've let you go…"

She let her words trail off. My head was a jumble of thoughts. Lisa continued.

"Stay the weekend. Sleep on——"

"No, Lisa. I can't put you to all that trouble." I stood and paced to the door at the back of the room. Beyond it, I observed the small utility room, complete with washing machine and dryer. Beyond that, a half-panelled glass door led to the modest back garden, a small square of lawn surrounded by neglected flower beds. Lisa obviously wasn't a keen gardener. As she replied, I turned to face her.

"It's no problem. I have two bedrooms. Admittedly, I'll have to clear yours out, but there is a comfortable bed in there. I'll pop into town in the morning and get you some clothes, you know, a couple of shirts, a pair of jeans and some underwear. If not, you'll be smelling quite bad by Sunday."

Fortunately, the police had found me a change of clothing from lost property at the station. I'd entered looking like a right prick; the oversized trousers and shirt I'd found in the wardrobe in the room they had held me in. My feet had been bare. I'd lost one shoe and discarded the other whilst running in the woods.

Despite all she'd been through, Lisa's smile was as infectious as ever. Cheeky, flirty, full of fun. She'd recovered quickly from Graham's heavy blow. It surprised me how swiftly she appeared to be recuperating from such an awful ordeal; much faster than me. However, being in her presence put me at ease, as it always had done, ever since the first day I'd walked into the office. I had to admire her tenacity. How could she be so considerate and downright upbeat following such a hideous turn of events?

"Thank you. You're a star. I owe you big time. I'll see you right once I get hold of my bank card."

"You owe me nothing."

Downing the remaining dregs of my beer, Lisa followed my lead. She retrieved two more from the fridge and placed one on the table before me. I nodded my appreciation.

"But seriously, Lisa." I couldn't let it go. "What do I do about my job? Do you think Mike may take me back once this is all out in the open?"

Lisa looked lost for words, suddenly despondent. I could have kicked myself.

"Hey, shit. I'm sorry. Mike let you go too. I forgot. Sorry."

It had slipped my mind. Before locking me away, Amelia had taken great pleasure in informing me that Lisa had been fired due to 'gross misconduct'. In other words, Amelia and Tracy had told Mike that she'd been seeing another member of staff: me.

"Yes, but I've been thinking about it. They couldn't sack me just for that. Could they? And it wasn't as though we were having an affair. Two nights at that hotel. That's it."

Graham must have known we spent those nights together.

Although I believed she had grounds to fight the dismissal, I knew that Amelia and Tracy all but ran that office. If Lisa insisted on a tribunal, the family would pin more on her. Missing documents, lost customers, and flirting with potential clients at the conference. They'd manipulated my emails once before, losing both myself and the company two high-profile accounts. From the look etched across Lisa's face, she'd quickly come to the same conclusion. Resistance was futile.

She showed me through to the living room and offered me a seat on one of a pair of faded two-seater sofas. After fetching me a third beer, she headed upstairs to prepare the spare bedroom. Again, I offered to help, or even find a cheap hotel, but Lisa insisted I stay. She declared she'd feel safer with somebody around. It made sense. She must have felt incredibly vulnerable considering the past day's ordeal.

Once she'd disappeared, I tried to relax and take in my surroundings. The living room was in stark contrast to the relatively new and expensive-looking kitchen. Had she spent all her money on one room? As well as the washed-out sofas, threadbare and shiny along the arms, the carpet appeared worn too. Patches of spilt liquid dotted the perimeter of the seating areas. The wallpaper was a painted woodchip, the same as my parents had when I was a child. Lisa's room looked just as old. Along the back wall lay an old sideboard, polished lacquered wood with brass handles. An ornate mirror was fixed to the wall above it, the glass speckled and blackened around the edges. The room felt odd, like stepping back in time. It gave the impression that it hadn't been touched for years. And the pièce de résistance? An ancient electric fire, set in the centre of a hearth surrounded by browny-yellow tiles. The fire itself contained two cylindrical heating bars, confined behind a rusting chrome cage. Two switches faced outwards, and I resisted the urge to check if it worked. A chill washed over me. Placing my beer onto the circular coffee table, I sat back and folded my arms, holding onto any warmth which remained in my body.

The sound of the doorbell made me leap out of my seat. One of those original *ding-dong* chimes, associated with advertisements and sitcoms from the nineteen-seventies.

"I've got it!" shouted Lisa. She bounded downstairs, sounding as though taking two steps at a time. Was she expecting somebody? If she had been, she sounded disappointed as soon as she opened the door.

"Oh. Chief Inspector. Detective Sergeant. To what do we owe the pleasure?"

Lisa's sarcasm hadn't been lost on DCI Small.

"Bad timing?" he replied.

Although I didn't hear Lisa invite them in, the DCI appeared at the entrance to the living room. Directly behind him, stood his sidekick.

"Aha, Matthew. We thought you'd be here."

Resisting asking, 'what the fuck is that supposed to mean?', I instead stood and nodded in acknowledgement.

"Go in, go in," Lisa instructed, hidden somewhere in the hallway behind her uninvited guests.

"Thank you." At least DS Paine had a civil tongue, and no doubt felt some sympathy with what we'd been through.

"Take a seat," Lisa continued, sounding somewhat flustered. "Tea? Coffee?"

DCI Small stood in the centre of the tiny room, taking in what I'd been doing moments before. He raised his hand to Lisa before his eyes rested on me.

"No, but thank you. We won't keep you long."

Why the hell do you keep looking at me like that?

"I'll come straight to the point."

Lisa looked at me, folding her arms into a defensive pose. She needed to relax. Deciding it best if the attention lay on me, I spoke first.

"What's happened?"

The DCI ushered his partner to step forward. They stood together, acting like there was some kind of strength in numbers.

DS Paine removed a small notepad from his inside

pocket. I'd always wondered if they were a gimmick for TV cop shows. Apparently not.

He explained forensics had already recovered fragments of bone from the unmarked grave. He said they would need to go to the lab to establish identity, but they were confident that my account of events would hold up. DS Paine also confirmed that Katrina had confessed that she'd witnessed Graham striking both Ryan, some years earlier, and Lee Blackmore that afternoon.

Lisa's eyes widened as I glanced at her. Could Katrina really have said such a thing? She'd only told me she'd seen me kill Lee a few hours earlier. Her mind was all over the place and surely the police wouldn't accept her as a sound witness?

Once the DS had finished, DCI Small apologised for taking up more of our time. Adding some light-hearted remark regarding the murder of my aunt too, he suggested Graham would go away for a long time. I resisted asking what he found so amusing.

Eventually, they turned to leave. We followed them into the hallway, desperate to see the back of them.

As soon as Lisa opened the door, the DCI stopped in his tracks. He turned to face me.

"Just one thing we can't understand."

I thought there would be.

"Yes?" I replied, my voice slightly raised.

"We've heard from the hospital. It's about Graham's condition."

Get to the fucking point.

"The doctors have put him in an induced coma."

"What does that mean exactly?" Lisa sounded frightened, as though he might pay her a visit as soon as he came round. It did sound scary, the thought of Graham waking again.

"I'm no medical expert, but I know it's a temporary type of coma. It's used to protect the brain from swelling and the patient receives a controlled dose of anaesthetic."

Neither Lisa nor I dared ask the question. DCI Small read our thoughts.

"It could last up to a month, but the doctor informed my colleague that he doesn't expect to keep Graham Meadows in an induced coma for more than a week."

Again, as he turned to leave, he halted once more.

"My prediction is he'll be awake and ready to interview within the next few days."

4

THE WEEKEND DRAGGED. Monday morning had been playing on my mind and the prospect of returning to the office to face Mike made me feel physically sick. I'd run Amelia's version of my dismissal over and over in my head.

'... *After the email debacle, Mike then somehow found out it was you who'd been sleeping with Lisa. Well, it gave him no choice. He didn't hesitate with his decision...*'

There could easily be other accusations made against me, whether or not they were true.

Would Amelia do such a thing, or more likely Tracy?

My only hope would be that once Mike realised what the family were capable of, he may reconsider.

The weather hadn't helped my mood either with steady rain and the temperature hovering a couple of degrees above freezing. We'd been stuck indoors, and it served as an excuse to spend most of the time lounging around in bed; Lisa's bed.

She'd been true to her word and made up the spare room. But as soon as the detectives had left, Lisa opened a bottle of red wine. We needed to relax, talk things through, and rationalise the facts from the fiction.

Had Katrina altered her confession of her own free will? Or could the family be covering something else, and if so, what? I shuddered at my question. The Reids were capable of anything and we knew we had to keep our wits about us.

The bottle of wine soon materialised into a second. As Lisa reappeared from the kitchen, instead of returning to her sofa, she sat next to me. I didn't object. A combination of delayed shock, alcohol and a desire to be close to her led to an unspoken consent. Pouring us each a fresh glass, Lisa tucked her legs underneath her bottom and snuggled by my side. Her head rested on my shoulder. Reciprocating, I placed my arm around her, pulling her closer still. Just as at the conference a few weeks before, I knew it was inappropriate. Amelia could never discover that we were close, even if her suspicions were well set. I needed a conflict-free separation, leading to a harmonious divorce. Any proof of foul play would play directly into the arms of my wife and her family.

However, the weekend couldn't be described as akin to two teenagers finding each other for the first time. More comparable to two traumatised adults desperate for comfort whilst trying to come to terms with their current situation. We'd been through so much, in such a brief space of time, and we'd become dependent upon one another.

My plan to visit Mike on Monday morning never materialised, that would happen two weeks later. I'd woken early, insisting Lisa stay in bed. She didn't complain as I promised a tray of fresh coffee and breakfast.

Once in the kitchen, I called Mike from Lisa's land-line. I knew the office number from memory and I wanted to make sure he would be at work. His reply stunned me. Although he didn't dismiss my plea to see him, Mike still came across as cold and callous.

'Can you hold on for a couple more weeks?' he'd proposed rather abruptly. He stuttered and scrambled for the correct words, as if somebody may have been with him, instructing him what to say.

I wonder who?

Mike continued with his excuses and indicated the police needed to give him the all-clear before he could see me. It all felt underhanded and contrived. I politely enquired if Amelia or Tracy had returned to work, but he remained non-committal. Surely if the police had asked for me to stay away, the same would apply to my wife and her sister? Somehow, I already knew the answer to that.

During the following two weeks, whenever the police phoned or called by, I became more frustrated with their dismissal of each accusation I raised against the Reid family.

Despite initially agreeing that they fully expected the bone fragments to belong to Ryan Palmer, they seemed adamant that anything else I told them could still be open to interpretation. I'd even doubted my own version of events.

They had searched the Reid house for any signs that they had held me against my will.

"Tied to a bed and drugged, I think you mean?"

DCI Small ignored my sarcasm and instead reeled out

a list of what they had *not* found. None of the bedrooms contained ropes or belts or string. In fact, the room I'd described as being held captive in didn't contain a bed at all.

"They've removed it," I insisted. My complaints fell on deaf ears.

The detective moved on and explained that a thorough search had taken place for drugs. Drugs that wouldn't otherwise belong in an ordinary household. Again, apart from a larger than usual amount of over-the-counter type medicines and ointments, nothing stood out.

"What about the pills they give Katrina?"

"Yes," admitted the DCI, "we asked to see those. And yes, she is on a drug. We've had them checked out with our medical team and both her prescription and dosage are commonplace for someone with her unfortunate condition. It keeps her mood swings under control. All very normal, Mr Walker."

"So, you think I've made it all up? I jumped from a window for the sheer hell of it?"

"No need to be facetious," DCI Small said. He carried the expression of somebody who'd heard it all before, heard all the excuses, all the made-up stories, to have the blame shifted elsewhere. "The thing is, the family are quite concerned for your well-being too. I believe Tracy Reid is an ex-nurse..." He looked to his colleague. DS Paine nodded to affirm. "... and she suggested you see a GP, maybe somebody else. Amelia, your, erm, wife, also told us you'd been suffering from bad dreams. Sleep walking too. And, what's her name?"

"Katrina, sir," DS Paine filled in the blanks.

"Yes, Katrina said she'd seen you roaming in the

woods a lot. What would you be doing in there on your own, Matt?"

Glaring from one detective to the other, I didn't know whether to laugh or cry. After attempting to exonerate myself by claiming it was all bullshit, DS Paine made a note in his little book and they stood to leave.

"Is that it?" I asked incredulously. "Surely you're not just taking their word for it all?"

The DCI cleared his throat and his tone mellowed. It sounded like sympathy.

"You've been through a lot. A hell of a lot. I can understand your animosity towards the family, especially given what you witnessed from Graham Meadows on numerous occasions. However, believe me, the family are just as shocked as you by his—"

"Bollocks!" I shouted.

Is that why the family had instructed Katrina to confess against Graham? If they could pin everything on him, did that absolve them of all crimes?

DCI Small ignored my protest.

"...by his behaviour. They did not know he was capable of such things and they have offered their apologies to you. They hope, soon, you'll be able to meet them again."

That time, I did laugh. I couldn't help myself. Days and days of pent-up frustration came crashing to the surface.

Once they left, I returned to the kitchen. Lisa sat at the table, cradling a half-empty mug of tea. She looked forlorn. I'd noticed a subtle change in her behaviour during the past few days. Crestfallen, as if they had finally sucked all the fight out of her.

"Did you hear all that?" I asked, still fuming and ignoring her apparent lack of interest.

"They're clever, Matt. Maybe you have to be clever too."

What does that even mean?

She stood, rinsed out her mug and placed it in the dishwasher.

"Where are you going?" I called after her. She stopped in the doorway.

"To lie down. I'm tired. Exhausted."

"I can't believe you didn't back me up in there."

My temper still flared despite Lisa showing no sign of joining me.

"There's nothing to back up. That family have an answer for everything. Can't you see that? Even the bloody bed you claim they tied you up in doesn't exist."

"Hold on. What do you mean, 'claim'? Are you saying I *have* made it up? How can you not accept what happened in that house when you know exactly what kind of people they are?"

Lisa's expression was full of remorse.

"It doesn't matter what I believe, or what I have witnessed. They've covered every single track. If they could have got Graham away with it too, I'm sure they would. But he's the sacrifice this time. Ryan was the sacrifice all those years ago."

Although she could be right, I still couldn't comprehend Lisa's attitude.

"So, what are you saying? Give up, accept it, carry on as normal?"

"All I'm saying, Matt, is just be pleased it wasn't you."

5

FROM THAT NIGHT ON, we slept in separate beds. It had been Lisa's idea. She suggested we cool things between us and respect each other's privacy. She was right. I'd already considered it to be the best course of action, but it still hurt to hear it. I'd presumed she had never contemplated 'each other's privacy' before, which made it harder to accept.

From the first night in individual rooms, losing Lisa being so close hit me hard. I felt isolated and more vulnerable. But I respected her too. After all, it had been me who had dragged her into the whole situation.

The following morning, I forced myself out of bed. Lisa wasn't up, and I made as little noise as possible. Forgoing a drink, I walked into town, grabbed a coffee and then found a mobile phone store.

With a fresh Americano in my hand, I asked a passer-by if there were any suitable shops nearby. She informed me I had a choice of two and promptly pointed me in the right direction. Apparently, they were next door to one another.

Stepping inside the first, a lad approached me. He looked young enough to still be at school. I hadn't even closed the door when he addressed me.

Slow day, mate?

"Good morning, sir. How can we help you?"

Stop being so bloody chirpy for a start.

"I need a phone."

Did he just grin?

"You've come to the right place. Apple or Android, sir?"

"Apple. Nothing expensive. It's a stop-gap. I lost mine, and…"

I trailed off. Even mundane chat was beyond me. I wished I'd stayed in bed after all.

"No problem, sir."

Following him across the shop floor, I glared at a wall. It displayed many iPhones, made up of all colours and sizes. The newest models sat prominently in the middle, on stands, the very latest of which spun slowly and silently on a revolving base.

"Any particular model in mind, sir?"

"Please, stop calling me sir. It isn't necessary."

The young lad went bright red.

"Okay," he mumbled, his previous enthusiasm extinguished within a second. Having no time for guilt, I cut to the chase.

"Listen, I'm in a rush. Do you have any older models in stock? I need a phone today."

"Sure." He tried to recover. "iPhone 6, 8? We've got them all out the back."

A short while later, he returned with both versions. I'd only nodded in response and he realised he had to act quick to clinch a sale. At least he showed intuition.

Settling for the iPhone 8 — there was no difference in

price — I had fifty pounds' credit added. I'd have to thank Lisa again for lending me some cash. As soon as the young sales guy had asked for a home address, I realised I couldn't set up a contract. Where the hell is my address? Where will I be this time next month? Next year? The thought depressed me and the reality of my situation hit hard.

Lisa wasn't in when I returned, but fortunately, she'd left her old burner phone in its usual place in the kitchen. After sending a message to her main mobile – she had that number stored – I spent the next few minutes copying contacts to my new phone. There was only a handful on there and one stood out. Realising I must have given it to Lisa at some point, that very person had been on my mind for the past few weeks. Quickly, I composed a text.

```
Hi Julia — it's Matt. I'm on a new phone.
Just wondered how you are? If you want to
talk, let me know. Take care x.
```

Unsure whether I was doing the right thing, I hit 'Send' before I could change my mind. What harm could it do? Besides, I had a genuine interest in whether she was okay. Julia had made it clear Graham bullied her, although I didn't know to what extent. Verbal or physical? And now he was out of the way, I wanted to know if she was alright and if she had any plans. It had been her who had begun the entire process of me becoming entangled with that family. But I didn't blame Julia; she would have had no choice.

As I waited for the message to deliver, my mobile

rang. Hoping it would be Lisa, my enthusiasm became short-lived as the phone displayed the caller's name.

How the hell did he get my number?

"Hello?" I answered, in a questioning tone.

"Matthew Walker?"

"Yes. Who is this, please?"

"It's DCI Small here. I've just called your landlady, erm, Lisa. She gave me your new number. I hope you don't mind me intruding on your day?"

I only bloody texted her ten minutes ago.

"No, it's—"

"Besides, Mr Walker. Or can I call you Matt?"

You've already decided that.

"I told you to inform me of any change of address or contact details. This is an ongoing investigation, if you haven't forgotten."

Even on the phone, the guy riled me. I felt like shit and he was speaking to me like a child.

"Yeah, sorry. Only picked up the new mobile an hour ago. I'm just adding the numbers—"

"Okay. But make sure you're readily contactable."

Just tell me why you've called.

I intended my silence as his cue to continue. He didn't require a second invitation.

"I thought you'd be interested to know that Graham Meadows has awoken from his coma."

Shit.

The idea of that man breathing by his own means, no longer reliant on a machine, sent shivers down my spine. Ever since the DCI had informed me they had put him into an induced coma, I'd had aspirations of visiting the hospital in the early hours and switching off the apparatus at the socket. And then I'd stand there, waiting for him to take his final breaths. He'd open his eyes one last time, and see me hovering over him, smiling as he slipped away.

"Matthew?"

"Yeah, sorry. I'm here. It's a bit of a shock, that's all."

"Yes, it must be. Anyway, we'll be visiting him later. Ask him some initial questions and get his version of events."

"What do you mean, 'his version of events'?"

Surely anything but an open and shut case couldn't be possible? There were three key witnesses, including his niece, however unstable she may be. All the evidence pointed towards him. Two dead bodies in the woods and the police had already concluded he'd murdered my aunt. What could he possibly say to persuade them different?

"As I said, it's an ongoing investigation. We need to hear what he has to say. Hopefully, he'll confess to everything and it will be a matter of crossing the t's and dotting the i's."

"And if he doesn't?"

The blood drained from my head, and my palms began to sweat. Already feeling like crap, this was taking my mood to a whole new level.

"Let's just cross that bridge if and when we come to it, shall we?"

He was right. Calm down, Matt. This is just standard procedure. But DCI Small wasn't finished.

"Unless something is bothering you, and he won't corroborate your version of events?"

My heart skipped another beat. I steadied myself against the kitchen wall.

"No, no." My attempt to laugh sounded pathetic to me, so goodness knows what the DCI thought.

"Okay. I'll let you go. Please keep this phone available at all times. Hopefully, next time I call will be to tell you good news and you are free to get your life back on track. I realise this can't be easy for you."

Get my life back on track? It's that simple, is it?

Taking two or three deep breaths, I tried to compose myself. Feeling dizzy, I knew my oxygen levels were low.

"Yes, yes. That would be great. That's exactly what I need to do."

Not wanting to make it obvious I needed the conversation to end, I stood still and remained quiet, silently praying that the DCI would say his farewells.

"Oh, Matt. Whilst you're still there, there was one other thing."

Oh, fuck, no. Just go away.

"Erm, yes?"

"Are you in a relationship with Miss Ingram, Lisa?"

What the....?

"No, no," I stumbled. "Why do you ask?"

He knew exactly how long to hold his silence.

"No reason. Just curious, that's all."

6

THE SHRILL of the alarm clock announced that Monday morning had arrived. I'd barely slept, apart from the final two hours. One of those deep sleeps after your body finally waivers and caves in. The prospect of visiting Mike and begging for my job back had been at the forefront of my mind, notwithstanding who else may be in the office.

Lisa hadn't helped my mood, she had remained distant all weekend. She'd returned home late on Saturday afternoon, feigned yet another headache, and only appeared once to eat a snack. I'd left her to it, not wanting to cause any upset. At that moment, Lisa was all I had, and I needed to keep her on my side. I'd already decided that once I received my share of the inheritance, I could tell her I intended to move out.

As I slowly made my way to the underground station, I contemplated all that had taken place since Christmas. It had only been six weeks ago. What had happened to my life? Even though our fate had probably been decided, Amelia was still my wife. The same woman I'd fallen head over heels in love with eighteen months before. We'd planned on buying our own home together, a cute little cottage, complete with a long, narrow garden. I recalled Amelia deciding what vegetables she would grow and what flowers would go where. Inside the house, she'd settled on the wallpaper she wanted, where the furniture would sit and what style of kitchen she envisaged. All those plans, just a few short months ago.

It also hit me that the house could still be ours. How had we left it? A list of unanswered emails from our solicitor? I'd hoped if we didn't reply, it might go away, disappear without a trace. But is that how property buying works? Surely we would receive a final warning, or whatever the term is, to inform us the house would go back onto the market? Had we? Or had she? Over the weekend, I'd unsuccessfully attempted to log onto our email account. 'Account temporarily suspended'. Why?

'They're clever, Matt. Maybe you have to be clever too.'

The tube felt claustrophobic, crowded and edgy, as commuters jostled for position. More people clambered aboard at every stop with relatively few leaving in return. It soon became standing room only, the entire aisle of the carriage packed with passengers wearing headphones or attempting in vain to read the free morning newspaper. Although I knew I should have offered my seat to somebody less able, I instead plugged in my earphones and faked ignorance. Who, or what, was I becoming?

Eventually, I left the stuffy underground. Opacy's offices were close to Covent Garden. The crisp, still air had never smelt so good.

Taking a deep breath, I set off. But immediately, an overwhelming sensation of being watched engulfed me. I stopped, much to the annoyance of a spectacled gentleman who bumped into the back of me.

"Sorry," I offered as a weak apology.

Muttering something under his breath, he straightened his jacket and stepped around me.

Spinning a full three hundred and sixty degrees, I searched for any eyes that might be watching me. All to no avail. The awareness of somebody hiding in the shadows left me feeling extremely vulnerable. And then, out of the corner of my eye, a flash. I spun once more. There, to my right, at the tube station entrance, a figure descending the steps. Far too quickly to distinguish.

Should I go in pursuit? No. You can't be sure. It could be anyone. Your mind is playing tricks.

With my heart thumping, I once again set off towards my destination. Soon, I passed the café, the coffeehouse where Lisa and I would often escape from work. They made lovely coffee — better than the vending machine crap at the office — but, towards the end, it had also acted as our secret meeting place, a getaway to discuss plans, avoiding prying eyes and ears. Amelia knew we went there, but she'd never said as much.

Although it had been several weeks since I'd last stepped inside the office, it felt like months, years even. Recollections of my first day flooded back. My disappointment at Amelia not coming in until lunchtime. How welcoming everybody had been. My brand new laptop and the list of company cars to select from. A new start, a new life.

Mike had left a note with reception informing them he had been expecting me, and I took the elevator up unattended. As I stepped out into the office, my mouth now unwittingly dry, I couldn't help but notice how quickly the noise levels dropped. A nudge on the arm, a nod of the head. Just as I'd feared, all the attention was bestowed upon me.

First, I noticed Mike. An incredibly sheepish-looking Mike, still wearing his old-fashioned, shiny blue suit. His hair was slicked back and he appeared to have gained weight in the brief space of time I'd been away.

However, Mike Whelan didn't hold my attention for long. I'd been expecting to see him. But, even though I knew it was inevitable, the shock of seeing Amelia and Tracy glaring nonchalantly at me made me feel both nauseous and light-headed in equal measure.

Grabbing the closest chair, I sensed the room spin around me. A gasp brought me back to the present.

Tracy Reid remained seated, but my wife, Amelia, rushed across the office to my aid.

"Come here. Sit down. Tracy, fetch Matt a glass of water."

Allowing Amelia to guide me, more in fear of falling than any kind of loyalty, I gingerly sat on the closest chair. I realised all the colour would have drained from my cheeks and, already feeling rough through a combination of anxiety and lack of sleep, the shock of seeing those two had rendered me dumbfounded.

Tracy returned with a drink. At least she had the decency to appear uncomfortable in my company. The same couldn't be said for my wife.

"Take your time. Have a drink. Whatever came over you, darling?"

Darling? What the...

I glared at her, slowly finding the strength to think for myself.

"What are you two even doing here?"

Standing abruptly, I knocked the glass of water from Amelia's grasp. It somersaulted to the floor, somehow bouncing but not smashing when making impact with the ground. The cheap carpet tiles acted as a sponge and quickly soaked up the spilt liquid. Looking around the room, my eyes eventually settled on Mike. He'd remained seated, his elbows perched on the desk and his chin resting in the palms of his hands. He appeared mesmerised by the antics taking place before him.

"You'd better come with me," he said, beckoning me to follow him to a meeting booth.

Glancing over my shoulder, I noticed Amelia smiling. Unable to decipher whether she was being affectionate or conceited, I could only offer a shake of my head in return.

"Come in, Matt, sit—"

"What the hell are they doing here?"

"You need to calm down. Now, sit and listen."

I'd never seen Mike look so serious. Following his cue, I sat opposite and listened intently to what he had to say.

He explained that Amelia and Tracy had a right to be at work. The police had been in regular contact with him over the past two weeks and said there was an ongoing investigation taking place. However, they were confident that their brother-in-law had been the primary culprit, the *only* culprit.

"That can't be right," I intervened. "That family…" I pointed through the glass wall, "…that family tied me up, drugged me and made me sign over half of my money to them. How the hell can Graham be the *only* culprit?"

Mike ignored me. He repeated that the police were investigating, and they had given him their word that as far as they could tell, neither Tracy nor Amelia had done anything wrong. His words echoed those of DCI Small. Absolving all guilt from the family apart from Graham himself.

Have you imagined the whole thing?

"What about Katrina?" I continued. "Tracy's daughter. She's so screwed up, that the only way they can keep her in check is by filling her with pills. Then there's Graham's wife—"

"Matt, Matt. Calm down. There has obviously been a major disagreement between you and your family over the past weeks. Maybe longer for all I know. Now, that's none of my business. But what is my business is people turning up for work and doing their jobs." He leant forward, his arms resting on the table. I spotted small flecks of dandruff resting on his shoulders. "And I have to admit, I'd already detected the downturn in your performance. What about those emails? You lost some good business, Matt."

"That's because they fucking planted them!"

I noticed Tracy and Amelia glance up before returning to their work. The sheer audacity of the pair of them. Mike's eyes had followed mine.

"Those two have reported in every day. They, alongside Don, are keeping this side of Opacy Property Management going."

Don was the other property portfolio manager, and Tracy was his personal secretary. Don rarely visited the office, but whenever he had, I barely spoke to him. He had a reputation for grabbing all the top accounts. As soon as any reached a certain turnover, Don would suggest to Mike that he handled them. Mike always agreed. It didn't help that Amelia and Tracy were in cahoots too, and as soon as I made significant headway with a client, Amelia told Tracy, Tracy told Don and Don informed Mike.

"Amelia told me you were unwell, but you never answered your phone. I tried emailing—"

"Mike. They drugged me. What bit don't you understand?"

What had Lisa said?

'Even the bloody bed you claim they tied you up in doesn't exist.'

Am I really losing it?

"Don't get facetious with me, Matt. I've only your word for all of this nonsense. I can't believe your wife could carry on so professionally if any such thing had been going on under her roof."

You don't bloody know them.

Ironically, Amelia smiled just as I looked up again. Like some kind of mind reader. She said something to Tracy, who glanced over too. They both laughed, enjoying their little in-joke. It took all my inner strength not to storm out of the meeting room, run over, and choke one of them to death.

"And it's not just the emails, is it? I know about you and Lisa. There are other things too. Both of you—"

I'd heard enough. As I'd expected, they had conspired against me — against us — and I'd be wasting my time trying to put across my side of the story.

"Is this it, Mike? The end of me working here?"

He stood, indicating the meeting was over.

"Security are on the way up. They'll show you out."

The café was as busy as ever, but fortunately, the table at the back was free, the small, two-seater table that Lisa and I used to frequent. I recalled our previous tête-à-têtes, the passing of the burner phones we'd used to communicate in secret, and our grand plans to finally bring down the Reid family. Had it all backfired? Had I played any sinister part in it all?

Get a fucking grip, Matt.

The sight of a red, double-decker London bus stopping outside caught my attention. As it pulled off, the café door opened and in stepped Amelia.

What's she *doing here?*

She stood on tiptoe, her eyes scouring the room. She spotted me.

Pausing at the counter, ordering herself a drink, she gestured to me if I needed a refill. Politely as I could muster, I shook my head. I wanted nothing from her.

"Mind if I join you?" She half-smiled, already sitting down.

"Do I have a choice?"

"Oh, come on. Don't be like this. After all, we *are* still married."

Leaning across the table, desperately trying to keep my voice low, I spoke through gritted teeth.

"What's your fucking game, Amelia? You had me tied to a bed a few weeks ago, and now you're acting as though we should move back in together."

She sat back, slowly peeling the plastic lid from her cup. Taking a sip, she exaggerated a sigh as the liquid trickled down her throat and the caffeine no doubt gave her the initial buzz.

"I do not know what you are talking about—"

"You—"

Holding up her free hand, she stopped me before I could launch into my next tirade.

"And neither have the police."

My eyes narrowed. I felt myself strangely intrigued to hear her side of the story. But what she said came as no surprise, I'd heard it all before.

"They searched the house. Didn't find a single thing. No evidence of anybody being tied up. No trace of drugs." Amelia smiled and leant a little closer. "Come on, Matt. It's been a very stressful time, but it's all over now."

Making a scene would be pointless. I needed to take my time and stay in control, however difficult I may have been finding it.

"Brilliant. I thought as much after DCI Small came to visit us. He said—"

"Us? Did you say, us?"

Feeling myself redden, I grabbed my cup and took a large swig of my drink. The coffee had gone cold, and I instantly regretted it as it slid down my throat. I thought I might be sick. Amelia continued.

"Oh. You've shacked up with that slapper, Lisa, haven't you?"

"Where the hell do you think I should stay? On the streets? If you remember, we did plan on buying our own house, but I guess even that must have fallen through by now."

She took her time. Another few sips of her piping hot drink. Watching enviously as she devoured the beverage, the steam rose and disappeared up her nostrils. Secretly, I wished I had taken her up on the offer of a refill, but I hadn't wanted to give her the satisfaction of accepting.

And then Amelia changed; her whole demeanour, like the flick of a switch. She painted on her nicest smile, the same smile which had melted my heart many times before.

"Well, funny you should say that, Matthew."

"Stop calling me Matthew. You never have done before. Only your mum called me that."

"You mean Mother. But that's not important right now. She still talks about you, by the way."

Amelia appeared to be doing her utmost to not only maintain the peace but somehow attempt to rekindle past emotions. I had to stay on my guard.

"Can we get this over and done with, please? Funny I should say what, exactly?"

"I mean, you mentioning the house? The cute little cottage that we nearly bought."

"What about it?"

My patience was wearing thin, but Amelia remained steady, willing to win me over.

"The solicitor called on Friday. He said he'd been trying to contact us for months and wanted to give us one last chance to say yes or no to the purchase."

My pulse raced and I leant forward once more.

"And what did you say?"

Following another dramatic pause, a huge smile spread across her face.

"I said we were finally coming into the money we had been expecting and…"

I could only glare at her, knowing what was coming, but equally dreading hearing it.

"…that we would love to go ahead with the sale."

My eyes widened and my fists clenched.

"Matt." She beamed with excitement. "We can carry on exactly where we left off."

7

AMELIA WAS DEADLY SERIOUS. I knew her too well. In any other situation, I'm convinced I would have burst out laughing. The sheer audacity. But what struck me most, even in the heat of one of the most surreal situations I'd ever found myself in — and there had been plenty of those recently — I couldn't help but admire the beauty of my wife.

Whilst she allowed me time to absorb her incredulous proposition, Amelia sat back in her chair, her infectious smile not once threatening to dissipate. Her hair had grown since I'd last seen her. Shiny black, stretching down her back. Standing at five foot seven, Amelia carried herself perfectly, her posture, her conduct, everything I found attractive in a woman. And those eyes. The darkest, brownest eyes I'd ever seen; her most distinguishing feature. I'd fallen head over heels the first time I'd spotted her, and sitting in that café, at that precise moment, I realised the initial spark had never really gone away.

Stay in control.

"What are you talking about? Carry on where we left

off? What, me tied to the bed in a spare room drugged out of my skull? Oh yeah, show me the way."

Amelia sat forward. Slowly. Deliberately. And somehow, still holding onto that irresistible smile. She gave the impression that she perceived the current situation as a mere difference of opinion. Nothing we couldn't resolve over a cup of coffee in a crowded café.

"No need for the sarcasm," she replied, upbeat. "Come on. We've got the inheritance money coming in. Graham is somewhat incapacitated, and I know—"

"He'll recover quickly. He's as strong as an ox. And then what?"

She remained unperturbed.

"He'll go to prison, of course. Those detectives more or less told us it's an open and shut case. Both you and that Lisa woman witnessed it. Even Katrina confessed to what had happened. Add that to the evidence of him visiting your aunt's place. He hasn't got a leg to stand on."

Letting the derogatory comment about Lisa go — my energy levels were depleting by the minute — I still couldn't shake a nagging feeling that Graham would somehow find a way out of it. Before I could respond, Amelia read my mind.

"I know how much you despise him. We all do now. We only did what we did because he told us to. You were right, Matt. Graham is a bully. He threatened us if we didn't comply. Threatened to have Katrina taken away. And we did not know he could have been responsible for the death of Ryan, we just assumed he had disappeared, run away."

"Give over. There's no way you couldn't have—"

"How could we have known? Graham never told us. However, he said that you had indicated you were on the verge of running away. And that you had no intention of signing the solicitor forms if I had access to half of the money. You realise I couldn't comply with that? We *are* a married couple, after all. You said your vows in church alongside me."

My words faltered. Could she be telling the truth? She sounded so convincing.

"So, how do you explain Katrina's behaviour? She witnessed Graham killing Ryan, her own father. Surely she must have mentioned that? It's why she acts the way she does. She could never have been like that without some kind of dramatic event tipping her over the edge. Tracy drugs her daily to keep her calm. She's disturbed, Amelia. Off her—"

Amelia leant further forward and placed her arms on the table. Her hands stretched out, her fingertips inches from mine. I fought my inner self not to reach out, touch them, hold them, and squeeze them once again. Images of the past cascaded through my mind.

"There's something you should know. About Katrina."

Amelia explained that Katrina had shown traits of very odd behaviour from an early age, maybe as young as two years old. She'd suffered from disturbing nightmares, often waking in the middle of the night, screaming, her pyjamas drenched in sweat. Frequently, she told Ryan and Tracy of seeing someone in the room. Sometimes, this person would carry a knife and threaten her, whilst on other 'visits' — that word unsettled me more than any other — he would climb into bed with her, stroke her hair, and sing a quiet lullaby until she drifted off back to sleep.

Surely not? Not him?

By the time she reached five years of age, a child psychiatrist had recommended Katrina be homeschooled.

She'd tried in vain to understand Katrina's behaviour. Some days, she would act normal and hold a decent level of conversation, but that was counteracted with levels of aggression the psychiatrist had never witnessed before. She'd diagnosed her with dissociative identity disorder.

"Katrina has multiple distinct identities."

"But she still watched Graham brutally killing her father."

"Maybe she did, maybe she didn't. She may have told you that, but she's certainly never told her own family."

"So, why hide the drugs when the police searched your house last week?"

"We *hid* nothing. Her prescription antidepressants were in the kitchen. You know, behind the cereal boxes. The police, quite rightly, didn't see that as any kind of evidence. Katrina is on medication prescribed by professionals."

I recalled the night when I'd tricked Amelia, Tracy and Melissa to go into town for a meal. Told them it would be my treat, and I'd look after Katrina in return. I'd seen where Tracy kept the drugs and I'd overheard her ordering Katrina to come down just before bedtime to get a glass of water and take her pills. They were kept behind the cereal boxes.

Although I didn't want to believe a word Amelia said, I couldn't find a hole in her story. Her version of Katrina's behaviour fitted perfectly. However, there was still one issue they couldn't pin on Katrina, Graham, or anybody else.

"And what about the family trees? The curricula vitae attached to each one? Scribbles, your writing, Tracy's writing, your mother's writing, all over them. Prospective employees, who one day would be worth thousands of pounds from dead relatives. Ryan had come into money after his wife had suddenly died of cancer. The next thing Tracy had moved in and swept him off his feet. And then my aunt Edith. I'd never heard of her, but you had. You'd circled her name in red ink. Marked me nine out of ten as the perfect fit."

Finally, Amelia went on the defensive, her confidence appeared to momentarily dissipate. She sat back, folded her arms and tucked her hands inside each elbow. A sure sign of defence. But she still had an answer. A pre-prepared response. She only had to stay calm, unflustered. And she pulled it off with textbook precision.

"Everything you say is true, Matt. But whilst you're putting two and two together, you're making five."

Again, she leant forward, the confidence oozing back through every pore of her body.

"The whole curriculum vitae and ancestry thing was Graham's idea. Well, alongside his wife, Julia. She is a genealogy wizard. She does it for other people. They pay her for her services. So, when she unearthed that a few individuals might one day inherit a fortune, or indeed already had done, she told Graham. And that's when he approached me, Tracy and Mother."

Although she remained calm and unruffled, her story lacked the same level of credibility as Katrina's illness.

"So, Graham just told you three to go along with his plans? Only consider people with the potential to land you with serious money one day?"

"Don't be flippant, Matt. Yes, I admit, he aroused our interest, but we knew we couldn't simply *pretend* to like someone because they may one day be worth money. When Tracy met Ryan, she knew his wife had died, and she knew he was worth a lot of money. However, she also fell head over heels for him."

"I bet she did," I interrupted with a fake snort of laughter. Amelia ignored me.

"She was heartbroken when he left. Searched for days, weeks, months for his whereabouts. Not once did any of us know Graham had followed him into the woods and—"

Realising I could be in danger of actually believing her version of events as she was so convincing, I stood to leave.

"I've heard enough."

Amelia grabbed my arm, but my dominance in stature gave me brief self-assurance.

"So, why did Ryan run away if he had the ideal wife in Tracy?"

"We don't know, Matt. It's as simple as that. We now believe Graham threatened him, just like he did you. Graham is clever. He knows what we want to hear as a family, and we had no inclination of how he would manipulate you guys behind our backs."

Amelia played the perfect part, whether she was telling the truth or not, it sounded plausible. However, it also somehow reeked of bullshit. She beckoned me to sit down.

"And me?" I asked, perching myself on the edge of the chair. "I saw my CV. Big red circles around my aunt's name. And don't forget, I watched Tracy and your mother work on all the other CVs, constantly on the search for the next fall guy."

"Matt."

She paused as her fingers stretched further and touched mine. Although I flinched, I didn't withdraw.

What the hell are you doing?

"Matt. I fell in love with you the very first moment you stepped out of that elevator on your interview day.

Any knowledge of rich aunts, long-lost parents or a pot of gold stashed away somewhere secret meant nothing to me. It was you who I fell for, and it's you I still love."

Stop this, Matt, stop this!

Instinct made me pull my hands away. All the words and movements threatened to overwhelm me. Still, Amelia continued.

"Mother loves you, Tracy admires you, and Katrina..." she paused, "...well, Katrina worships the ground you walk on."

I stood again, momentarily catching Amelia off guard. A brief expression of sorrow emanated from those wide brown eyes.

"No. This is all wrong. We're finished. It's over. I must—"

She reached for my hand, grabbed it, and attempted to pull me back down.

"Sit down. Please, Matthew."

Like the proverbial rabbit caught in headlights, I did as instructed. My heart raced and my mind did somersaults.

"What is it? We need to put a stop to—"

For the first time, Amelia raised her voice. Not aggressively, but forcefully enough to keep her authority. Her next words hit me like a hammer blow. I immediately felt breathless, my whole life spinning and twisting in another unknown direction.

"Matthew. I think I'm pregnant."

8

It wasn't so much as Amelia announcing her delight that she may be pregnant, it was her following threat which penetrated most.

"You need to come back home," she said. "Otherwise, you'll miss your first, and maybe your only, child growing up."

Suggesting it was tantamount to bribery, and I protested she had no right to intimidate me that way. But Amelia fixed on her cutest smile and told me to at least consider it.

A conversation we'd had at the beginning of our relationship sprang to mind. Fearing I may have dreamt it, I kept my mouth shut. It would only add to the confusion and tension.

An imaginary haze shrouded my journey back to Lisa's house. Unable to see straight, let alone think, I subconsciously went about my business. Catching underground trains, manoeuvring ticket barriers and riding escalators without even thinking. People moaned and cursed as I barged my way past, desperate to be alone, yet aware I had to speak to someone, somebody I could trust.

I'd asked Amelia how certain she could be. She'd said she was two weeks late. I then quizzed her on when it had happened, again having no recollection of events. 'Over Christmas', she'd told me. I racked my brains. Yes, we had slept together over the holiday period. Stopping short of asking if it was definitely mine, I left her outside the café with a solitary hug. Unsure why, it felt like the correct thing to do.

It wasn't until the final approach to Lisa's house that I stood still, my boundless urgency to get inside and lock myself away finally abated. First, I saw the front door open, and, carrying something in his hand, out stepped a guy wearing a polo shirt and chinos. I noticed he wore spectacles too. He looked as though he could be in his mid-forties.

Darting into an alleyway, I watched as he spoke to someone inside, no doubt Lisa. She didn't appear, but I saw an arm reach out and she shook the gentleman's hand. As soon as he left, the front door closed with a thud.

Who the hell is that?

Deciding not to pry as I couldn't bear any further drama, I doubled back and walked towards the main shopping area of town. Earlier, as we'd parted outside the café, Amelia had returned my bank card along with a bag of clothes. At least she'd considered my situation and realised I'd soon be broke as well as having nothing to wear.

Despite my reservations, Amelia had even gone to the trouble of checking my balance, a derisory two hundred pounds. 'Our joint money is in the savings account', she'd added with a sarcastic smile. She also confirmed that the inheritance would arrive within the next two weeks, directly into our account, as I'd instructed the solicitor on the day I'd signed the papers. It would be futile trying to cut Amelia from the windfall. We were a married couple and the solicitor had witnessed me signing the entire amount to our joint account. I'm not sure I would have denied her a fair share anyway.

Three dead people, a murderer recovering from a coma, me temporarily out of work, living in an interim home and my wife potentially pregnant. Without looking, I stepped onto the road. A car horn blasted, and the tyres squealed.

"What the hell are you doing?" the driver protested. He got out of his car and stood several metres along the street.

"Hey, sorry. I'm really sorry. I don't—"

"Just watch where you're going, you idiot. You could have killed us both!"

Bit of an exaggeration.

"Yeah. Sorry," I repeated.

I need a drink.

As I approached the high street, the overwhelming feeling that I wasn't alone struck me once again. My mind rushed back to leaving the tube station at Covent Garden. Someone had definitely followed me. It had slipped my mind, but now, the sensation came rushing back, grabbing me by the throat, threatening to strangle me.

Spinning from side to side, my eyes searched every alleyway, each shopfront. Nothing, although I knew somebody was out there. Call it intuition, or call me plain crazy, but I knew.

With a desire to be amongst people, I hurried my

pace. The prospect of going back to Lisa's house filled me with fear. Should I tell her about Amelia? Maybe not. She'd probably offer me advice, maybe advice I didn't want to hear, but knowing I would act upon it. I had to think for myself and stop involving Lisa.

Spotting a pub on the opposite side of the road, I made a conscious effort to look out for traffic. Once at the door, I took another quick glance over my shoulder. Eventually, I stepped into the relative safety of a traditional London public house.

On first impressions, it appeared quiet, even for late Monday afternoon. This was still London, and pubs always filled up once people left work. They would remain busy for an hour or so before customers inevitably made their weary way home.

At least with the pub being half empty, there were a few tables to choose from. However, once I'd spotted the bar, which took up almost the entire length of the far wall, I knew where I would take up residence for the next couple of hours.

There must have been over twenty stools, equally divided to sit comfortably along the bar. Only half a dozen were occupied, and I soon found a free one at the far end. Far enough away from anyone attempting to make polite conversation, but also close enough to ensure I felt safe. It also enabled me to see the entrance, although I hadn't been expecting anybody.

"Yes, sir?"

I didn't notice the barman approach.

"Oh, hi. Pint of bitter, please."

"Which one?" and he reeled off a choice of four or five beers.

Settling for the only one that had registered, I finally took my place on the bar stool and allowed myself to breathe easier. The beer tasted great, and I soon ordered a second.

"Got a thirst on, sir?" enquired the barman.

"Yeah. Been a bit of a day, if you know what I mean?"

He grinned and nodded his head in acknowledgement. I hoped he didn't push for further details and the inevitable small talk. Fortunately, as he returned with a card machine, the entrance door swung open, allowing the sounds of the streets to seep in. The spring shutter snapped the door back into place and closed off the outside world once more. Two couples entered together. They were dressed smartly, no doubt making their way into the city and stopping off for refreshment before the tube ride. The barman took my payment and sauntered off, acknowledging his latest arrivals.

By the time I'd ordered my third drink, the pub had filled up considerably. Only two or three bar stools remained unoccupied, the latest taken by a man at the far end. I'd noticed him glance over at me once or twice. Possibly solidarity for lone drinkers, but it felt more than that, as though he somehow knew me, or at least recognised me.

I placed him in his late sixties. Although he had a good head of hair, his face was weather-worn and wrinkled, maybe ageing him above his years. Speckles of grey broke his wavy brown hair. He was well-tanned, far too brown following a winter in England. Greying stubble gave him a distinguished look, and I guessed he must have been quite the ladies' man back in the day. Maybe he still was given the lack of a wedding ring on his finger.

Whilst the barman poured my next drink, I discreetly asked whether he'd seen the guy before. He glanced over his shoulder — a little too obvious for my liking — before returning with a shake of the head.

"No, gov. Never seen him. Want me to ask who he is?"

"No!" I replied, resisting the temptation to reach out and grab his arm. "Just thought I recognised him, that's all."

Trying my utmost to remain discreet, I vacantly looked around the pub, allowing myself quick glances towards my fellow solo drinker. And each time I did, his eyes were fixed on me.

Finally, he drank the dregs of his beer and stood to leave.

Carefully pushing his barstool back into position, he offered a nod of his head towards the barman.

And as he turned to leave, he offered the identical gesture to me.

9

DURING THE NEXT couple of weeks, I became a regular at the pub on the high street. I invited Lisa to join me, hoping to cheer her up, but she always declined, citing she wasn't in the mood. Purposefully, I'd avoided mentioning the news of my impending fatherhood, or should I say, *possible* impending fatherhood. Lisa's attitude was changing, her moods deepening and her appearance spiralling. The only time she made an effort would be on the odd occasion she left the house.

"Where are you going?" I'd ask, although I was always met with a similar response.

"Out. Shouldn't be too long."

After a while, I stopped asking Lisa to accompany me to the pub. Instead, one evening, I left her alone in the kitchen. She was preoccupied with her ironing which appeared to temporarily lift her spirits. At least she's making an effort, I thought, and I said my goodbyes. Lisa turned and offered a vacant smile in return.

"You sure everything's okay?" I double-checked, more out of politeness than anything else.

"Huh, huh."

"Listen, if there's anything wrong——"

"There's nothing wrong, Matt. Just enjoy your drink."

Knowing it was futile to ask any further questions, I made for the front door. As I left, I heard Lisa shout after me.

"Just be careful out there."

What does she mean by that?

For a few brief seconds, I contemplated going back, but I knew by her recent behaviour I'd get the same emotionless response. Besides, the pub beckoned and a drink always helped with my mood. I'd been in a state of shock since my last meeting with Amelia, and I'd frequently questioned my sanity. The last thing I needed was to play carer to Lisa too.

The handsome stranger hadn't been in since I'd seen him, at least not to my knowledge. Part of me felt disappointed. He'd intrigued me, maybe intimidated me too. I'm convinced he somehow knew me. However, if he showed up again, I'm not sure if I would have had the courage to approach him, or indeed what I would say.

That evening, I only stayed for two beers. Something bothered me and I hadn't been able to settle since leaving Lisa alone. Even alcohol didn't have its usual calming influence. Lisa's words persisted to play on my mind.

'Just be careful out there.'

As I turned into Lisa's street, I broke out into a jog. Ominous thoughts gathered at the back of my mind.

Something didn't feel right, and when I reached Lisa's house, it didn't *look* right. The front door lay slightly ajar. The tiniest of gaps. Only visible once I stood adjacent, key poised in my hand.

Tentatively, I pushed it open. Glancing over my shoulder, I took a quick look up and down the street before stepping inside. Immediately, I sensed the house lay empty. No sound, just an eerie silence. An overwhelming sensation of abandonment enveloped me. It didn't have the same feeling as other occurrences. 'I'm popping out to the shops', or 'I shouldn't be too long'. Something more untoward, more sinister.

An inner perception led me directly to the kitchen. That had been the last place I'd seen Lisa and instinct told me that's where I might find my answer. The note on the table stood out, like a neon sign drawing my eyes instantly to it.

Maybe I'm inheriting some of Katrina's sixth sense?

The message looked as if someone had scribbled it in lipstick, or eyeliner. It certainly didn't look like a normal writing implement.

Matt

I'm putting the house on the market. I need to move on. I suggest you do the same. Details of my estate agent are on the table. He does rentals too. Please use him to find yourself a flat.

Everything is fine. I just didn't want to make a scene. Please don't contact the police. It's nothing for anybody to be concerned about, and they know where I am.

Oh, and please don't try to contact me. I might be gone for a while, but I'm safe and well.

Lisa x

PS In the meantime, please help yourself to any food or drink in the fridge.

What on earth was going on? How long is 'a while', and where the hell could she have gone to? Don't call the police? Lisa knew me too well, as that would have been my first course of action. She didn't want me to contact her either.

'*I need to move on.*'

The events in the woods must have scarred her for life, much worse than I'd originally expected. When we were checked over at the infamous scene, a member of the medical team had told us it could take a while for the effects to wear off.

'*The shock may take days, weeks or sometimes months to come out.*'

Her mood had changed, and she barely communicated.

And now she would sell the house. I recalled wondering whether Lisa could afford to keep the house on now she'd lost her job. Maybe not, but it was obvious she needed to move on. This was her way of handling everything.

'*I suggest you do the same.*'

Picking up the estate agent's business card, another piece of the jigsaw clicked into place. Of course, the spectacled guy leaving the house in the polo shirt and chinos. He had an iPad in his hand. He'd been measuring up, taking photographs, gathering the property details.

Kicking myself for not staying with her earlier, I walked from room to room, looking for any kind of clue to her intended destination. Even though she told me not to contact her, I needed some kind of reassurance she would be okay.

Her bedroom was the last place I checked. I felt uneasy about going in there as I hadn't been in her room for weeks. Lisa's bed was unmade, the duvet thrown back from first thing that morning. Her head print still dented the centre of the pillow. A few clothes scattered on the floor. Checking her wardrobe and chest of drawers, it at least appeared as though she'd taken enough belongings with her. Dashing back downstairs, her pile of ironing was now removed, but the iron remained plugged into the socket.

She must have waited for me to leave and packed as fast as she could.

'*I didn't want to make a scene.*'

Without her presence, the house seemed cold, desolate. I suddenly felt extremely lonely.

Not only had I relied on Lisa being around as my punchbag, but I'd also regarded her as my only real friend. Somebody to chat to, small talk. The trivial things in life. Despite the downturn in her mood, she had still been there, under the same roof. Whenever I woke in the middle of the night, a regular occurrence, it reassured me she was just along the landing.

Instinctively, I went to the fridge. The contents felt like my life, empty and thoroughly depressing. Half a dozen eggs, an opened carton of milk, a block of half-eaten cheese and some curled-up ham.

'*Help yourself to food in the fridge.*'

Fuck me. It would be difficult to rack up a single meal from those offerings, let alone keep me going for a while.

Lisa had prepared most of our meals. My 'speciality' had been ordering a takeaway, but she'd insisted on cooking most evenings.

At least I found some beers. A four-pack of ice-cold lagers. Grabbing one, I popped the top and made my way to the lounge, still in a daze. Within minutes, I'd returned to the kitchen to open a second.

After pacing the room for several moments, I suddenly felt vulnerable. I'm not sure why I considered myself to be in any kind of danger, but something nagged me that it wasn't far away. My mind played all kinds of tricks on me. Who wouldn't be suffering from a similar fate, given what I'd been through?

Lisa had made her excuses and got away. Who knows where, but maybe I needed to do the same. But how far could I go? With my wife expecting, I had to do the decent thing and hang around. Or did I? Should I take my share of the money and run? But the police had clarified that wasn't even on the agenda, for the time being at least.

I heard my mum's voice imploring me not to be so selfish. What she would have given to see a grandchild being born into this world. Swallowing the lump in my throat, I fetched another beer.

Is that a tear in your eye?

Forcing myself not to drink the last lager, I instead grabbed a shower. The urge to sober up and think things through became paramount.

After ordering food to be delivered, along with four more beers – just in case – I found myself sitting on one of the tired sofas.

'... *please don't try to contact me...* '

Returning to the kitchen, I inevitably helped myself to the last beer in the fridge.

There'll be more there soon.

Grabbing the estate agent's card from the table, I read it over and over, spinning it continually between my finger and thumb. Lisa was right. I had to move on too. Especially if she was putting her house on the market. Knowing London, it wouldn't take long to sell. Returning to the lounge, I propped the card upright on the mantelpiece, a reminder to call the very next morning.

The doorbell made me jump.

It's just your food.

Ensuring the door was securely locked behind the

delivery driver, I again found myself in the kitchen. I must have walked the entire house ten times over since returning from the pub.

Placing the carrier bags on the work surface, my eyes drifted to the note.

Slowly, I spun the sheet of torn-off paper until the writing faced me.

After a while, I could recite it word for word.

So why did I keep reading it?

10

ANOTHER WEEK PASSED BY. Amelia had sent me a text and asked me to go around to the family home the following evening, on Friday, after she'd finished work.

She had sounded upbeat, and I feared the worse. That house scared me.

There must be further developments.

Despite my protestations, I knew I had to see her. I'd asked to meet somewhere neutral, but Amelia had insisted we met at hers. She'd added that the rest of my belongings were there to collect, should I decide not to stay.

Decide not to stay?

To be fair, she added that she didn't expect a rash decision, and told me she respected my initial desire to think things over.

During those seven days, Lisa hadn't responded, despite me sending several messages. I'd neglected to say that I hadn't contacted the estate agent yet, more in hope that the door would burst open, and Lisa would run into my arms full of apology. But as the days passed by, I knew

I had to accept that she wouldn't be returning, however sad it made me feel.

On the Friday night, I took the overground train to Epsom. My heart pounded and my palms perspired as I neared my destination. Once I stepped onto the platform, I had an overwhelming desire to cross the bridge and wait for the next one to take me straight back home. Ever since Amelia's invitation, I knew we wouldn't be alone. No, the whole damn family would have to be involved. However, with the impending news and the necessity to discuss money, I *had* to make the visit. A tiny part of me actually wanted to.

On what should have been a familiar walk from the station to the Reid household, it instead turned out to feel somewhat alien, like a journey I'd made another lifetime ago. Although it had only been two months since I'd left — escaped — the memories were already becoming hazy. Maybe a hidden psyche within had tried to banish it from my thoughts?

Maybe it's all in your head.

As I made the final approach, I noticed the mailbox at the end of the drive. The same mailbox Graham had erected so I could no longer chat with the friendly postman. After a few months of living at the family house, I'd taken to drinking my morning coffee on the bench outside. The original reason had been to escape trivial conversation, but after a while, I'd struck up a cordial repertoire with Bob the postman, talking about anything from football to politics. After a while, he'd probed me about the family and, in return, he'd recollected stories of his own. Bob told me of how the previous postwoman had asked to be moved to a fresh round, such was her dismay at the strangeness of the occupants. They had also accused her of tampering with their post.

Graham didn't like my chats with Bob, and subsequently bought a new mailbox. He erected it as far away from the house as possible whilst remaining on their land. I considered it petty, but I soon realised it was because he didn't trust anyone. He didn't want me to hear anything that might undermine the family.

Allowing myself a wry smile at the reminder of such rash behaviour, I continued to walk along the broken paving slabs, which completed the last steps to the Reid house. And then I heard the swing.

Squeak... squeak...

Like a pendulum on a grandfather clock, with each iteration, the rusty chain would catch against the bracket at the top.

Diverting my route, I took a few steps to my left. The land rose sharply up an embankment on that side of the house. I'd never explored where it eventually led to but had recollections of Amelia telling me it backed onto more houses as the village forever expanded westward.

Katrina squealed before I'd seen her. After knowing her for more than a year, Katrina's behaviour still put me on edge. She still scared me.

"Uncle Matthew!"

She smiled broadly, her yellowing teeth on display, crooked and uneven. On the swing's descent, she stretched her legs as far as they could go, propelling herself higher and higher. But not once did her eyes leave mine.

"Hi, Katrina. How are you?"

As always, she ignored my question.

"Are you coming to live here again?"

Climbing the short mound, I stood next to the swing

and held onto the frame. With the momentum that Katrina had built up, the squeak wasn't so evident.

"No. I've just come to visit Aunt Amelia."

Katrina giggled.

What's so funny?

"I know that, silly."

Of course you do.

"Well, you enjoy yourself," I added, turning to leave. Experience had taught me that Katrina had to be in a certain mood to get any genuine sense from her. That evening wasn't one of those occasions.

As I scuttled down the bank, I heard Katrina giggle once more. I turned and smiled. But the look of cheerfulness had left her face, replaced by a much more sinister expression.

"Be careful," she said, barely moving her mouth, her voice suddenly deeper.

Jesus. What's wrong with her?

"Sorry? What did you say?"

I may have sounded brave and in control, but I could feel a chill run along my spine. Dragging the toes of her shoes along the ground, Katrina abruptly stopped the swing. She stood, effortless, her hands remaining on the chains behind her. The long white dress appeared dirty at the knees, something I hadn't noticed before. And her hair stood up at the back, like someone had administered an electric shock. She was freaking me out and the desire to run almost overwhelmed me.

"They know."

What the hell?

"Who, Katrina? Who knows what?"

Like the flick of a switch, her voice returned to normal. Well, normal for Katrina. Her everyday tone resembled a small child, often accompanied by laughter or a giggle.

"They do, silly."

And as if being released from a trance, Katrina ran. She swooped past me, her dress flowing in the wind. Giggling and squealing, she ran for the woods, not once stopping to look behind.

A chill swept over me, as if Katrina hadn't run around me, but straight through me. I watched my hands shaking.

"Matthew!"

Hearing my name made me flinch. I was a nervous wreck.

"Matthew." The call came again. Recognising my wife's voice, I desperately tried to compose myself. Stepping around the corner, I noticed her standing on the doorstep, arms folded, a look of concern on her face.

"Ah, there you are. We saw you coming up the footpath five minutes ago. Thought you'd got lost."

Amelia laughed, her attempts to keep the opening encounter as light-hearted as possible.

We! Did she just say we?

"Just saying hello to Katrina. That's all."

As soon as I stepped inside the house, the memories came rushing back, the wide staircase leading directly to the dark forbidding landing above. That part of the building had always given me the creeps. Like something from a horror film. Dark shadows and an elongated walkway led to the far side of the house. Katrina's room. Tracy's room. Melissa's room. And the room where they had held me against my will.

"Matthew! You're home!"

Home? Don't fucking kid yourself.

Melissa beamed. Age defied her. I'd always thought as

much. Despite approaching seventy years of age, Melissa could quite easily have passed as somebody twenty years her junior. Her jet black hair — Amelia had certainly inherited that gene — now complete with greying streaks, but she carried it perfectly. And just like her youngest daughter, Melissa had the darkest brown eyes. I'd often wondered what she'd looked like forty or fifty years ago. Quite the catch for any young man I'd always assumed.

"Hi, Melissa. Please don't think I'm staying. I'm just here to—"

Tracy appeared from the lounge doorway. Her face was the least welcoming, full of disdain and hostility.

"Just here to what exactly, Matthew?"

The smile disappeared from Melissa's face too. Had she really expected me to walk back in with open arms?

Finally, Amelia reappeared from outside. What had she been doing?

"Come on, you two," she addressed both her sister and Mother. "I said we are at an early stage. Matt is here this evening to talk to me and to fetch some clothes. We have to give ourselves time."

It felt like walking onto a stage in a pre-rehearsed play. Amelia sounded so wooden, without the slightest intonation in her voice.

"But you're pregnant, darling." Melissa looked crestfallen. She turned back to me, doing her utmost to force a smile. "Surely you'll want to be around your child, Matthew?"

"Mother. Enough. Now let us talk in private. Please."

I'd never known Amelia to be so assertive where her mother had been concerned. Maybe she had been right. Now the domineering influence of Graham was no longer on the scene, could she be more relaxed, more decisive?

Tracy pushed past me and joined Melissa in the kitchen. She quietly closed the door behind her. I had visions of the pair of them on the other side, their ears pressed to the wall.

And then a banging sound. From overhead. Like something being dropped.

I glared at the ceiling and then back at Amelia. She looked momentarily unsettled, a glitch in the well-rehearsed play.

"What was that?" I asked, looking back up at the ceiling.

"Katrina? Who knows? This house carries many sounds. As you well know, Matt."

Amelia recomposed herself. She walked to the lounge, silently beckoning me to follow. I couldn't help but take one last look up the staircase and towards *that* landing, all the while, ensuring I kept up with Amelia's every step.

11

"So, you're definitely pregnant, then?"

I'd waited until Amelia had closed the door with an audible 'click'. At least it put some distance between us and the prying family beyond. However, it wouldn't have surprised me had they bugged the room, or Amelia somehow recorded our conversation for late evening entertainment.

"Yes," she replied, in a surprisingly unemotional manner. She sat on the chair in the corner. Graham's favourite chair. I recalled how he would play with Katrina's hair. It would be at the end of another long and painful evening where we sat around making polite, yet incredibly boring, conversation. He'd stroke her hair, touch her neck, and massage her shoulders before his hands wandered lower. I shuddered at the thought.

"You okay, Matt?"

"Oh, yeah. Good thanks. I thought you might be expecting. You seemed convinced when we met in the café."

We discussed due dates — mid-September — as well as agreeing to meet up on a semi-regular basis until the child was born. Although I offered no resistance, it came as a surprise when Amelia suggested we meet in the café near her work instead of her house. That suited me fine.

Following the arrangements, she told me the money from my aunt's inheritance had been paid into our joint account. She had already taken the liberty of arranging half to go into mine which I could expect within three working days.

A few moments of awkward silence ensued. I just wanted to leave and try to take it all in, and then Amelia addressed the elephant in the room.

"Have you given it any more thought yet? You know, if, or when, you might return home."

I'd expected it from Melissa, but not from Amelia. It caught me unawares, and I mumbled a reply.

"To be honest, I'm not sure what I'm going to do yet."

Her reserved expression gave way to something more animated. I could see her struggle to control her emotions.

"What's that supposed to mean?"

Stroking the palms of my hands along the chair arms, exasperating her further, I attempted to keep my reply reflective rather than negative.

"Well, it's a lot to take in. And given everything that happened here…" I glanced at the ceiling. "…I had promised myself a fresh start. You know, new job, new life. The announcement of a baby has knocked me sideways, to be honest."

Amelia would have known that I'd received my redundancy letter in the post from Mike. She, or more likely, Tracy, had probably typed the bloody thing herself. I'd be allowed around three months tax-free pay. Apparently, it was a little higher than the legal requirement, but it had been a further kick in the balls, especially given that I'd been the innocent party.

But the prospect of becoming a father had scuppered any initial plan to move on with my life. I'd genuinely had some fresh ideas, and had been considering moving abroad. However, I now had additional responsibilities. I'd never given parenthood much thought, and at thirty-eight, recognised my time to become a dad had probably passed. Even though people were having children later in life, I'd always considered it a younger person's duty. Maybe late twenties, early thirties. However, once I found myself in that situation, I had to admit to a tinge of excitement, along with dreaded trepidation.

"Are you saying you were thinking of moving away? Leave the area altogether?"

Her attitude shifted with each sentence. I'd never seen Amelia act like that before. She liked to be in control but obviously hadn't been expecting my response. Knowing I had to keep a balance between trying to appease her and getting what I wanted, I did my best to remain non-committal.

"Yes, that's what I originally thought. Well, until the police told me I have to hang around until the trial is over. But now, well now you're pregnant, now I'm going to be a father, I obviously want to be around."

A glimmer of a smile from Amelia.

"But that doesn't mean moving back here. I honestly couldn't do that after what has happened."

"How about we go after that little cottage again? It's back on the market and now the money—"

"No, Amelia, no." I stood and paced the room before

turning back to face her. "It's all too much right now. I'm just thinking of the baby."

It was as though she'd stopped listening. She'd heard 'I obviously want to be around' and that was enough to pacify her, for the time being, at least. Something to work on. A flicker of hope that somehow she'd perceived as, 'yes, one day, I'll be back'.

"Maybe not *that* cottage, then. I guess it is quite small. You never know, once we've had one, we'll probably want to adopt a baby sister or brother."

Adopt?

Amelia stared out of the window as she spoke, almost as if she'd forgotten I was there. Sitting back down in the chair, I became mesmerised by her excitement and reverie. Amelia continued to talk, gibberish about swings in the garden, birthday parties, Halloween and family Christmases.

When she finally returned from her trancelike state, she gazed towards me, smiling, convinced that I'd agreed with her every word. Had I?

What just happened?

The only response I could offer was to nod my head. But I didn't agree to anything. If I'd uttered a single word of acceptance, she'd have taken it as the gospel that I'd be going back. However, I realised I hadn't bluntly refused. Not only would it destroy her, but it would also be detrimental to my own interests. I wanted to keep her sweet, on my side, until the baby came along. I still couldn't quite believe it.

As soon as Amelia opened the living room door, the kitchen door simultaneously sprang open. I'd half expected Melissa to fall to the floor, such was her haste to greet us.

"Everything okay?" she asked, as casually as she could muster.

"Yep, all good. Wasn't it, Matt?"

"Huh, huh."

Melissa's smile dissipated. Tracy appeared from the kitchen too. She'd obviously interpreted my response with all the plaudits it deserved. Her scowl told me all I needed to know.

"Have you got my bag of clothes and stuff, Amelia? I should get going."

"Sure. I'll fetch them."

She remained full of energy and incredibly upbeat. We watched her bound upstairs. Once out of earshot, Melissa took a step closer.

"If you want to be part of your child growing up, you'll think long and hard about what your wife wants."

Just as I opened my mouth to reply, Amelia reappeared at the top of the stairs.

"Got it!" she squealed, like an excited school child, and descended the stairs, sliding an oversized sports bag behind her. Melissa's expression changed like a switch.

"Well done, darling. I'm sure Matthew will take that from you." She nudged me on the arm. "Go and help your wife, Matthew."

Instead of Amelia's broad smile, she was in floods of tears.

I'd been shouting at Amelia, explaining it was all over and I would marry Lisa instead. Melissa joined us, desperate for me to listen to her daughter's side, that everything would be okay if only I returned home. But the more I said no, the angrier she became.

By the time I found myself at the front door, Tracy too had joined the confrontation. Amelia attempted to reconcile with me. Her eyes repeatedly focusing on mine, begging me, pleading with me. Full of tears, full of sadness. She came across as genuine, which made leaving all the harder.

Once outside, Melissa and Tracy didn't hold back, despite the protestations from Amelia.

"You'll regret this for the rest of your life!" shouted Tracy.

I could detect sheer hatred emanating from each. Melissa's face twisted, disguising all the beauty I'd witnessed when I'd first arrived. Her eyes narrowed, pupils glaring straight through me. The ultimate 'if looks could kill' stare.

In an attempt to raise my voice above their shouting, I addressed Amelia. She stood in the background, appearing lost and crestfallen.

"I'll be in touch," I said. "We'll work it out. Don't worry. And thanks for these." I held the holdall full of clean clothes aloft. Amelia attempted a smile, whilst her hands lay spreadeagled across her stomach. She was trying everything she could to riddle me with guilt. If it hadn't been for her crazy sister and deluded mother, I may have capitulated under pressure. But I had to get away. To rebuild my life. Still, Melissa wasn't finished.

"Matthew!"

Turning again, I walked backwards, desperate to increase the distance between myself and them.

Melissa's voice changed. Like the flick of a switch, the stream of vitriol abated, as if that particular soul had left her body. She began to somehow float towards me, gliding over the broken footpath, gaining on me with ease.

In return, it felt as if I was walking in treacle, my feet dragging, my speed restricted. Out of the corner of my eye, I saw something flash. The woods were to my right. And there, on the edge of the dense foreboding tree line, stood Katrina. Her white dress fluttered in the wind, her hair swishing and swaying. She smiled as she slowly outstretched her arms, beckoning me forward.

What's happening to me?

And as I became acutely aware that Melissa was gaining on

me, Katrina appeared to float too, her feet leaving the pine-clad ground beneath.

Turning once more, as quickly as I dared, I tried to focus on the road ahead. The line of houses within reach. Safety.

Melissa whispered. So quiet, it amazed me I could hear her at all. But her words sounded crystal clear, as if she stood only a step away.

"You need to come home, Matthew. It's where you belong."

No... no.

"We'll find you, Matthew. We always do."

Suddenly, Katrina was by my side.

How the...

She smiled and reached out for my hand. Although I tried to resist, I couldn't help but lift my own to hers. Her fingers felt icy cold as they intertwined with mine.

"Come home, Matthew," she whispered.

Laughter from somewhere behind. Tracy.

"We're your family. You belong with us."

Snatching my hand away, I ran, immediately stumbling and losing my feet.

More laughter. Tracy, Melissa, Katrina.

Resisting the temptation to bend over and throw up, I stood and ran, but I made no headway. The harder I ran, the more the ground moved backwards, like a giant treadmill beneath me.

Again, the laughter. Tracy, Melissa, Katrina. And then somebody else, but not Amelia.

I spun around. Despite my hallucinations, I had somehow put some distance between myself and the house. My three antagonists stood shoulder to shoulder at the edge of the pathway, like an invisible boundary halted them from following any further. Looking beyond them, I hoped to see Amelia. But she'd left the doorway, just an open dark abyss leading into the hallway, the landing.

'This house carries many sounds. As you well know, Matt'.

My eyes followed the line of the staircase within, my attention drawn by some imaginary force inside.

And there, at the window at the top of the turret, stood a figure. A darkened silhouette. Broad-shouldered, powerful, intimidating.

And he laughed. Audible, even from that distance. A deep, booming, and repulsive laugh.

12

WAKING WITH A START, drenched in sweat, I threw the duvet off me, allowing my whole body to breathe. Clambering to the window, I attempted to drag the bottom frame upwards. It complained, gripping tight against the upper.

Just like the sash windows at the Reids' house.

Instinctively, I thought of Lisa, and if the noise might wake her, before remembering I was in the house alone. I needed air. The nightmare left me feeling incredibly uneasy and queasy, as if I may be physically sick. The window finally gave way, and I hung my head outside. Studying the street below, I sucked in lungful's of damp air. It felt so good, momentarily revitalising me.

Reluctantly, I returned to bed. It was just after seven o'clock, but, as usual, I had no specific plans.

The sheets were moist and cool, so I instead lay on top of the covers. I'd left the window open, despite the chill pouring inside. Small droplets of moisture circulated the room, as if a fog had let itself in before settling over my body.

With my breathing returning to normal, I tried to think about what could have triggered the dream. As if I needed to ask myself.

Attempting to push the nightmare aside, I stared at the ceiling and contemplated what had *actually* happened once I left the Reids' house the previous day. Melissa's threat wasn't far from my thoughts.

'If you want to be part of your child growing up, you'll think long and hard about what your wife wants'.

Surely she wasn't threatening me? Did she not realise that the law of the land would be on my side? But that family didn't go by the law, they had their own rules. Could she honestly stop me from seeing my child? The look on Tracy's face had indicated they would do all they could if I didn't conform to Amelia's wishes.

And when I had left the house, I genuinely saw something flash in the distance, not just in my dream. But trying to distinguish reality from fantasy had become a challenge.

The woods to my right. There, on the edge of the dense, forbidding trees, stood Katrina. Her white dress fluttered in the wind, her hair swishing and swaying. She smiled as she slowly outstretched her arms, beckoning me forward.

The front door had clicked shut behind me. Amelia and her mother disappeared back indoors. I imagined the conversation. Melissa and Tracy grilling Amelia about what had been said. Would they be planning their next move? Would they be able to contact Graham and ask his opinion? Or had Amelia been genuine, and he was now out of their plans and no longer part of their family? She had remained upbeat, trying to convince herself all would be okay once the child came along. Could she be right? If it weren't for the others, would I go back?

Get a grip.

"Uncle Matthew."

Shit.

Katrina had stood right by my side. How long had I been standing there?

"Blimey, Katrina. You almost gave me a heart attack."

Katrina giggled.

"You can't have a heart attack, silly."

She walked away, back towards the woods. Despite everything screaming inside and telling me not to, something compelled me to follow her.

What the hell are you doing?

With a glance towards the house, I convinced myself I wasn't being watched. I walked after Katrina. Struggling to keep up, I had to jog every few steps. How could she move so quickly?

Katrina appeared to float, her feet leaving the pine-clad ground beneath…

Once on the periphery of the dense trees, she stopped and turned.

"Are you coming back home, Uncle Matthew?"

Gathering my breath, I needed to keep the conversation light.

"I'm not sure yet. Would you like me to?"

She giggled.

Why can't you just answer one of my questions?

"Aunty Amelia wants you to."

"Does she? Has she said so?"

Katrina walked along the footpath, the trail that meandered the entire woods, eventually reaching the steep hill which led to the village on the far side. And if you veered off towards the end of the path, it would lead you to where Ryan's body had been exhumed and Lee Blackmore had reached his pitiful end. I hadn't been back since. Neither had I contemplated going anywhere near it. But again, something dragged me forward.

She sang. One of her tuneless numbers. I'm sure she made them up, words from a variety of songs she'd heard and jumbled them all together.

'Katrina has multiple distinct identities.'

Could she have been like that since birth, as Amelia suggested, or had witnessing her father struck dead with a shovel tipped her over the edge? The family dismissed the latter – of course they did – citing they never even knew that had happened. Katrina was on regular medication, confirmed by the police. But what exactly is *regular* medication? They made it sound so normal, but Katrina was far from normal. Still, she intrigued me, and I had a particular fondness for her.

Maybe you do have parental intuition, Matt.

"What are you smiling at, Uncle Matthew? You look silly."

Unaware I had been smiling, I gawked awkwardly at Katrina.

"Nothing. Just happy to be walking with you. Listening to you sing."

She giggled, this time placing her hand over her mouth.

We walked deep into the woods, not once deviating from the footpath. Although I didn't know it as well as Katrina, I still felt comfortable with my surroundings, recognising fallen trees, larger roots strewn across the path and the sounds of rustling leaves so high above. It surprised me I didn't feel afraid. I'd never ventured so far into the woods before and not felt at least a tinge of anxiety. Normally, I'd be looking over my shoulder, every snap of a twig or flap of a bird's wing would make me jump from my skin. But not that time. I was in control, merrily following my leader.

My leader?

My apprehension hadn't abated because of the familiarity of my surroundings. No, it was because of who I was with. Katrina. She owned the trees. This was her domain. The Queen of the Woods.

Shit. Who is she?

My mind had become so detached in thought that I hadn't realised we'd turned off the main footpath. Only when I tripped on some overgrown brambles, did I become conscious of where we were heading.

"Where are we going, Katrina? I don't think we should be here."

Would the area still be cordoned off? Police tape surrounding the space where they had both met their demise?

Katrina didn't reply. She just kept walking. Effortlessly, through thick brambles, upturned tree roots and low-hanging branches. Struggling to keep up, I scrambled after her, losing ground with every step.

And then she stopped. I knew exactly where we were. The very spot where Lisa and I had sat waiting for the police to arrive, a few feet from the unmarked grave.

Blue and white tape remained at the scene, but it flapped unattached in the breeze, no longer forming a barrier. The grave had been exhumed and refilled, a couple of fresh weeds breaking through the recently dug earth.

Once I caught up, I realised Katrina wasn't interested in where she used to come and speak to her father. Instead, she was on her hands and knees, lifting two large rocks.

"What you looking for, Katrina?"

Her head spun, defying the normal elasticity of human neck muscles. At one point, I thought her head would turn a hundred and eighty degrees. She smiled. That hideous smile where all of her teeth appeared at once. Yellowing, crooked and uneven.

Yet again, she didn't reply. Instead, she returned to the task at hand. Eventually, she stood, holding something aloft in her right hand.

"That's my phone!" I exclaimed, a little too brashly. I immediately regretted snapping.

Katrina stared at me. She hated anybody shouting, especially *at* her. I thought she might run.

"It's my phone, Uncle Matthew. I found it."

Standing perfectly still, realising one step further could make her dart off, I smiled, trying to keep things calm.

"I think I must have dropped it there. When the police——"

"Mother said whatever you find belongs to you. I found it, and now it's my phone."

Holy shit.

"Does Mother know you've got it?"

She giggled.

"Of course not, silly. I'm not allowed to have a phone."

"Why is that, Katrina?"

She said nothing.

"Can I have a look, please?"

Gingerly, she handed me the mobile. I pressed the power button, but it was dead. I passed it back to her.

"I'll tell you what. If I can find the charger, why don't you keep it?"

Her eyes lit up. You'd have thought I'd just promised her a never-ending supply of chocolate.

"I already have the charger. You left it in Aunty Amelia's bedroom, silly."

Then why haven't you charged it?

"But it would have to be our secret. If Mother found out, she would take it off you."

Katrina nodded.

"Do you have anywhere in your bedroom you can hide it, keep it safe without it being found by anybody else?"

She thought, desperate to hang on to the best gift she'd ever received. Suddenly, she nodded her head, exaggerating the response.

"Yes! Under the floorboards. It's where I keep my secret diary."

Immediately, she knew she'd said too much. The look of excitement dissipated. I had to keep her sweet.

"Well, why don't you keep your new phone with your secret diary? We can be mobile phone pals. I can send you a text with my number on it. You do know how to use it, don't you?"

Once more, her face lit up. The prospect of being 'mobile phone pals' had obviously struck a nerve.

"Of course I do, silly. I set up Grandmother's phone all by myself. She can't use them at all."

Having no idea whether we would ever make contact, it felt good to have a secret that the rest of the family knew nothing about.

13

"Wow. You look like crap. Whatever's wrong?"

'Crap' was as close to actual swearing as I could ever recall Amelia using. More importantly, it hadn't gone unnoticed that her primary concern had been for my health. She looked genuinely worried. My head throbbed and an icy trickle of sweat ran along my spine. Maybe I was coming down with something?

We were in the café, three weeks after she had confirmed her news. The first of our pre-arranged meetings to keep in touch throughout the pregnancy. The neutral ground suited me, and I held a genuine interest in Amelia's gestation period. Who wouldn't?

"Nothing. Just been feeling a little under the weather recently. Lack of sleep and all that."

It wasn't far from the truth. My sleep had become more erratic, the prospect of somehow becoming a father finally hitting home, but that wasn't the crux of it.

"Isn't it comfortable at Lisa's place, then?"

Although the content of her retort could have been construed as sarcastic, Amelia no longer appeared to hold the same vitriol towards me living there. She wouldn't have known Lisa had gone away, and I hadn't mentioned the house being on the market. I put her mind at ease, anyway.

"Actually, if you must know, Lisa has put her house up for sale. She's gone to stay with friends, I guess, until it's sold. You'll be pleased to hear that I'm no longer with that *slapper*, as you so eloquently called her before."

Amelia opened her mouth to respond, but I hadn't quite finished.

"I'm going to search for a flat of my own. I just needed the money to come through and decide where to go next. Happy now?"

Although difficult to read her expression, it appeared to contain a mixture of relief and sorrow.

"You know you're more than welcome to——"

"We've been through this, Amelia. I'm not ready for that yet. I need my space. For a while."

The prospect of me not completely dismissing moving back seemed to appease Amelia. She looked as though she was clinging to the word 'yet' and offered a brief smile, a ray of hope all was not lost. I didn't correct her. Her eyes remained fixed on mine, reading my thoughts. After a few moments, she changed the subject, my appearance obviously still concerning her.

"You sure you're okay, Matt? You really look ill. In fact, we all thought you did when you came around the other week. You left in such a hurry, as if…"

She left the sentence hanging. There was nothing I wanted to add, even though she waited for me to fill in the blanks. Once she realised I would not reply, she instead reached out and took both of my hands in hers.

Unsure why, I made no effort to remove them. It felt good, maybe too good.

We remained silent for a few brief moments, both lost in our own worlds, but no doubt holding similar thoughts. What might have been, and how had it all gone so wrong? Eventually, I removed my hands and sipped my coffee, desperately trying to think of something to say.

"When does it start to show?" I asked, nodding towards her stomach. Amelia laughed. She always found my naivety on such matters a sweet and innocent distraction.

"Between sixteen and twenty weeks according to Tracy."

Bloody Tracy again.

"Although it can be a little later until the bump is very noticeable."

She wore a baggy sweatshirt. She'd worn the same item when I'd been around to the house weeks earlier. It was impossible to tell if she'd grown at all.

"Okay."

More silence ensued, although it soon became apparent that Amelia had something on her mind.

"What is it? You can tell me."

Amelia adjusted herself on the seat and bought herself some time by taking a few sips of coffee.

"The thing is, Matt, you've seen our house. Well, your house too, if you come back."

"Go on," I replied, ignoring the invitation but dreading where the conversation may be heading. My mind flashed back to the time she had used our joint money to buy her mother a new cooker and Graham a new car. They had been Christmas presents from both of us as a way of saying 'thank you' for all their help. Oh, the irony.

"The house is damp, as you well know."

I knew it.

"Apart from the kitchen and living room. It's impossible to keep the place warm." She looked me in the eye whilst resting her hands on her stomach. "Do you want your child being raised in such an environment?"

She was good, clever, and manipulative.

"There's no way you're having all the money. I can't survive with—"

Amelia reached and grabbed my hand for a second time.

"I'm not asking for *all* the money, silly. I'm just saying it's not a place to bring up a baby in its present condition."

"So, why don't you buy a flat with your share?"

Realising how stupid the question was, I raised a hand in acknowledgement. Prising her away from Melissa and Tracy was akin to somebody taking her child away.

"Sorry. So, how much are you talking about?"

Amelia produced a piece of paper from her handbag. I pulled at the neckline of my T-shirt, stretching it out of shape. My fingers felt damp and cold against my skin.

She carefully unfolded the note before spinning it around on the table and explaining her calculations. After a few moments, I blanked out the reasonings and my eyes flicked to the figure circled at the foot of the page.

"Is that it?" I asked, pointing.

She glanced over my shoulder, as if somebody might be interested in our conversation.

"Are you being facetious? I'm only thinking of our baby. It's not for me, it's not for Mother and it's certainly nothing to do with Graham."

"Calm down, will you? I just need to make sure that is the definite figure." I tapped on the page.

The final sum wasn't nearly as bad as I'd been expecting, and I could see things from her point of view. Deep down, I knew she was right. The house was cold and damp, no place to raise a child, *my* child. If I gave her the money, and she agreed that would be the final amount, then it would leave me enough to move on with my own life, if that's what I really wanted. It would cover the cost of a small flat or at least a large deposit on a more expensive one. I would have to eventually get a job, anyway.

Taking out my phone, I logged onto online banking. Completing the security checks, I transferred the agreed amount to her individual account.

Once I finished, I could see a faint trace of a smile etched on her face. It left me feeling a little nauseous. Surely she planned to use the money for the intended purpose?

"I do hope you'll keep all the receipts, darling?"

Before she could respond, my phone rang.

"Not going to answer that?" Amelia enquired, ignoring my sarcastic remark and appearing strangely intrigued at who might call me.

Holding my phone at an angle, I glanced at the caller ID. DCI Small.

"It can wait," I said, placing the device onto the table as soon as it stopped ringing.

We sat in silence for a few more minutes. I found the situation uncomfortable again, and I needed some fresh air.

"I'm just popping to the gents," I announced, standing rather abruptly. "Okay if I meet you outside?"

"Sure, Matt. I need the ladies, too." Amelia appeared equally happy that I was calling an end to the meeting. "And I need to get back to work."

Pushing my chair underneath the table, I avoided the possible underhanded dig that she had a job. The redundancy still irritated me.

Once outside, the air wasn't as fresh as I'd hoped. We had reached the onset of springtime, and the heat of the city was rising. Momentarily, I struggled to catch my breath. Propping myself against the wall, I waited impatiently for Amelia.

Hurry up, goddamn it.

Finally, the door opened. I couldn't be sure, but Amelia appeared to have been crying. Her eyes were slightly red around the rims, and she bowed her head before retrieving a pair of sunglasses from her handbag. Once she looked back up, I couldn't help but admire her beauty. Just seeing her wearing those wide-rimmed glasses provoked many pleasurable memories. She could look like a model, in my eyes at least, and as the sun caught her skin, it sent me back to our honeymoon in Corfu. The endless days around the pool, the evenings strolling around the marina, choosing which restaurant to eat in before returning to our apartment and spending each night in new marital bliss.

"You forgot this," she said, handing me my phone whilst snapping me back to the present.

"Oh, shit. Thanks. Not sure what's wrong with—"

"Just be careful what you're doing, Matt."

What's that supposed to mean?

She stood on tiptoe and kissed my cheek. Her lips felt warm against my cool, damp skin.

With my back still propped against the wall, I watched as Amelia strolled back towards her office. Convinced she wouldn't be able to resist taking one last look around, I felt disappointed when she turned the corner and disappeared out of sight.

Without thinking, I glanced at my mobile screen. A second missed call.

But this time, it wasn't DCI Small.

Julia had tried to contact me.

Inadvertently, my eyes drifted back along the street and retraced Amelia's footsteps. I'd left my phone on the table when I'd visited the gents.

Had she seen who had called me?

'Just be careful what you're doing, Matt.'

14

ANDY COLEMAN WAS YOUNGER than I'd first thought. When I'd seen him leave Lisa's house, I'd put him in his mid-fifties, but once up close, I realised he must have been around ten years younger. He didn't have his spectacles on, although he wore a very similar polo shirt and chinos.

"Yes, sir?" he asked, standing, as I approached him. A nameplate with the title, 'Sales Adviser', sat at the front of his desk.

"Matt Walker. We spoke on the phone earlier."

"Ah, yes. Thanks for coming in, Mr Walker."

"Matt, please."

A week or so before, after I'd left Amelia at the café, I visited the Apple store in Covent Garden and treated myself to a new MacBook. I'd been unable to operate without a computer. They were as important to me as a phone, and it felt as though I'd lost a limb without either device. Once I returned to Lisa's house and set it up, I noticed the estate agent's business card propped up on the mantelpiece. As the latest updates downloaded on the laptop, I gave Andy a call. He sounded especially pleased to speak to me. Maybe business was slow?

Later that same day, I'd had a visit from DCI Small and DS Paine. I'd completely forgotten about his missed call. It would have been early evening, maybe around six thirty.

Opening the door just enough to see into the outside world, I first noticed DS Tom Paine. He offered me a brief smile, almost by way of an apology for being there. And if DS Paine was present, I knew who else would be. Pushing the door a little wider, DCI Small came into view. He didn't smile. His face was pensive, solemn.

It transpired they had dropped by for two reasons. First, to give me a gentle reminder to return their calls whenever they contacted me — I was 'still a key part of their investigation' — and second, to inform me when Graham's trial would take place if I wished to attend the court case. Nothing could be further down the list of places I'd want to be. At least he confirmed I didn't need to give evidence

"Just let me know the outcome," I politely asked as they left.

Following introductions, Andy completed an online form, tapped a few more keys, and my registration was complete. He clicked the mouse a few more times, before looking up at the girl sitting at a desk behind us. I'd somehow missed her on the way in. Maybe she hadn't been there, or more likely, my mind had been elsewhere. I put her in her early twenties. Fresh and keen.

"I'll do it," she said, sarcastically, before joining us and taking over Andy's mouse actions. She then stomped to the printer and returned with two A4 sheets. She rolled her eyes behind Andy's head before returning to her desk.

"Thanks, Katie," he said, without looking up.

Andy then spun both pieces of paper on the desk between us to face me.

Shit. Is that the best you've got?

Trying not to appear too downhearted, I attempted to sound upbeat. Both properties were local to Ealing. Maybe, subconsciously, I'd already decided I wanted somewhere fresh. Away from Epsom, away from Lisa's house too. Maybe Lisa would want that as well?

"Yeah, they look okay."

Andy laughed.

"I can tell you've not fallen in love at first sight, Matt. Tell you what. Why don't you take a look at them, see what you think, and then we can take it from there?"

Although unconventional, I found myself warming to Andy Coleman. His down-to-earth approach suited me fine. None of the usual bullshit about being in a highly desirable area or the neighbours are all fantastic, just a 'do you like it or not' kind of attitude.

Two days later, I viewed both flats. I didn't stay at either above five minutes.

The first one left me feeling incredibly disheartened; a tiny studio apartment, one room containing a living room, kitchen and bedroom as an all-in-one open-plan affair. The only interior door led to a tiny bathroom. Fortunately, the second flat was at least a little larger. It came at a higher price, but to have a separate bedroom and kitchen made it feel semi-homely. However, it still wasn't for me.

As I returned to the agent's office, a wave of fear rose

over me. What would I do? The thought of living with Amelia, our new baby and *that* family didn't warrant thinking about. But could I live with Amelia elsewhere? After viewing the two flats, I realised I couldn't live in a place barely big enough to fit two people, so what would I do? Andy's enthusiastic smile at least gave me a glimmer of hope.

"No good?" he asked. I'd hardly stepped inside the door when he greeted me from halfway across the office. With his hand placed in the middle of my back, he guided me to his desk. I glanced at the girl, Katie. As before, she rolled her eyes.

"They're a bit small, Andy. Nice, but a bit——"

"Yeah, yeah," he interrupted, without looking up from his computer.

A few moments later, he spun his monitor around to face me. He tapped the glass with the tip of his pen. The girl coughed behind me.

"What about this one?"

The apartment on his screen looked like an entirely different proposition than the two I'd just viewed. Bright and clutter-free. A large open-plan living kitchen area, two bedrooms — one double with en suite, the other a single but big enough for a home office — and a generous bathroom complete with both shower and bath.

"I can't afford that," I said, unable to take my eyes off the screen.

"Hundred pounds a month more expensive than the second one you've just viewed."

Andy's confidence visibly grew. He sat back in his chair, his monitor still pointing towards me.

"How is that possible? It looks ten times better."

He leant forward again. He had me hooked and was on a roll.

"It is ten times better. Just come on the market. The landlord wants it filled, so he's offering a fantastic price. You know what, Matt?"

He tapped the monitor with his pen again.

"I'll not let anybody else see this until you've had a chance. I can get you in this afternoon at four o'clock."

I couldn't help but smile at his bullish flamboyance. I was his puppet, and he was pulling all the strings.

"Where is it?"

"Earl's Court. Our other branch took it on, but I'll tell them I've got somebody lined up. Great location. Right near the tube, shops, cafés, and trendy restaurants. You'll love it."

Andy had been right. I did love it. As soon as I stepped out of Earl's Court tube station and past the old Police Box — a replica from the British TV series, *Doctor Who* — I felt I could be happy there, *happier*, at least.

Didn't you want a fresh start?

The flat was a ten-minute walk from the station. Not only did I find the area exactly as Andy had described, but it would also give me the anonymity I desired. I'd never been there before, and nobody would need to know where I lived. It gave me an opportunity to move on, but still maintain the option of commuting when I looked for a job. It would also be just as easy to meet Amelia in the city. Hell, I'd even have two bedrooms. Maybe I could set up the smaller one as a nursery and have my son or daughter come and stay with me.

Aren't you getting ahead of yourself?

The apartment turned out to be even better than the photographs had suggested. As I looked out of the large bay window in the living room, I called Andy. He said he'd get Katie to draw up all the paperwork and would let me know when I should visit the office to sign along the dotted line. At the end of the call, he said I could move within a couple of weeks, if I so desired. "Not worth putting off the next chapter of your life, is it, Matt?"

That evening, on my brand new laptop, I ordered new mattresses for the supplied bed frames, a fridge freezer, a washing machine plus new kitchen appliances. I'd arranged for everything to arrive at the new place either on the following Saturday or within a day or two of moving in. It felt good to be active. It also felt good to have money in my account, although I knew it wouldn't last forever.

Finally, I sat down with a beer. However, guilt washed over me in an instant. Lisa had left her property because of the situation I'd put her in, and here I was, ordering stuff over the internet like some spoilt brat.

Picking up my phone, I sent another text.

Hi Lisa
    Just to let you know, I've found a flat. I move in two weeks, so you can come home if it's bothering you me being here.
    Please let me know you're okay.
    Take care.
    Love, Matt xx

After a couple more beers, I relaxed. I revisited the agent's website and checked the photographs and details of the flat at least a dozen more times.

Finally, with a glimmer of hope, my spirits temporarily lifted.

15

_____

IT WOULD BE another week when I finally received a reply from Lisa.

I'm okay. Staying at Mum's house. Is everything alright there? Thinking of you. L x

It felt so reassuring to eventually hear from her, and an immense relief that she was okay. I replied with a couple of kisses and immediately wished I could see her in person.

And since accepting the apartment, Julia had tried to call me too. However, she went cold again after I'd left a message. Maybe I needed to visit her at home, check she was okay?

Glancing at the clock, I saw it was four thirty in the afternoon and decided I desired a drink. It had become a habit. But I knew three days later I'd be moving into my new flat. It would banish the temptation of my local pub. I'd start afresh, settle in for a week or two and then get my curriculum vitae updated and circulated around a few agencies.

Curriculum vitae — bring back memories?

I'd also been to see Andy and signed the paperwork.

It wasn't until I opened the pub door that my few days of optimism took a downward turn.

Who is he?

Determined not to let anybody ruin my mood, I confidently strode towards the bar. Taking my usual stool at the far end, I fixed on my cheeriest grin for the barman.

"Yes, sir? Pint of usual?"

Usual? Wow, how often have I been coming in here?

"Erm, yes, please."

Although I tried to avoid eye contact with the handsome stranger, I knew he hadn't taken his off mine since I'd arrived. It must have been at least two months since I'd first seen him, although the barman told me later that he had been in a few times during the past few days.

The barman placed my pint in front of me, the thud making me jump.

"There you go. Pint of bitter."

"Thanks. I'll pay by card, please."

"No need, sir. The gentleman at the end of the bar has got it in for you."

Shit.

"Oh, okay."

Realising I had no choice, I lifted my glass to acknowledge him. But he'd moved, the bar stool now stood empty.

How the hell?

Just in time, I saw him leave, before the spring shutter snapped the door back into place.

Should I go after him?

"He left you this too."

The barman passed me a beer mat with scribbled red writing across it. It contained a name, Patrick, and a phone number underneath. Quickly, in an attempt to banish him from my thoughts, I pushed it into my back pocket.

The following day, I kept my promise and paid the estate agent the required deposit. The experience with Patrick had left me even more eager to move on.

After he'd left the pub, I'd ordered another pint and a large whisky chaser. I knocked the latter back with one gulp, the burning liquid sliding down my throat and onwards to my stomach like molten lava. It had its desired effect and the neat alcohol calmed my rising anxiety. Quickly, I ordered another. Who the hell was Patrick? I deliberated calling the police but realised I had nothing to tell them.

'A guy bumped into me in the pub and left me his phone number and I'm not sure who he is'. I could just imagine DCI Small's face.

Once I returned home, I called Julia again. How many messages had I left for her now? At least this time, her phone rang before the inevitable answerphone cut in. My previous calls had gone directly to voicemail, a sure sign that her mobile was out of signal or, more likely, switched off.

Following my trip to see Andy, I took the Piccadilly tube line to Earl's Court. Not only had I felt vulnerable on the streets near Lisa's house, after all, Patrick had somehow found me, but I also wanted to familiarise myself with my new surroundings in West London. It was a fine crisp day, with not a cloud in the deep blue sky, and I tried my utmost to keep my spirits raised.

First, I walked to the flat. Andy Coleman, strictly against company rules, had lent me a key, two days before my actual moving date. Katie protested it wasn't legal and would break the contract, but Andy brushed her aside. I didn't argue. Maybe he'd taken pity on me when I'd said how desperate I was to move.

Leaving the tube at the Police Box exit, I turned right and made my way towards Old Brompton Road. Turning right again, and then first left, I arrived at my new accommodation. The building was in keeping with almost every block in the neighbourhood. Painted white, I counted six storeys high. My flat was on the fourth floor, complete with a small balcony to the front.

Although my actual apartment was neat and exemplarily clean, the building's interior looked in need of some general repairs. Paint peeled along the stairwells, the wooden balustrades desperate for a fresh coat of varnish and the carpeted areas were old and frayed. But it hadn't been the common spaces which had attracted me.

As I removed the key from my jeans pocket, the handle to the adjacent property turned and the door opened. Feeling exposed, as well as knowing I shouldn't be there, I found myself in two minds about whether to turn and run or try to get in and close the door behind me. Hesitating, it quickly became apparent that I'd been too slow to do either. A woman awkwardly made her way out of the door. Stepping backwards, she dragged and bashed a suitcase on its wheels behind her. She flinched when she saw me.

"Oh, allow me," I offered, stepping behind her and holding the door ajar.

"Thank you," she said, still concentrating on the suit-case. Her accent wasn't local, sounding more akin to the West Country. Somerset, Devon? I couldn't be sure.

Once she'd navigated herself out onto the landing, she locked her door and turned to face me. All of my instincts cascaded to the surface. I recalled Lisa mocking me for fancying every woman I ever set eyes on. Of course, it wasn't true, well, not entirely.

Instantly regretting not making any effort with my appearance, I tried in vain to flatten my hair and pull my creased T-shirt taut. I must have looked ridiculous attempting to put right several days of neglect in a matter of seconds.

"I'm Francis," she said, at least having the decency to avoid my antics.

"Hi," I mumbled.

Shit. I can't even speak to women anymore.

"Do you have a name too?" She chuckled.

When she laughed, two deep dimples appeared in her cheeks. I noticed her teeth weren't perfectly aligned, but they somehow added to her attractiveness, a flawed beauty. Her eyes were olive green, underlined by her pale skin. I could make out tiny freckles across the bridge of her nose, which continued their journey a short distance either side. The only thing I couldn't see was her hair, apart from the ponytail escaping through a gap. Her pink baseball cap carried a well-known sports logo on the front, a tiny tick to the left-hand side. The headgear made it difficult to age her.

"Yeah, sure. I'm Matthew. Matt. Everybody calls me Matt."

Francis let out another suppressed laugh.

"Are you going to be my new neighbour?"

Looking at the key in my hand, as if to remind myself of why I was there, I blushed.

"Yes, I am. I move in this weekend."

"On your own, or is there a Mrs Matt?"

Wow. Is she flirting with me?

"On my own. Definitely on my own," I repeated, a little too bullish.

"Oh, okay. I will be back by then."

We both glanced at her suitcase before she continued.

"Just going to visit my mum," she added. "She needs a hip replacement. Always going on about it, but waiting for the NHS is killing us. It'll be the most boring two nights, but it has to be done."

She laughed for the third time during our brief encounter. Although she carried an outer appearance of confidence, there seemed to be an air of introversion surrounding Francis. Something I couldn't put my finger on, but the giggle didn't come across as entirely genuine and she looked at the ground when she spoke. In the meantime, I'd composed myself.

"And is there a Mr Francis?"

Blushing ever so slightly, I noticed more freckles on the sides of her cheeks.

"No. Well, there was. But there isn't anymore."

"Hey. I'm sorry. I didn't mean to pry."

"It's fine. Honestly. It was a while ago. Anyway, I must dash. Got a train to catch."

And with that, she went. Just as I felt awful for putting her on the spot, she called after me from somewhere down the stairwell.

"See you Saturday," she shouted. And laughed again.

.   .   .

Keeping my promise, I returned the flat key to Andy before he closed for the day. He appeared relieved to see me before sarcastically smiling at Katie. Breaking the rules obviously hadn't sat as comfortably with him as he'd originally made out.

"Oh, Andy."

"Yep?" He had his back to me, replacing the flat key in a lock-up drawer.

"I had a look on your website, you know, to see if you had anything else suitable."

Andy slowly turned. He glanced over my shoulder to where Katie sat, appearing uneasy with where I might take the conversation.

"Oh right. Is there a problem with Earl's Court then?"

"No, no. It's nothing like that. It's just, well…"

My phone rang. Andy raised his eyebrows.

It was Julia.

"Excuse me. I have to take this."

Answering at the same time as I closed the office door, I noticed Andy watching after me.

"Hi, Julia. How are you? I've been trying to—"

"Can you meet me?"

"Oh, yeah, sure. When would be—"

"Tomorrow. Somewhere safe. Somewhere they can't find me."

16

Russell Square wasn't busy. In fact, I couldn't recall it ever being particularly bursting with activity. A few benches circled the centre island of the small park, whilst others were sporadically placed around the periphery. I'd told Julia I would arrive around ten o'clock and find a suitable seat away from prying eyes. She reluctantly agreed.

Her call had scared me. Her voice sounded so shaky. Although I wanted to ensure she was okay, her tone made me think I could be making a mistake.

Why do you have to get so involved?

"Hi," I said, standing to greet her whilst stunned at her appearance. Neither of us smiled, I'd already assumed it wouldn't be a meeting for hugs and merriment.

"Hello," she responded, keeping her voice low. Julia nervously glanced over her shoulder before reluctantly joining me on the bench.

I tried to recollect the last time I'd seen her. It had been when she had confessed to being married to

Graham. She was the ancestry expert, and the family had manipulated her skills, especially her husband. She had all but admitted that he threatened her. Julia denied knowing anything about how the Reid family used the family trees to manipulate people. Graham would ask, or instruct, her to find the next victim, somebody with money, or at least due to come into money. She sought the information and blindly passed it on. It was almost perfect.

"Have you been followed?" she asked.

Her eyes darted everywhere, her hands constantly on the move, from resting on her thighs to brushing her fringe and then tucking her hair behind her ears. And what had happened to her hair? It used to be shoulder length, fair and straight. But now, it looked unkempt and greasy, as though it hadn't been washed in days. She wore the same baggy cardigan from the last time I'd seen her, and, as on that occasion, she continually pulled it tight across her chest. As soon as she let go, it draped back open.

Her jeans were dirty, especially along the thighs, most likely because of her hands constantly rubbing along the surface. That's when I noticed her fingernails. Not so much the dirt underneath, but the quicks around the edges. Raw and thick with congealed blood. As if on cue, Julia bit at one on her left hand. A horrible snapping of her teeth as she attempted to grip the loose skin between them.

What is wrong with her?

"Followed where, Julia? Here, now?"

Apart from gnawing at her nails, Julia finally sat still, her free hand now drawn into a fist on her thigh, the whites of her bony knuckles protruding. She looked extremely unwell, her skeletal-like features exaggerated in the harsh reality of the unbroken sunshine. Her skin was translucent, as though she hadn't been out of the house in weeks. Blue veins stood out along the backs of her hands, like rivers trapped under her skin, meandering down to the top of her fingers before disappearing deeper underground.

"Is he in prison then? Or at the police station? Don't tell me he's on the run?"

Struggling to keep up, I realised who she meant.

"You mean Graham?"

"Yeah, yeah. Of course, Graham."

Resisting the temptation to take her hands in mine, I took a deep breath, knowing I had to keep her calm. She looked as though she might stand and dash off at the slightest hint of concern.

"No. He hasn't escaped. He's awaiting trial. The police have told me he's admitted to everything."

"Oh, shit, no."

She stood and paced the width of the footpath, back and forth, three or four times, before sitting back down.

"Isn't that good news?"

Her head snapped sideways, her eyes boring into mine. She appeared out of control, almost out of her mind.

"And he hasn't contacted you?" she asked.

"Me? Why? How? You're not making sense."

"He's going to escape. I know he is."

Julia frantically tried to grip any loose piece of skin from each finger. It would have looked comical had it not been so bloody scary.

Reaching out, I placed my hand on her shoulder. She squealed, jumped off the bench, and stepped forward until she stood on the grass.

"Listen, please," I pleaded. "He's not going to escape,

and he's never going to get out to find any of us. He's admitted to it, Julia. That's the end of the matter."

Julia nodded before repeating her now annoying routine of pacing to the bench and back to the edge of the path.

"Please, sit down. You're making yourself look conspicuous."

Not understanding if she looked conspicuous or not, it was the only thing I could think of to stop her from making me scream. Fortunately, she sat down and fidgeted with her hair again instead, allowing her time to take it all in, and her breathing eventually regulated.

Once she'd calmed down, I told her the news about Amelia being pregnant. Julia looked non-committal. Such had been her lack of reaction, I asked if she already knew. Maybe that's why I'd confessed, to see if she'd had contact with the family. She denied knowing anything.

"I don't speak to any of them anymore. The last time Tracy called, I told her it would be her last visit. I told her I'm giving up on the ancestry and I don't want any further contact."

"When was that?" I asked, intrigued.

"Don't know. Last week. Last month. I'm not sure. I don't go out anymore."

"Are you sure you're okay? Are you eating?"

Her cardigan fell open again. She looked desperately thin. The night I'd met her in the hotel, Julia had been slightly overweight. She'd told me she needed to up her exercise, get out more, and start walking. I doubted she ever had. But now, she had lost a lot of weight.

Maybe she's ill?

"Yes, yes, I eat. You sound like them."

"Who?"

"Them. All the others." She stood without warning. "That's why you're here, isn't it? They sent you."

I looked around. Fortunately, the park was almost empty. I beckoned her to sit back down.

"You invited me. Not the other way around."

Julia's eyes flickered from mine to her fingernails. We remained in silence for several more moments.

"So, you're going to be a father?"

The return to the subject from minutes earlier took me by surprise.

"Yes. Yes, I am. Scary isn't it?"

Finally, she managed a wry smile.

"You're not thinking of going back, are you?"

"No way. I couldn't, not now."

"Not now? So you had been thinking about it?"

"Not really. Far too much has——"

Julia grabbed my hands, halting me mid-sentence.

"Matthew, you can't. You mustn't. They're mad. Crazy."

Look who's talking.

"But Amelia has been nice to me."

"You've met her?"

The shock in Julia's voice scared me. I could feel her hands trembling within mine.

"Of course. She had to tell me about being pregnant. Then we had to discuss money. It's not as simple as cutting myself off."

Still, she held my hands, gripping harder, her bones threatening to pop through the skin.

"You must promise me you'll never go back, even if they find Graham guilty and lock him up forever. They can't be trusted. Look at Ryan."

The memories of the shallow grave in the woods came flooding back. Katrina and her handmade cross, two twigs held together with strands of green wool. Her father. Tracy's husband. Julia continued.

"Why do you think he ran? What was he running from?"

"Julia. It's alright. I'm not going back. Okay?"

I regretted ever trying to contact her.

Silence ensued once again. A squirrel ran across the freshly mown grass, busying himself looking for any scraps of food the public may have left behind. An elderly couple walked by, the man briefly nodding his head in acknowledgement. As soon as they were out of earshot, I asked Julia another question. Something I hoped she wouldn't know the answer to.

"There is one other thing."

She looked at me as if on the brink of collapse, unable to cope with much more.

"There's a guy who's been in my local pub. I think he's purposefully tracked me down. Says he knows the family. Grey hair, mid to late sixties. Good-looking chap. Do you know of anybody?"

Julia stopped looking at me and stared ahead instead. Had she even heard me?

"You're like me, Matthew. You're going crazy with it all."

Yet again, she bit her nails. Pulling herself to the edge of the bench, she made her intentions clear.

"I'm sure you're imagining being followed," she continued, rushing her words. "That's only natural. I get the same feeling too. And I'm sorry, I don't know of anybody else. Whoever this person is, who you met in a pub."

Julia's mood changed, and she suddenly looked disinterested, bored and itchy to get away.

"Okay. Thought I'd ask."

She stood, looking around, ready to leave. I became annoyed.

"So, why did you ask to meet me today? You haven't said."

Her eyes rolled upwards, the whites almost filling her sockets. I thought she might pass out. A slight grin spread across her mouth, her lips twitching at either end.

What the hell is happening to her?

And as quick as it started, she snapped out of her trance and walked away. At least she turned, as if to placate me.

"What's his name?" she asked, totally oblivious she'd just scared the living shit out of me.

Trying to recompose myself, I kept my eyes steady on her.

"Who?"

Julia tutted nonchalantly.

"This guy in the pub?"

"Oh. Said his name is Patrick. That's all I know."

I'd lost interest and wanted to get away too. Standing, I watched as she shook her head.

"Name means nothing to me. Sorry."

I instantly knew she was lying.

17

FRIDAY NIGHT, my last night at Lisa's house, would be the worst so far.

After reluctantly leaving Julia, I genuinely became concerned about her welfare. Outside Russell Square, I'd suggested I bought her a meal. 'Somewhere safe', I'd said, 'somewhere around that part of London where nobody would know we were there'. But she'd declined. Said she had to get home.

As I walked her to the tube station, I asked what her plans were from now on. She said she had no intention of leaving the house. Despite my protestations, she declared she had no money. The house was in Graham's name alone. She hadn't worked for years, had no income and no savings. 'Where could I possibly go?' she asked. Had it been an underhanded plea for me to take her in? I doubted it very much, and the prospect of harbouring Julia under my roof didn't cross my mind, even if I did fear for her safety.

Without ever understanding why she'd asked to meet,

we said our goodbyes and Julia scuttled down the station steps. Underground and to safety.

Watching her disappear, I realised I had to move on. Until I cut all ties with that family, apart from Amelia, I knew I could never bury the past. Meeting Julia had further cemented my concerns. If it wasn't because I could be a father in four or five months, I believe I would have moved abroad. Fled to Spain. The Andalusian hills. A white sugar cubed retreat in the wilderness. I had money, enough for a modest place. What could I do? Something online. Use a dropshipping company maybe. Buy and sell merchandise. I would never have to handle stock, just run a business from my new MacBook. The more I thought about it, the more entertaining the prospect became.

But then there was the baby. I knew I had to hang around. Until the birth, at least.

First, I needed time, time to contemplate the future. Move into the new flat, maybe even start the online business from there and see how things panned out. And just as importantly, wait for Graham to be trialled and sent away. Despite Julia's warnings that the rest of the family could never be trusted, I seriously doubted that any of the daughters, or indeed their mother Melissa, could be capable of killing.

Back at Lisa's, I found myself triple checking all the locks. The curtains hadn't been opened in days and I could see dust dancing across the living room as the sun broke through the tiniest of cracks. Promptly, I walked over and pulled them tighter still, ensuring no peeking eyes could see anything within.

As I opened the fridge door, the solitary ready meal stared back at me. Lasagne. Retrieving it, I studied the cooking instructions. *Microwave on full power for seven minutes. Let it rest for one minute. Careful, the contents will be hot.*

Yeah, right. Blah, blah, blah.

Tossing it back inside, I closed the fridge door and reached for the bottle of Scotch instead. There was just over half a bottle left. As I made my way back to the living room, I glanced in the mirror hanging in the hallway, bottle in one hand, glass in the other. The image stared back in disgust at my behaviour. Amelia's words echoed loud.

'You look like crap, Matthew. Whatever's wrong?'

My drinking was getting out of hand. It had to stop. I could do myself irreparable damage.

Still, may as well finish this bottle, eh?

I sat in the threadbare armchair until after dark, drinking every last drop. At one point, I must have attempted the lasagne. A half-eaten plate of food lay on the coffee table.

By the time I went to bed, my head spun and throbbed. The hangover had kicked in even before I'd stopped drinking.

Another glance in the hallway mirror. My eyes were sore, red, and watery. Had I been crying?

Sleep it off. Tomorrow you move. One last night.

One last night of hell.

The knock on the door made me sit bolt upright. Remaining as still as I could, I desperately tried to wake myself by rapidly opening and closing my eyes. Thinking it unwise to put the light on, I cautiously reached out my arm and felt for my phone. But it wasn't there. I must have left it downstairs.

Shit.

Knock, knock, knock.

Three more times, each one increasing in volume.

The darkness wrapped itself around me, refusing to let go.

Slowly, I peeled back the duvet. The air felt so warm. As hot as the bed had been under the covers.

Spinning on my backside, my legs reached over the edge of the bed and my toes made contact with the fake wooden floor. As I stood, I felt the soles of my feet stick to the laminate, and with each fragile step, they made a disgusting sound as my sweat clung to the surface.

Knock, knock, knock.

Louder still.

I'd never noticed it before, but the bedroom door opened with a slow, elongated creak. At least, once I made it onto the landing, a sliver of light filtered upstairs. Maybe from underneath the front door, the streetlamps spewing their orange glow through every available crack. It allowed me to see my progress, rather than feel it. Some minor comfort.

Taking every step as though it might be my last, I gingerly made my way downstairs. Pausing at the bottom, I stood statue-like, praying the banging had been a figment of my imagination.

Knock.

A singular, loud thud. The door rocked in its frame.

Shit.

Creeping forward, my heart thudding in my chest, I reached for the door handle.

"Who is it?" I whispered.

Knock.

"I said, who is it?"

"It's me. Lisa. Let me in," *she murmured, barely audible despite no other sound being distinguishable from outside. No traffic, no voices. Just the still of night.*

What time is it?

Why would Lisa be knocking on her own front door? It made little sense, even in my sleep-induced state.

"Where's your key?"

Lisa raised her voice.

"For God's sake, let me in, Matthew! He's here. He's coming!"
No!

Fumbling for the key, my hand shook violently as I attempted to turn it.

Bang!

Lisa's fist connected with the door, her impatience boiling over.
"Hang on, hang on," I pleaded.

Eventually, my hand gripped the key, and it clicked into place. Standing back, I waited for Lisa to come bounding in.

But nothing.

My heart thudded louder still. Sweat dripped from my brow.
"It's open," I said.

I couldn't be sure if I had actually spoken, as if I'd lost the ability to talk.

Nothing.

The still of the night surrounded me, suffocated me.
"Lisa!"

That time, I shouted, loudly. It would have been impossible not to hear.

Nothing.

Stepping forward once again, I steadied my hand as it reached out for the handle. My fingers trembled as they grabbed claw-like around it. Slowly, ever so slowly, I turned it until it reached its limit.

"Lisa. Are you there?"
Silence.

Gradually, I pulled the door inwards. As soon as the slightest of cracks appeared, I leant the side of my head against the inner wall and strained to see outside. But it wasn't open far enough. So, cautiously, I opened it a little more, until I had a clearer view of the street.

From my position, I could only see one side of the road, to the left, towards town. It was as quiet as I'd ever known it. Apart from a continual line of parked cars, it appeared deserted. The glow of the streetlamp illuminated the houses opposite. There wasn't a single light on in any property as far as I could see.

You need to look the other way, Matt.

Taking a step back, I steadily pulled the door further open until the gap was wide enough to step outside. With my hand remaining on the handle, I allowed another few moments to pass. Still nothing. Where is she?

Forcing myself forward, I stepped out onto the pavement. The coolness of the concrete immediately soothed the soles of my boiling feet.

Looking to my right, the street resembled what I'd witnessed to the left. A symmetrical scene of parked cars, orange streetlamps, and an otherwise uninhabited neighbourhood.

Instead of having a calming effect, the lack of any movement had the opposite. I'd heard Lisa on the other side of the door. As clear as day. So where was she?

Deciding to investigate further, I walked along the street. Dressed in only a pair of shorts, I felt vulnerable. Hurrying, and ignoring the particles of grit sticking to my feet, I jogged twenty or thirty paces to my right, doubled back, and ran the same distance the other way. There wasn't a single movement or sound.

Half relieved and half disconsolate, I returned to the house. Closing the door with a click behind me, I leant my back against the icy wall of the hallway.

The following morning, exhausted, hungover and tormented, I begrudgingly forced myself out of bed and trudged downstairs to fix myself the strongest coffee. As I walked past the living room doorway, something caught my eye.

Retrieving my mobile phone from the sofa, I tapped the screen to check the time. Eight thirty-seven.

But that wasn't all I saw.

One missed message.
From Lisa.

Hi Matt. Hope you are well. Have you left
my house yet?

With my thumbs poised over the keypad, the sound of
traffic outside distracted my attention. As soon as I
reached the hallway, the reason became apparent.

The front door lay slightly ajar, and as I stepped
forward to close it, something stabbed into my sole.
Balancing myself with one hand on the wall, I lifted my
leg by the ankle. A few particles of grit were stuck firmly
into the bottom of my foot.

18

I SHIVERED INVOLUNTARILY. A sheen of cool sweat formed around the nape of my neck. After brushing the grit away, the dream came flooding back.

Had the knocking on the door been part of it at all? A nightmare, so lifelike, so vivid, I'd run along the street, whilst the text from Lisa had been the real calling. The feeling of inner intuitiveness freaked me out.

My fingers trembled as I tapped on *Reply*.

Are you coming back soon? I'm leaving your house today. x

The message sent and my eyes remained static until the status changed to *Delivered*. However, it didn't change to *Read*.

Although relieved that Lisa was fine, and safe, with her mum, I couldn't help but feel a little irritated at the abruptness of her question.

. . .

Have you left my house yet?

But I guess Lisa had every right to know. It was her property. For all she knew, I could have turned into some kind of squatter.

Pinching my arm to confirm I was actually awake, I ran upstairs to find a T-shirt and some jogging bottoms. The shirt reluctantly slid down my damp back. Next, I walked to the bathroom and splashed my face with cold water, wiping the residue through my hair. Finally, I stood and examined myself in the mirror.

Shit.

My eye sockets were dark and hollow. My hair stuck up at angles, the combination of grease, sweat, and fresh water holding it in place. The stubble on my chin had manifested into something resembling a proper beard, I'd barely noticed it growing over the past few days. Being the kind of guy who'd obsessed with his appearance, it shocked me how much I was letting myself go.

Back in the kitchen, I tried to keep myself occupied by stacking the dishwasher. Guilt suddenly enveloped me. This was Lisa's house, and she'd left me in charge. Allowed me to stay out of the goodness of her heart until I found somewhere of my own. And how had I repaid her? By showing no respect, thinking only of myself. Now she wanted me out, and I couldn't blame her.

Has she been back and seen what a mess this place is?

With the dishwasher whirring and the kitchen surfaces cleared and wiped, I carried the rubbish and empty whisky bottles to the back door. The first glimmer of sunlight filtered through the two panes of frosted glass at the top. It already promised to be another sunny day in London. Spring had arrived, but the prospect of enjoying it felt a million miles away.

As I opened the back door, a cat bolted from one of the abandoned flower beds. Catching my breath, I watched it sprint the width of the garden and, in one gracious movement, leap to the top of the fence. From its new vantage point, it turned to face me, as startled as it was, its tale standing vertical. I made that sound through pursed lips, the sound that everybody makes when talking to cats. But it wasn't interested in my apology and instead turned, jumped and disappeared to the other side.

Once I'd dealt with the rubbish, I concentrated on the living room. Then, the bedrooms. Tidying up had its desired effect, diverting my mind and giving me a sense of purpose. Carrying my phone in my joggers' pocket, I periodically checked for new messages. The last one to Lisa remained at *Delivered*.

Unsure what to do with the linen, I left it where it was and remade the beds to the best of my ability. I did the same with the towels, replacing them on the relative holders in the bathroom. Although not perfect, I at least hoped Lisa would appreciate my efforts.

When I'd eventually packed my bags, the time was fast approaching midday. Andy Coleman said I could pick up my new flat keys after lunch. Just before I left, I sent Lisa another message, informing her I was leaving and would drop off my key at the agents.

Pushing the key into the lock, I noticed a card half hidden at my feet. It had got caught underneath the door. Once inside, I turned and bent down to retrieve it. A pair of pink training shoes outside in the corridor made me jump.

"Hey, welcome, Matt."

As I stood, holding my heart, Francis's expression changed from delight to shock.

"Blimey," she added before I could reply. "Are you okay?"

Francis carried a box, her arms clasped around it and hugged tight to her chest. The label, pointing towards me, had my name and address printed on it. I glanced at the card in my hand. 'Missed delivery' and 'left with neighbour at number 404', scribbled roughly across it.

"Hi. I take it that's for me?" I replied, nodding at the parcel.

She looked slightly offended. I'd ignored both her cheery greeting and subsequent question. Maybe she'd been more concerned that somebody looking so rough could move in next door. Had I changed that much in five days? I hadn't exactly looked a picture of health then, but her expression told me all I needed to know.

"Yes," she said, handing it to me. "There's a couple more I've taken in too. They arrived yesterday."

"Oh, right? I thought I'd arranged all deliveries after lunchtime today. I'll get onto them—"

"Not to worry. At least they've turned up," she interrupted. "I'll leave you to it. You're obviously busy. Come and collect the others when you're ready."

Clearly pissed off at my abruptness, Francis turned on her heels and stomped back into her flat. She didn't exactly slam the door, but it wasn't subtle either.

Great, Matt, great. Just the start you needed.

Dumping a bag of clothes on my bed, I opened the box that Francis had brought. It contained the new sheets, pillowcases and towels. As I contemplated going next door to apologise, my intercom buzzed. It was a dull sound, almost as if it couldn't be bothered to alert anyone. I pressed and held down the small white button.

"Yes?"

"Grocery delivery," came the reply.

Taking the stairs two at a time, I greeted a guy in a dark blue uniform. He had three plastic trays at his feet, full to the brim with food. He carried two whilst I grabbed the spare one. After signing, I filled the cupboards and stockpiled the fresh stuff, ready for the impending delivery of the fridge. Despite all that was going on, it felt good to finally have my own space. I'd lived a bachelor's life since leaving home at eighteen, until I met Amelia, of course. Maybe it had always been my destiny?

Roughly two hours later, my new fridge freezer arrived, along with a brand new kettle, toaster and microwave. I'd also added a TV to my electrical order, a treat in an attempt to cheer myself up. Shortly after, the mattress arrived too. I spent the next two hours setting everything up. Once finished, I unpacked my relatively few clothes in the supplied wardrobe and chest of drawers. Finally, I arranged my bathroom essentials along the shelf provided.

Sweating and feeling dirty, I took a shower. It took me a while to work out the two controls, one for the flow and the other for the temperature. Standing with my head tilted backwards, I allowed the steaming flow of water to wash over my face and down my body. It felt so good, invigorating.

Click.

What was that?

Twisting my neck outside the stream of water, I strained my ears to listen.

Nothing.

Convinced my mind must have once again been playing tricks, I returned to the relative sanctuary of my boiling waterfall. The bathroom became immersed in steam, the far side invisible in a fog-like haze.

Click.

That's a door opening, closer than before.

Shit.

"Hello?" I shouted, feeling defenceless.

The sound of shuffling feet.

"Is somebody there?"

Another door closing, this time farther away. The front door again?

After gripping the wrong handle, the water instantly turned freezing cold.

Bollocks.

Panicking, I turned the other as fast as I could. Feeling like an eternity, the flow of water eventually halted.

Tentatively, I pushed the cubicle door open and stepped onto the bath mat. Grabbing one of the new towels, I quickly scrubbed at my hair before drying the majority of water from my body. Wrapping the towel around my waist, I opened the small window to allow some of the steam to escape. As I finally reached the bathroom door, I noticed it was already open, ever so slightly ajar.

Had I shut it completely?

"Hello?" I repeated, much quieter this time.

Not a sound.

Stepping into the living area, I first checked the front door. Closed. I confirmed each window was fastened, before realising how foolish it was considering I lived on the fourth floor.

After convincing myself I'd imagined the whole thing,

I decided I needed a drink. Retrieving a fresh bottle of whisky, I found a glass in the cupboard and poured myself a generous measure before knocking it back in one. Refilling the glass, I left it on the work surface before returning to the bedroom to dress.

As I crossed the living room, I spotted a box on the sofa.

A parcel.

Had it been there before?

As I retrieved it — another expected arrival from Amazon — I noticed one or two shoe prints on the laminate flooring. Then a couple more. Across the room, to the bathroom door, and back again.

Surely a delivery driver wouldn't let themselves in? But if not, who would?

It was time to go next door and make that apology.

19

"Oh, hi."

Francis didn't appear overly impressed by my impromptu visit. Holding out a bunch of flowers I'd bought from a stall holder just along the street, I fixed on my friendliest smile. Although the whisky had given me a shot of confidence, I knew I may stink like a failed recovering alcoholic.

"These are for you. My way of saying sorry. You know, if I came across a bit, well, grumpy earlier on."

After taking the flowers, she looked me up and down, as if judging me as suitable to enter her home. The smile returned, her dimples deeper still. Like the flick of a light switch, Francis transformed into the person I'd met earlier that week, cheery, friendly, and welcoming.

Not another bloody schizophrenic.

"Come in, come in." She disappeared inside.

"Only if it's convenient," I called after her, stepping inside her immaculate apartment. I found out later Francis preferred 'apartment' to 'flat'. She thought it sounded grander, and less like a tower block. Francis could be quite the snob.

"Come through. I'm in the kitchen."

"Lovely place," I genuinely commented as I admired her faultless taste in furniture and fittings.

The living room gave a spatial appearance, despite it being no bigger than my own. An L-shaped leather sofa clung to two walls, leaving the rest of the room clutter-free. Despite a rectangular coffee table in the centre, and a modest-sized TV fixed to the wall, the lack of any large furniture allowed for much easier manoeuvrability. A huge multi-coloured rug covered the laminate flooring, giving the entire area an appearance of opulence. But the living room was nothing compared to the kitchen. The island in the centre stood prominently, elegant chrome and leather stools tucked neatly underneath. The jet black granite work surfaces were accentuated by the equally expensive-looking ivory units. Top-of-the-range electrical appliances completed the scene, alongside one of those large American fridge freezers. It looked as though a family of four could easily live there. The arrangement made Francis look a little lost standing on the far side of the island.

She had her back to me, arranging the flowers in a vase.

"What did you say?" she asked, continuing with the task.

"I said, lovely place. It's immaculate. Makes mine look a little depleted."

Maybe my initial presumption had been right. She could quite easily have been concerned with my appearance. Did I meet the criteria of clientele she would allow into her showroom apartment? Finally, she turned, the flowers looking much healthier than they had wrapped in cheap cellophane.

"Thank you." She placed the vase in the centre of the island. "I'm sure we can work on yours too. Given time."

We?

Forcing a smile, I felt somewhat out of my comfort zone.

"Drink?"

Can she smell it on me, or do I look desperate? Maybe both.

"Erm, yes, please. Whatever you're having."

"Wine okay?"

Francis bent down and retrieved a bottle of red from her side of the island. She effortlessly removed the cork with a 'pop'. Reaching above her head, she slid two large glasses from a rack and placed them in front of us. Half filling both, she collected the drinks and beckoned me to follow her into the lounge.

With an outstretched arm, she showed where I should sit. Placing my wine onto a small table hidden behind the end of the sofa, she sat down opposite. Finally, Francis tucked her legs underneath herself whilst holding onto her wine.

It all felt very formal, especially compared to living at Lisa's. I'd been used to leaving empty glasses and beer bottles on the carpet.

"Cheers," she said, holding her drink aloft.

Nodding, I retrieved my own and swallowed a huge gulp. I then watched in horror as Francis took the tiniest sip in return. She placed her glass on the table between us. Embarrassed, I put mine down too, despite an over-whelming sensation to neck it in one and demand a refill.

I'd noticed Francis hadn't giggled the same awkward laugh as she had the day we first met. Maybe it had been nerves after all. Did she feel more secure on home territory?

"How was Mum?"

Francis appeared at a loss.

"The other day. You were going to visit her?"

This time, she laughed.

"Oh, as expected. Totally boring. But it's over and done with for a while."

Francis laughed again before retrieving her wine. She took a longer drink. It didn't take a second invitation for me to follow her lead.

Slow down.

"So, tell me more about yourself, Matt."

Feeling myself redden, I took another drink to compose myself. Before I realised, I'd emptied my glass. I held onto it uncomfortably.

"Another?" Francis asked, jumping up from the sofa and mock jogging into the kitchen.

Get a grip.

"Sorry, I didn't mean to guzzle it so—"

"Nonsense," she said, returning with the bottle. She took my glass and refilled it. Giving me a more generous shot, I guessed she may have considered whether I had a serious drink problem. "It's what it's for, isn't it?" she added, sitting back down. Whilst her back was turned, I took another quick drink.

"Well, I'm thirty-eight. I work near Covent Garden for a property management firm," I lied, "and—"

"You weren't working last Thursday then, when you came to look around your flat?"

Shit.

Blushing again, I took another drink of my wine.

"Okay, I *used* to work near Covent Garden for a property management firm. It's kind of a long story."

Francis nodded, smiling sympathetically.

It was pointless lying. She'd soon find out that I didn't go out to work.

"Anyway," I continued, "I'm married, but separated."

"I'm sorry," she interjected.

"It's okay, for the best, given the circumstances, shall we say?"

Francis looked intrigued. She stood up, walked over, and refilled my drink. This time, almost to the brim. The glass was huge and there must have been over a third of a bottle in there. I took a long swig, conscious of spilling the contents onto the expensive rug beneath.

"Want to tell me more?" she asked, sitting back down and retrieving her drink. "There's plenty more where this came from."

Sensing the alcohol relaxing me, I knew I shouldn't share too much information. We'd only just met, and besides, I wanted to talk about something different with Francis. The appeal of us being friendly neighbours felt good, much better than another punchbag to vent my anger.

"There's not much more to tell," I lied for a second time. However, realising that any attempt to conceal the impending birth would prove almost impossible, I stammered my words whilst feeling my cheeks burn.

"Well, actually, you'll need to know this too. My wife, well, ex-wife, is expecting our baby. Soon. September, I think."

Ex-wife? Why are you calling her that?

"Wow," she said. "That is quite a lot of information, Matt."

Although Francis smiled, I found it difficult to gauge what she actually thought. Did she imagine me as some selfish husband who had walked out on his wife after getting her pregnant? Or maybe I'd been kicked out for being a drunk before the child even arrived?

"It's not like it sounds," I replied. "A lot has gone on in my life in the past year. A lot more than I wish to divulge, if you don't mind?"

"Hey, none of my business," she said, raising the palms of her hands.

An awkward silence ensued. Keeping myself occupied, I looked around her room whilst continually sipping at my wine.

"One moment," Francis said, standing. She disappeared into the kitchen before returning with a fresh bottle. Positioning it in front of me, Francis nodded, implying I help myself.

Is she trying to get me drunk?

Making a conscious effort to slow down, my head had already begun to spin, and I caught myself slurring one or two words. If I had much more, I knew I might divulge far too much information.

"Tell me about you then," I said, tempted to place my glass on the table. Not for the first time, Francis appeared to clam up.

"Oh, you know, not much to tell."

"Nonsense. Do you work? Where are you from? Kids? Husband beater?"

At least she laughed.

"Okay," she replied. "In order. No, I don't work. I'm originally from Oxford, moved to London when I was twenty-six. I have no children, and yes, my ex-husband is buried in the woods."

The glass slipped from my hand, slow-motion-like. Twice, I tried to catch it, only resulting in sending it spiralling through the air, the dark red liquid breaking free in multiple directions. Finally, it landed with a soft bounce on the multi-coloured rug below.

"Oh shit, bollocks…" I shouted, standing, but with no idea what to do.

Francis jumped from her seat and ran to the kitchen. Almost immediately, she returned with a damp cloth. She knelt and dabbed frantically at the dark stain.

"So sorry, Francis. I don't know what happened. It just—"

"Shh, Matt, shh," she said, glancing up at me. "It's okay. Accidents happen."

A short while later, I made my excuses to leave. Francis convinced me to stop worrying about the rug. She'd removed the stain. If it hadn't been for the damp circle, you wouldn't have known anything had been spilt.

She made a joke about burying me in the woods if I ever did it again. A tiny part of me considered telling her the real reason I'd almost had a heart attack, but I held back.

Francis promptly leant forward and kissed me on both cheeks as I stood in the doorway to leave.

"Oh, by the way," I said. "I remember why I came to see you."

She remained silent.

"It was to say thanks for dropping off the other parcel earlier today."

Francis looked puzzled.

"Sorry, Matt, but I don't know what you're talking about."

20

ANOTHER MONTH PASSED BY, and later one Friday, I was due to meet Amelia at the café for a usual catch-up. In the meantime, I'd received a further message from Lisa thanking me for leaving the house and being so understanding. She added she would be in touch soon.

Julia had responded too, albeit with a *Yes, I'm okay* note, and nothing more. I'd also socialised with Francis on two more occasions, once for a coffee in my flat and once at the local Costa on Old Brompton Road. She had joked that although the wine stain had completely disappeared, I would have to drink from a plastic beaker in the future. It felt good to have a new friend. Somebody who was exactly that, a friend with no attachments and very little knowledge of my history.

The weather had remained pleasantly kind, so I secured a table outside the café and waited for Amelia to join me.

"Hi," she said, air-kissing both of my cheeks. I found it difficult to gauge her level of commitment. She had clarified that she wished for us to start over, but some days she appeared reluctant to get too close. Deep down, I preferred it when she came across as overtly friendly.

Having not seen her for a couple of weeks, I'd become impatient to see how much the baby had grown. However, when she arrived, the only thing I could do was stare at her ridiculous outfit. With the temperature reaching the low-seventies, she turned up in an oversized, thick woollen jumper. Despite never expecting our current situation to arrive, I had always considered Amelia as a stylish person, and I certainly expected decent maternity wear.

"You not hot?" I enquired, as politely as I could. She pulled out the chair opposite before awkwardly sitting down. One hand remained on her stomach throughout, causing her to lose balance once or twice. It didn't fit her demeanour at all, and I couldn't help but stare.

"A bit," she laughed, "but it's difficult finding maternity wear at this stage of pregnancy."

A woman glanced over her shoulder and smiled at Amelia. But just as I had, she gawped at Amelia's outfit. Her eyes opened wide before quickly turning back into her seat. Although I couldn't be certain, I'm convinced she stifled a giggle. Fortunately, Amelia had her back to the woman, and hadn't seen, or heard anything.

"How many weeks are you now?" I asked, half interested and half wanting the ground to swallow me up. Who on earth would dress like that? Sweat dripped from her forehead.

"Twenty-two. Over halfway there."

My eyes inadvertently diverted to her stomach. Her hands cradled the bump underneath the thick jumper. I could see another layer, maybe a sweatshirt below? It made me light-headed just looking at her.

"Amelia?"

She looked at me quizzically.

"I've not been to see the doctor with you yet. I'd like to be more involved."

Amelia appeared taken aback, as if such a suggestion would be ridiculous. She picked up a sachet of sugar and rolled it between her fingers.

"The thing is, Matt," she said without looking up. "The thing is, Tracy has been coming with me, you know, to see the obstetrician."

Is that what they're called?

"Why, is she the father?"

The woman who had looked around earlier laughed. Amelia glanced over her shoulder before rolling her eyes in disgust.

"Don't be facetious. You know full well she's a qualified nurse." Amelia hunched herself closer and lowered her voice. "And if you can't be bothered to come home and be with your family, then I'll need all of her help in the future." She threw the sugar sachet onto the table. "Won't I?"

Desperate to not cause a scene, I asked what she'd like to drink. It came as no surprise when she requested a bottle of cold water. "Out of the fridge," she added.

When I returned, an envelope lay on the table. It had my name written on it, nothing else, just my name.

"You asked for copies of the receipts for the work I'm having done in the nursery."

"Ah, okay."

Passing Amelia a bottle of water and a glass full of ice, I retrieved the envelope. She immediately changed the subject.

"We need to know where you are living," she continued, as I struggled to open the letter. "I assume you're still living at that Lisa's place?"

Stopping what I was doing, I studied Amelia.

"Why would you *assume* that?"

Amelia busied herself. She removed the screw top from the bottle before filling her glass to the brim. Her hand shook slightly as she helped herself to half of the contents. She licked her top lip before refilling the glass.

"It's just that I have a right to know where you're living, and who with. After all, I am expecting *your* baby."

She raised her voice. The woman sat close by, shuffled awkwardly on her chair, desperate not to turn around but equally determined to hear the conversation unfold behind her.

Without giving her the satisfaction of knowing where I was living, I changed tack again. As I slid my finger underneath the flap of the envelope, I noticed Amelia studying me, no doubt awaiting my reaction. The headed notepaper from 'Dean's Home Improvements' looked amateurish.

Is that a smirk on Amelia's face?

"Thanks," I said, dropping the letter onto the table. "Has *Dean* done a good job?"

Amelia didn't even attempt to disguise her enjoyment.

"Dean has done a remarkable job. He's quite the hunk too."

Amelia still held all the cards, and I felt she was playing me like a fool. Once again, I retrieved the letter and read the figure at the bottom of the page. I did not know whether it was a genuine amount for the work he'd carried out.

"By the way," I asked, attempting to sound a little more upbeat whilst returning to my earlier subject. "When is your next scan at the hospital?" I nodded nonchalantly towards her stomach. Her hand remained resting whilst she sipped at her cold water.

"Why do you need to know that?" she asked.

"Because, as you rightly say, you're expecting *my* baby."

It had always felt good whenever I held the upper hand over Amelia, or, more to the point, any member of her family. It wasn't something that happened very often. The woman on the chair sneaked another quick look over her shoulder, her interest suddenly rekindled.

"I went last week, actually," Amelia replied. "Everything is fine and, as I said, Tracy travelled with me. It's the one in Epsom. You've no need to get involved at this stage."

"But what if I *want* to get involved?"

Amelia was annoying me, but the thought of being included in the hospital visits hadn't entered my head before. The power she held over me, the baby, checking if I'd left Lisa's house, the redundancy. She had the capability to shape my entire future, and I knew if I wasn't careful, I would allow it to happen. I'd accepted the prospect of being a father, something that somehow excited me, but I needed everything else to be my choice, my direction in life. I just had to remain as amiable as possible until the day arrived.

"You've made it pretty clear that's the exact opposite of what you want, darling."

Darling? Did you just call me darling again?

"So, I think it's best all round if we keep our regular meetings here, and I keep you in the loop on the health of our baby. Don't you?"

"Whatever you want. If you think the sister being present instead of the father is normal, that is."

The woman in the chair stifled another laugh. She'd become my stooge, and each time she reacted, I could feel my chest puff out a little further.

"Grow up, Matthew," Amelia said, standing to indicate the meeting was over.

We air-kissed our goodbyes, and I didn't hang around to watch her head off back towards the office. Instead, I needed a drink, and I knew exactly where I'd be heading. I'd spotted a pub opposite Earl's Court tube station twice before. Despite all that was going on, I briefly felt a little ray of optimism. Impatiently, I made my way back to the underground.

Soon after I'd ordered the first pint, my phone vibrated in my pocket. The number was withheld, and I answered with trepidation.

"Hello?" I asked, two or three times in succession. But whoever called did not speak.

All I could hear was an indistinct murmur and the rustling of leaves in the trees.

21

FOLLOWING our most surly meeting to date, I rose early and forced myself to get ready for the day ahead. It had been over a month since I'd left Lisa's house and Amelia questioning whether I still lived there had reminded me I should keep an eye on the place. I presumed the mail would be piling up on the doorstep, and the thought of anybody breaking in had also occupied my thoughts.

Ignoring my hangover – I'd stayed at my newfound pub opposite Earl's Court station for far too long again – I dragged myself into the shower. Following two cups of extra strong coffee, I left my apartment and began the descent of the four flights of stairs. Halfway down, I heard my name being called from above.

"Matt, wait."

Straining to see through the stairwell, I could just make out Francis leaning over the top bannister.

"What is it?" I asked, my headache subsequently turning to dizziness as I tilted my head backwards.

"Going anywhere nice?" she called back.

· · ·

Twenty minutes later, we strolled towards the tube station. Following Francis's polite enquiry, I'd reluctantly informed her I was heading back to my old place to pick up something I'd left behind. As soon as she asked if she could accompany me, I knew I'd have to think of what that *something* would be. However, I could always tell Francis to wait outside if I had to.

She admitted to being bored, and the prospect of spending the day alone had given her the perfect excuse to ask if she could join me. By way of persuasion, she promised me a free pub lunch. It made no difference to me if she came along. In fact, the idea of some company galvanised my spirits. And without admitting as much, I didn't feel entirely safe on my own, especially in an area where people knew I'd been living.

Francis wore the same pink baseball cap from the first time I'd seen her, her ponytail swishing via the hole at the back. With a bright white polo shirt, knee-length burgundy shorts and her favourite pink training shoes, she looked the epitome of good taste on a fine summer's day, and dare I admit it, beautiful too.

As she tapped her card on the pad and stepped through the barriers at the tube station, she turned and caught me admiring her. Francis did nothing to suggest any irritation.

Behave yourself.

We sat in silence throughout the journey. As always, I counted down the stations until the last stop. I had chosen wisely, moving from Ealing to Earl's Court, all on the same underground line, so no swapping of lines, and no inconvenience. After arriving at Ealing Broadway, we departed the station and less than ten minutes later, we found ourselves outside Lisa's house.

Inadvertently, I studied her property for any sign of

life, a curtain twitching, or a sound from inside. Once satisfied, I kicked myself for being so stupid.

Who are you expecting?

After politely knocking on the door a couple of times, I reached for the key in my pocket. I'd forgotten to hand it in to the estate agents. Maybe a sixth sense had told me to hang on to it, or, more likely, useless Andy had never asked for it.

Francis stood beside me. I'd somehow forgotten she was there. Suddenly, it didn't feel quite right that she should be with me. She sensed my hesitation.

"Want me to wait outside?" she asked.

"Oh, no, it's okay. I doubt she's been back since I left."

Expecting some kind of resistance from the pile of mail which Amelia had mentioned, I slowly pushed the door open. But there was no resistance, and there were no letters on the floor.

Maybe the agents have been in?

Francis had gone on ahead, and I quickly joined her in the kitchen. It looked immaculate.

"Lisa must have been back," I said with a smile, realising that had been the underlying reason I'd gone back. It amazed me how much difference a thorough clean could make. Although I'd tried, or at least made a token gesture, the kitchen was spotless. I recalled leaving the dishwasher running, but it now lay empty, its interior gleaming. Every pot, pan, plate and mug had been placed away in their rightful cupboard. The sink sparkled, and the taps likewise. All surfaces shone under the sunlight filtering in through the panes of glass at the top of the back door.

In a daze, I walked from room to room. The living room was spotless too, despite the ancient furniture and the well-worn carpet. The bed I'd slept in had been stripped of its linen and replaced with new sheets and duvet, the pillows plump and inviting. Lisa's bedroom was the same. And the bathroom had had a thorough spring clean too. The chrome taps sparkled and fresh towels hung.

"It's like a brand new place," I said to nobody in particular, unsure of Francis's whereabouts. She didn't reply, anyway.

As I returned to the kitchen, I noticed the back door open. Stepping outside, Francis appeared at the shed doorway, a look etched across her face that I couldn't read. Something didn't feel quite right, even though the place had only had a thorough clean.

"You okay?" I asked, joining her in the small garden. Someone had even tidied outside. The eight-foot square space of lawn had been freshly mown, the borders weeded and planted with colourful and bright bedding plants. Reds, oranges and yellows gave the area a summer feel. I could imagine sitting there, in a reclining chair, reading, or maybe grabbing an afternoon nap in the sunshine. However small, it was still a quintessential English back garden.

"You told me this place was a dump," Francis replied, taking out her phone.

Had I?

"Are you going to take some photos to prove me wrong?" I laughed. She ignored me and tapped away on her screen.

"There," she said, beckoning me to join her. "It's up for sale. Look. Newly listed this week."

Sure enough, Lisa's house was on the market. With a rough idea of how much property went for in the Ealing district, I thought it was pretty cheap for a terrace within a London suburb.

Curiosity had completely got the better of me, and I asked if Francis would accompany me to the estate agent.

"Oh, hello, erm…"

"Matt. Matthew Walker. You helped me find my new flat."

"Ah, yes. How are you settling in at Earl's Court?"

Andy Coleman seemed a little apprehensive. His eyes flickered between us.

"Yes, all good, thanks. Don't worry, I'm not looking for anything else."

Andy laughed, relaxing a little. His focus then fixed upon Francis.

"Not her either," I said, immediately filling in the blanks. "She's just a friend."

"Nice. Cool." He became a little flustered, either finding Francis attractive or my unannounced arrival catching him off guard.

"It's about Lisa Ingram, her house, the one on—"

"Ah, yes," Andy interrupted, glad of the change of subject. "You lived there for a while, didn't you?"

"I've just been back."

The agent's face changed again.

"Not inside, Mr Walker? You're not supposed to be going in there anymore."

I glanced at Francis, and then back to Andy.

"What do you mean, not *supposed* to be there? Lisa told me to use it as my own. Well, until I found somewhere else."

"And you have found somewhere else, Mr Walker.

Lisa told me that nobody else would have a key. Can I take yours please?"

Something much more authoritative had replaced Andy Coleman's initial nervousness. He actually appeared quite pissed off at me for even being there.

"I'm not sure what the problem is," I responded, trying my utmost to keep the conversation on a pleasant level. "I'm actually best friends with Lisa, and she said—"

"When did you last speak to her?" Andy interrupted once more. I could feel the blood rush to my face.

"Well, last week, the week before. I don't know. What does that matter?" And then I thought. "Actually, Andy. When did *you* last speak to her?"

He momentarily stalled. I realised Francis was standing next to me. When had she stepped so close? Her hand brushed against mine. A spark ignited somewhere inside.

"I've been in touch with her quite a few times. She phoned and asked if I knew of a reputable cleaning company. With all our rentals, we use a very good one based on an industrial estate near town. They've been in two full days this week. Looks good, doesn't it?"

At least I couldn't argue with Andy on that point. The house had looked very nice. Something I'd probably consider buying myself if I had a bit more money or a steady job to support a small mortgage.

"And she did all this by phone?"

Both Andy and I turned to Francis. She hadn't said a word before now. Andy noticed her hand against mine, envious and probably taken aback. Either way, he didn't look pleased.

"Yes, she's staying out of town. Why?"

"Well, doesn't she have to sign the paperwork? An agreement?"

"All via email," Andy responded, his confidence returning.

"I'm just surprised she hasn't been back to collect her stuff, and then come in and see you in person, that's all."

"Actually, she came and collected her stuff…"

He stalled again, as if he didn't know how much information he could divulge.

The door opened, allowing the busy sounds from outside to momentarily disrupt our conversation. Katie, the other sales assistant, entered carrying a bunch of keys. She took one look at us, smiled, and sat at her desk.

"When?" Francis wasn't letting up.

That was the spark for Andy to go on the defensive. His eyes rested on Francis.

"That's none of your business, madam, as you well know."

"Hey, hey," I intervened. "There's no need to speak to her like that. She's just asking."

Andy's eyes didn't leave Francis, and likewise, she held his stare. It looked like some kind of game, 'who dare speak next'.

Eventually, I tugged on Francis's arm.

"Come on. Let's go."

Reluctantly, she agreed, but she held Andy's gaze until we were outside.

"What was that all about?" I asked as we walked towards the tube station.

Francis shook her head as she spoke.

"I don't like that man," she said. "I don't like him at all."

22

LISA LOOKED pleased to see me. Her broad, infectious smile was evident, even from a distance. She stood in the woods, along the footpath which led to the grave. She'd called me earlier, asked to meet me. I'd eagerly accepted, although the choice of venue had somewhat shocked me.

As I approached, I became aware we weren't alone. From the dark shadows on either side of the path, people stepped forward. First came Amelia, smiling, beckoning me towards her with a strange and continual swish of her arms. She held something in her hands, but I couldn't quite register what. Then, from the other side, Melissa appeared. She carried a saucepan in one hand and a giant wooden spoon in the other. As she stirred the contents, she blew me kisses, an innocent kiss at first, but it soon transgressed into something much more suggestive. A snap of a branch made me switch sides again. Tracy stepped out of the dark, dense woods. She wore a white apron, covered in blood. Dark red smears mixed with congealed chunks of meat. When she smiled, blood dripped from the corner of her mouth, her teeth crimson. Finally, I reached Lisa. But Lisa hadn't been smiling at all, as I'd initially assumed.

Instead, the ends of her mouth had been cut, or more likely, *sliced, backwards. Two long rows of crude stitches stretched from the corner of her lips all the way back to the base of her ears. From behind me, a chuckle. I turned to catch Amelia laughing. And then I saw exactly what she held in her hands; a meat cleaver, its blade sparkling as a ray of moonlight caught its sharp edge. Blood dripped slow-motion-like, each droplet echoing around the forest as it landed on the pine-covered ground below.*

The sound of Katrina's squeaking swing came from somewhere far in the distance. And out of the shadows stepped Graham. He slowly raised his arm, his forefinger beckoning me forward. Resisting, I held my ground, but soon, the mother and her two daughters were directly behind me, nudging me, gently pushing me. Closer and closer to Graham.

At first, Lisa screamed, immediately followed by my own...

"Matt, Matt!"

My eyes sprang open, and I felt an instant dizziness inside my head. Just like my nightmare, a sliver of moonlight illuminated the room. My heart pounded, and I struggled to distinguish between reality and fantasy.

If I've been dreaming, then why aren't I in my bed?

Desperately trying to focus, I sat up and strived to recognise something, anything, around me. Not my duvet, not my furniture, not my room...

The chilly hand on my back forced a startled screech from my mouth.

"Matt, it's me. Francis. I'm here. It's okay."

She sat behind me, upright, her back against the headboard.

Was she naked?

What the hell?

"Where am I?" I stumbled for words, my breathing deep and irregular.

"It's okay. You've been dreaming. I'm here. You're alright."

As soon as I jumped out of bed, I realised I was naked too. Attempting to cover my modesty, I noticed Francis did nothing to cover her own. She remained still, sitting, her hands by her side, holding herself steady on the bed.

"But what, how?"

She too realised the situation and tugged on the edge of the duvet before pulling it up and over her chest.

"We had a bit to drink, shall we say?"

Allowing my heart to return to somewhere near normal, I sat on the corner of the bed, pulling my side of the cover over my knee. I tried to recall what had happened. Leaving the estate agents, feeling despondent about Lisa's house being placed on the market and the realisation that I may never see her again.

Francis and I had returned to Earl's Court and, instead of going home, we walked towards Hammersmith. She had bought me the promised pub lunch and we'd drunk wine. After that, it became hazy. Another pub? Maybe straight back to her apartment? More wine. Whisky too? A kiss...

Shit. Why can you never control yourself?

The sound of my phone ringing awoke me with another start. Waking twice in the same morning didn't agree with me and I momentarily lost track of what the actual day was. At least I found myself in my bed. Sunshine seeped in through every available crack of the curtains. A quick glance at my phone informed me it was almost lunchtime. What time had I left Francis'? Four, five in the morning?

Following my hideous dream, we sat in her bedroom, talking. She'd brought me a pint glass of icy cold water and appeared genuinely concerned for my welfare. She wanted to know more about my dream. At least it diverted the conversation away from anything that may or may not have happened in her bed. Although it came as a relief to avoid that particular subject, I found it equally disturbing to recall the awful nightmare. Francis suggested I lay off alcohol for a while, to see if that helped. Of course, she was right, but it was Catch-22, I drank to sleep, but the drink made me dream.

With a peck on her cheek, I dressed and left for my apartment. After downing another pint of water, along with three paracetamol, I retired to bed. It must have only taken moments to drop back off, thankfully into an undisturbed sleep.

"Hello?" I spoke into the phone, my eyes half open.

"Matt? Did I wake you?"

I sat upright, suddenly reactive. She sounded scared, her voice barely above a whisper.

"Julia. What's wrong?"

"Something has happened. Hang on…"

Pushing the phone tight to my ear, I could just make out the sound of faint footsteps. I heard curtains being drawn; closed or open? The click of a lock and a rattle of a door handle.

"What's going on?" I asked. Not understanding why I matched her low voice, I repeated the question at normal volume. She didn't reply, not immediately, anyway. Instead, I continued to listen. It sounded as though she was climbing stairs.

Speaking louder, I desperately tried to get her attention.

"Julia. Are you there? Are you at home? Is someone there? Talk to me."

Her continued silence infuriated and unnerved me.

Creeping around, closing curtains, locking doors. She must be in danger.

"Julia!" This time, I shouted. A few more seconds of silence ensued, and I deliberated hanging up and calling back to get her attention.

"I'm here."

Thank God.

"What is it? What's wrong?"

"I think he's here."

He? Who the hell is 'he'?

"Who's there, Julia? You're not making any sense."

The sound of banging on a door. Julia gasped.

"Julia?"

Clambering out of bed, I grabbed my boxers from the floor and paced the room. My phone remained tightly pushed against my ear. I prised open the blinds with my fingertips and bent down to peer outside. Everything looked normal. People milling around, busy. After all, it was Saturday lunchtime. A taxi drove past the far end of the road, pursued by a red London bus, both heading in the city's direction. I turned back to my room. The bed was a mess with scrunched-up sheets and one pillow had fallen to the floor. My clothes, after returning from next door, were abandoned and strewn across the carpet.

"Do they know where you live?"

"Who? What are you talking about, Julia?"

Silence.

"I'm coming round. You're freaking me out. This is—"

"Wait!"

Finally, Julia spoke above a murmur. I could hear her running down the stairs, the front door unlocking, the handle turning.

Then silence.

"Julia!" I shouted again.

A car whooshed by at her end, quickly accompanied by the front door closing. The sound of a key locking and a further rattle of a doorknob. I could only assume she'd locked herself back inside.

"Matthew. I think they know we met. Last month, in Russell Square. I'm sure they followed me."

"Who? Who knows? Who followed you?"

Annoyance surpassed my apprehension. Julia had phoned me yet had barely spoken a word, and when she did, she spoke in riddles.

"Listen," she eventually said, "I need to tell you something. But not on the phone. I don't trust them. We need to meet."

"Okay. When? Where?"

"Soon. Not yet. Maybe in a week or two. It's too dangerous. They know."

"Who knows what? You're not making—"

"Just wait for my call. Okay?"

I'd had enough. Even guilt couldn't hold my interest any longer.

"Yeah. Whatever. Think of somewhere you want to meet and let me know."

"Oh, I know *where* we'll be meeting."

Expecting her to suggest somewhere safe in public, I was astounded, and freaked out, by her suggestion.

"Where?"

"In the woods."

Oh no.

"What bloody woods?"

Surely she would not suggest *that* place?

"The woods next to the Reid house. I have to show you something."

23

A COUPLE of weeks after Julia's crazy call, I ventured out onto Kensington High Street, a thirty-minute walk from my apartment. I'd tried phoning her back several times since, but she hadn't picked up. However, she sent me two texts, both informing me she would be in touch soon. When the time is right she'd unnervingly added.

If she hadn't sounded so scared, both on the call and by the time I'd met her in Russell Square, I think I would have told her I wasn't interested. I'd had enough of that family. Only Amelia seemed anywhere near *normal*. But ever since Graham's arrest, Julia's whole demeanour had become irrational, both physically and mentally. Had I misinterpreted her situation? Did she actually miss *him*? Miss his 'control'? Had Graham held her together all those years? I worried she may head for some kind of breakdown. I also sensed an undercurrent, not just with Julia, but with events that were transpiring around me.

You only need to see it through.

.   .   .

During a half-hour stroll, Google Maps directed me via some lovely back streets of West London to Hogarth Road, before crossing the busy Cromwell Road and onto Marloes Road. I'd never been good at dating property, but the houses lining either side of the elegant streets looked Victorian. Or could they be Edwardian? It didn't matter to me, I just admired their style. Tall, four or five-storey buildings, bay windows, most of which were painted bright white. Some had pillared entrances, and many had black wrought iron fences, with steps between descending to the basements below.

Halfway along Marloes Road, I spotted a pub on my left. The Devonshire Arms. It looked so inviting, especially the beer garden at the front, surrounded by planters filled with pretty and colourful flowers. Four huge parasols protected the seating area from the sun, which had re-emerged during the past few days. Making a mental note, I continued to my original destination.

The barbers were unexpectedly quiet, and they offered me one of the large red chairs before I could sit down in the waiting area. Twenty minutes later, the transformation startled me. Gone was my beard – clean shaven with one of those cut-throat razors which always scared me to death – and I'd had an inch of hair cut or trimmed from my scalp. Leaving, I felt fresh and more like my old self.

With a renewed energy, The Devonshire Arms looked even more appealing upon my return journey. The sun was now high and offered considerable heat. The shade of a parasol and a cold beer almost pulled me inside, as if somebody had held a giant magnet at the door and dragged me in. I certainly didn't need a second invitation.

However, as I crossed the street, that hideous feeling of being watched threatened to overwhelm me again.

Stopping at the doorstep, I spun around. A few pedestrians were making their way along the main road, but nobody acting conspicuously. A black taxi, pursued by a white van, whizzed by. Everything was normal and, as expected. Scanning the windows of the nearby houses and flats was futile, most reflecting in the bright light, making it impossible to see inside.

"You going in or coming out, mate?"

"Oh, sorry," I said to a couple, who had crept up behind me and attempted to enter the pub.

With one last glance up and down the street, I followed them in.

Once I'd ordered my pint, I made my way out into the garden. Fortunately, one table of the four remained available. Grabbing it, before anybody else had the opportunity, I settled down to enjoy my beer.

Some ten minutes later, I'd finished, had the taste, and craved another. The garden had filled up, even during the time it had taken me to drink my first pint. Cursing that I hadn't brought a jumper or jacket with me to claim the table was occupied, I instead caught the eye of a girl sitting on the adjacent bench.

"Can you save my seat, please? I'm going to the bar and don't want to lose it."

"Sure," she said, grinning. I couldn't help but notice how pretty she was, even if she was at least fifteen years my junior.

Nodding my appreciation, I caught myself smiling as I made my way back inside.

Is there any female you don't find attractive? I heard Lisa whisper in my ear. A fresh wave of despondency washed over me.

Come on, Matt.

Not only had the garden filled up during the past fifteen minutes, but inside had become increasingly busy too. All four members of staff were serving and at least two more couples were waiting their turn to order drinks. Attempting to see outside, I hoped the pretty girl would be true to her word and save my table.

Just as I inched my way to the front, she appeared at my side.

"Oh, hi," I said. I soon replaced an initial feeling of disappointment that I may have lost my place with the prospect that she may have actually come inside to find me.

"Hi. You're taking your time." She laughed. A friendly and contagious laugh.

"Yeah. Kind of busy in here."

Instead of continuing the conversation, she pushed up alongside me and waved her phone towards a barman to get served.

What the…?

"Erm, I'm next," I said, suddenly pissed off with the girl who, seconds earlier, I thought may be flirting with me.

"Yeah," she said, turning her head slightly. "I know. Just trying to get his attention. You'll be here all day."

That laugh again. I felt confused.

"But what about my table?"

"Oh, yeah. Your friend is saving it for you. She wants a gin and tonic, please. Loads of ice."

I looked at the pretty girl with suspicion. Was she having me on?

"He's next," she said to the barman. I hadn't even noticed him approach us.

"Yes, mate?"

"Erm, pint of Pride and a gin and tonic, please."

"Loads of ice in the gin," the pretty girl added, giggling. "You'd forget your head, you would," she said, nudging me.

"Yeah. Maybe you're right."

"Francis. What a pleasant surprise."

If I hadn't sounded sincere, it was because I hadn't been. How did she know where I'd be? And had it been her who had been watching me when I'd entered the pub?

"Hello, you," she replied, taking her drink. "This looks lovely. And what a great pub you've found. I didn't even know it exist—"

"Did you follow me?"

Francis looked taken aback, hurt even.

"Follow you? No, I didn't. And I don't like to be accused of that."

The pretty girl had returned, carrying a tray of four icy cold lagers. She looked at Francis and back at me. She winked.

Bloody flirt, I thought, but it still made me feel momentarily good about myself again.

Francis must have noticed the wink too.

"Friend of yours?"

Quickly, I sat down, closest to the girl, nudging Francis along with my backside. At least Francis would have to look through me to see her at the next table.

"She saved my seat, that's all. Well, until you turned up, of course."

Fortunately, the din of chatter drowned out our conversation from any prying ears.

"Young enough to be your daughter."

Francis smiled sarcastically, pursed her lips and sucked childlike on the straw poking from the top of her drink. The clear liquid in her glass sank. Following her lead, I took a huge gulp of my beer. I wanted to steer the conversation back onto a more amiable course, but I failed miserably.

"How did you know I would be here? It's not as though we're close to home."

She answered, dropping the straw which she had been holding between her teeth.

"Didn't. I went to the bookstore on Kensington High Street and walked this way back. It's the fastest route. Then I saw you stand up in this garden and go inside. I guessed you were getting another beer. So, I wandered over and sat down." She nodded to the pretty girl behind me. "Your new girlfriend said it was taken, and that's when I told her to find you and tell you I wanted a G and T."

So, had she followed me or not? Her version sounded plausible, but I'd encountered so much bullshit during the past year that I couldn't tell the truth from a lie anymore.

"Anyway," she continued, "let's take a look at you."

Unsure of what she meant, I turned to face her.

"Hmm, quite nice too." She placed her hands on my cheeks and turned my head from side to side. "I liked your beard, but you look younger without it. And your hair…"

Francis could be quite the flirt too.

We stayed in The Devonshire Arms for another two hours, or more to the point, another four drinks. At one point, Francis ran across the road to a small grocery store and bought twenty cigarettes. I hadn't smoked for years, but the combination of alcohol and her insistence on me having one meant I couldn't refuse. The nicotine made my whole body, and mind, relax. By the time we arrived home, I'd completely forgotten about being followed, stalked or however else I attempted to label it.

Francis ordered a takeaway, and we sat around listening to music. We continued drinking and smoked the rest of the cigarettes. It must have been around midnight when we finally crashed out in bed.

And all the time that we'd been eating and chatting and drinking and smoking, I'd missed the text message on my phone.

The following morning, through blurry, hungover eyes, I reached for the mobile in my pocket to check the time.

One message.

Sent the previous evening at eight-twenty-four **PM**.

From Katrina.

```
I've seen your friend. She isn't well.
```

24

FRANCIS SLEPT SOUNDLY by my side, so I clicked reply and asked Katrina who she was talking about, although I already realised.

It had come as a surprise to hear from her at all. I'd sent her my number, but never heard back, so assumed she never had the charger.

'We can be mobile phone pals…'

My message was abrupt, and I knew I had to keep Katrina sweet to get any kind of sensible response, but, like Julia, I'd become more and more pissed off with her cryptic messages and having to step around her, as if treading on eggshells. It reminded me of the day I'd seen her on the swing. What had she said?

'… be careful… they know…'. I'd never understood who she meant, or what they knew. Perhaps I never would. But probably, as with many things Katrina said, it had meant nothing. She had followed it up with a familiar giggle before running away.

'Katrina has multiple distinct identities…'

But maybe Katrina *had* called me before? The one I'd

taken whilst sitting in the pub. I'd heard an indistinct murmur and a rustling of leaves, but nobody spoke. Had that been her calling from the woods?

You and your fucking mobile phone pals.

Quickly scrolling through my calls, I found the missed call matching the day and time I'd received it. But they had withheld the number. Katrina wouldn't have the know-how to do such a thing, would she? But why would she withhold the number, anyway? Her last text had her name brazenly displayed across my screen.

Yet again, I'd been left with a piece missing from a puzzle. But this was Katrina, and Katrina's puzzles always had several pieces missing.

"Morning."

"Jeez. You gave me a heart attack."

Francis laughed. She hunched herself up onto her elbows and trailed a fingertip down my back.

This is getting out of hand.

"Who are you messaging?" she asked, sitting up to see my screen.

Quickly, I pulled my hand down and hid the phone from view.

"Just something I need to take care of," I said.

"Oh, well. I'm sure she will let you know if it's important."

She?

"Anyway," Francis continued, "it's Sunday morning. Fancy a long lie-in?"

A few days later, I met Amelia. In the meantime, unsurprisingly, Katrina hadn't replied, but more worryingly, neither had Julia.

I'd saved us a table outside again. The weather had

become overcast, and the temperature had dropped a few degrees, but I didn't feel comfortable inside. Something about being indoors with Amelia made me feel claustrophobic.

We exchanged our usual pleasantries, and I asked about the baby. She told me there were only three months to go, but Tracy thought it may be born sooner.

"Shit, she's a qualified midwife too, is she?"

"She is actually, Matt. Didn't you know?"

Of course she bloody is.

Appearing smug, Amelia, in her now familiar pose, rested her hands on her stomach. Yet again, I couldn't help but stare at her attire. She wore a pair of denim dungarees, but, as with her oversized jumper, they were far too big. At least I could make out her bump though. Suddenly, it felt very real. Or, more precisely, surreal.

"Anyway, how is the baby?"

"*Our* baby, Matt. I wish you would—"

"Not now. Just tell me how you both are."

At that moment, I was unsure whether we could ever make things work out between us. Our meetings had become more subdued. Maybe it was because I was developing a friendship with Francis, if that's how it could be described, or my yearning to move on in life frustrated me. However, Amelia was my wife, and I respected her. Besides, we were in this together. In return to my renewed optimism, Amelia became a little more upbeat too. It sounds clichéd, but we were invariably in sync with one another.

There's still chemistry.

"Oh, he's a little fighter. Always kicking and—"

"He? Did you say he?"

Sensing my wife's embarrassment, she tried in vain to backtrack.

"He, she, I, well, I don't know——"

"You *do* know, don't you?" I interrupted again. At least Amelia had the decency to blush. She rarely got embarrassed, and if she did, it was a sure sign I had caught her out. It left her with no choice but to confess.

"Well, yes. I hope you don't mind. It was an accident. Came up on the scan. Please don't be cross."

Without making it obvious, I genuinely didn't care. I knew she should have told me before, but somehow it didn't matter to me. Also, I didn't want a scene, and I didn't want to make her feel bad. The only thing that pissed me off was that Tracy and Melissa would know too.

"No. I'm good. It's nice to know, actually. A little baby boy, eh?"

"Yes. It's exciting, isn't it?"

Again, my positive response rubbed off on her.

The situation gave me an opportunity to be involved. Something for just us two. Something the other bloody family members couldn't do for us.

"I want to be involved in choosing a name. I think that's fair, don't you?"

"Yes, sure. That would be, well…"

"You haven't already chosen a name, have you, Amelia?"

I hadn't needed to ask. Of course, *they* had chosen a name.

"No. We've had some ideas, but——"

"We? Do I even need to ask who *we* are?"

Aware I was raising my voice, I leant forward and placed my arms on the table. Fortunately, we were the only occupants sitting outside. However, the streets were busy as usual, and I didn't want anybody staring at an angry man sitting with a heavily pregnant woman.

"Don't be like that," she said. "If you were around, you could help choose. But you've decided to live away from me, from your baby, from your family."

"I want to help choose, Amelia. You have no right without my input."

She wanted to keep the peace and knew my request wasn't at all unreasonable, whatever the circumstances.

"Yes, yes, okay. Have a think. When we meet next time, we can chat about it then."

Still, I couldn't resist turning the screw.

"Are you going to tell me what names you and Mother have come up with?"

"Stop being so bloody childish. We've just got a baby name book and we've been going through them. It's only a bit of fun."

The conversation petered out, leaving an awkward silence.

"Have you heard anything from Julia?"

I'd deliberately sprung the question upon her to catch her off guard. Amelia spilt a small amount of her coffee over the rim. It landed on the leg of her dungarees.

"Oh, damn. Look at that," she said, standing quickly. It amazed me she kept one hand on her stomach without needing both arms to keep her balance.

Brushing herself down, she said she had some wet wipes back at the office and would sort it when she got back. She sat down, clearly agitated by the way the meeting was panning out.

"Well?"

"Well, what?"

I almost laughed.

"Have you heard anything from Julia?"

Amelia gave herself a few moments to settle.

"Why would I?"

"Because she's your sister. Because her husband is locked away awaiting trial for murder. Because——"

"Alright, alright."

She readjusted her backside on the chair and pulled her dungarees from underneath until she became comfortable.

"If you must know, Julia is seeing a psychiatrist."

What the....?

"A psychiatrist? What for?"

Although a rhetorical question, Amelia answered anyway.

"Because of those things you've just listed, Matt. Her husband being locked away has really disturbed her. She's gone off the rails."

"What a lovely way of putting it, darling."

Amelia smirked at me.

"Come on. Even you never thought that Julia was all there, did you? She just sat in that house, day after day after day. Never left the living room unless she had a call of nature or needed to eat or drink."

That's because Graham forced her to do all that ancestry shit and find your next unsuspecting husband.

"She's never been a mixer. Can you remember when you asked Graham where his wife was?"

'*My wife works for a charity, Matt. She spends months abroad at a time, around Africa, you know, dealing with orphaned kids and other stuff...*'

I nodded.

"Well, he wasn't lying."

That makes a change.

"In fact, early in their relationship, Julia spent a lot of time out of the country. She meant well and had a good heart, but when she eventually returned home, you know, for good, she had changed. Tracy and Mother think she met somebody abroad, had an affair. She was easily led, as you well know."

My moment of having the upper hand soon dissipated. Her confidence had returned. I found it difficult to find fault with anything she said, I could easily equate it all to Julia. She differed from her two sisters. Unassuming, and extremely vulnerable. I recalled meeting her in Russell Square. She never had told me why she'd asked to meet me.

'She's gone off the rails...'

And it was easy to imagine her abroad, in some village in the middle of nowhere in Central Africa. Away from everybody, especially Graham and the family. The idea suddenly felt very appealing.

"So, how do you know she's seeing a shrink?"

"What a lovely way of putting it, darling." She paused, allowing herself a wry smile. *That* smile. "But if you must know, we *do* still speak to her. She is family, after all."

Another dig. Amelia was loving it.

"Tracy calls on her now and then. Checks she's okay. She went round a few weeks ago, kept knocking on the door, but couldn't get Julia to answer, even though she knew she was in."

Something clicked in my brain. I didn't like the *few weeks ago* bit.

"How did she know that?"

"She could hear her. Tracy held the letterbox open. Heard Julia mention Russell Square."

'... I think they know we met. Last month, in Russell Square...'

Shit. It was the time she'd called me. Did Amelia know she'd been on the phone with me?

'... I think she's here...'

What else did Tracy hear? What else had we discussed? Bollocks. Meeting in the woods. Had she heard that part? Is that why Julia hadn't been in contact since?

"What did Tracy do?"

My voice had risen a few octaves. I'm sure Amelia noticed, but she saved me from any embarrassment.

"She went around the back of the house. Julia often leaves the back door open. That's how she found her."

"Found her? What does that mean? Found her?"

"Matt. Julia was sitting in her armchair. She had a bottle full of pills in one hand and a bottle of Scotch in the other. If Tracy hadn't found her…"

25

"Is she okay now?"

The thought of Julia being that depressed hit me hard, but could I trust Amelia's version of events?

"She's back home. For now. Until she's fully recovered."

"In her house, you mean?"

Knowing exactly which 'home' Amelia had meant, I still wanted to hear it from her mouth. The visions of being strapped to the bed and Tracy pushing giant-sized pills down my throat made me shake.

Could Julia be in the same bed?

"In the family home, Matt. She's in a spare room. The doctors are very happy that Tracy is looking after her."

Nodding my head in agreement whilst thinking the exact opposite proved difficult. Again, I wondered how much Tracy had heard of Julia's relatively incoherent phone call to me. Julia had spoken so quietly, so vaguely, I'd barely been able to decipher her words myself. The only time she had raised her voice was when she mentioned Russell Square, the part Tracy *had* understood.

What else had she said?

'*Have you been followed?*'

Julia had acted irrationally, nonsensically. Her behaviour had scared me. I recollected her appearance when we met. Greasy hair, a long baggy cardigan which she kept wrapping and unwrapping from her chest. And those fingernails, filthy and bloody. She had continually bitten at the quicks, hard skin which protruded at angles, like jagged edges. She'd stood and paced to the lawn, turned and then stepped back again, her eyes darting everywhere.

"Matt?"

"Yeah, yeah. Just trying to imagine what she's going through, that's—"

"When did you last see her?"

Shit.

"Sorry. I, erm, I do not know. Before Graham did what he did in the woods, I think."

Amelia didn't smile. She showed no emotion. But her eyes never left mine. A look of knowing something but not being able to quite prove it. Or could she prove it, but opted for politeness instead? Either way, she didn't ask again.

"She's psychotic. That's the diagnosis."

Even though I didn't really know what it meant, the word still scared me.

"Psychotic?" I repeated. "Is that even curable?"

"Apparently so. We need to get the balance of chemicals right in her head. Tracy knows about it."

Of course she fucking does.

"Will Julia go home again? I mean to her own place."

"Hopefully, soon. We don't really want her in the house. You know, with a baby on the way."

Although considering it a cruel thing to say, I'd half expected it. I even allowed myself a little smile when I considered how many bloody nutters were in that building already.

"But what if she doesn't recover before then? You can't throw her out onto the streets."

Amelia stood. We'd already spent longer in conversation than at any previous meeting. Although she didn't rub it in that she had to get back to work, she still couldn't resist one little dig.

"Maybe she could come and live with you?"

Once Amelia disappeared towards her office, I ordered another coffee and sat alone outside. I needed time to think, and take it all in. Could Julia *really* be psychotic?

Katrina's text.

I've seen your friend. She isn't well.

'*Your friend.*' Although I'd asked Katrina who she was talking about, I somehow already knew, she had meant Julia. It's why I hadn't heard from her. And Katrina would have witnessed Tracy administer the drugs. What state of mind would Julia be in?

As I made my way home on the tube, I tried to push Julia to the back of my mind, for the time being, at least. Instead, I focused on where I might find a job. Nothing stressful, and definitely away from the world of property management. However, I needed something to tide me over until the birth. But what could I do? Possibly look into the dropshipping idea I'd had? The money from the inheritance would keep me going for a long while, but it wouldn't last forever. Besides, the more I spent, the more I would eat into any form of deposit I'd need for my own place. But I was enjoying the freedom. The right to wake whenever I wanted. Meander around the West London streets. Take in Hyde Park, walk, sit and people watch. Drink copious amounts of coffee, or grab a beer or two if the urge hit me, which had been far too frequently. I thought of all the people who say, 'if I won the lottery, I wouldn't be able to give up work'. Are they mad? I'd hand in my notice the next day, desperate to get away. Then again, I'd never had that *dream* job, the one where you woke with a spring in your step. Although I enjoyed working in property, I realised it was a means to an end rather than a lifelong aspiration. But maybe that was the answer? I knew the property game well. Perhaps I could visit some local estate agents, and ask if they needed anybody on a part-time basis. Yes, that would be ideal. If I could cover my rent until the baby came along, then at least I wouldn't be haemorrhaging my savings, and it would stop me spending so much in coffeehouses and pubs.

The girl who sat opposite me on the tube looked away when she noticed me smiling to myself. She wore state-of-the-art headphones. Feeling myself blush, it came as a relief when we quickly pulled into Earl's Court Station.

Deciding to put my new-laid plan into action, I strolled purposefully along the principal shopping streets whilst still heading towards my apartment. I'd never paid attention to any estate agents along the route before but considered there must be at least three or four along such a busy street. Although dressed in a polo shirt and jeans, I still thought it okay if I popped my head around the door to make a polite enquiry. If any showed an interest, I would need to return with an updated curriculum vitae. The very idea momentarily halted my positive thinking. A curriculum vitae, maybe attached to my family tree?

Come on. That's all in the past, isn't it?

The first two I tried yielded no success. One had no vacancies at all, full or part-time, and the second told me to return in two weeks when the manager returned from holiday. The third, however, may have had exactly what I was looking for.

It was an independent agency. As soon as I stepped inside, a cheerful young lady greeted me. Once I explained the reason for my visit, a guy stood up behind her. He quickly introduced himself as the owner and asked me to join him at his desk. Thirty minutes later, I left with an offer of a part-time role showing prospective customers around local properties. It was, of course, subject to seeing my CV. The worst part, though, and something I hadn't previously considered, was that he wanted a reference, preferably from my last employer.

Could I contact Mike direct? I'd have to beg him not to mention it to Amelia or Tracy. Surely he would understand if I explained the circumstances. The big problem would be trying to speak to him without the intervention of the sisters. I knew they saw his emails, they saw everybody's bloody emails. And a letter would land on their desk before his. How could I get to Mike without them knowing? Maybe Francis could help?

With a renewed skip in my step, I called at a convenience store and picked up two bottles of wine. Hoping Francis would be up for a celebratory drink, I eagerly made my way to her apartment. However, as I ascended the last flight of stairs, I heard voices. They came from behind her closed door.

Gingerly, I made the final few steps on tiptoe.

Sure enough, there *were* voices, one hers, the other a male. Did I recognise him?

"You shouldn't even be here," said an animated Francis.

Another door closed with a thud, somewhere behind me. It made me jump.

Everything went quiet in Francis's apartment.

Once I turned, I recognised the older lady standing outside her door, her key hovering at the lock. I'd seen her and exchanged pleasantries before. This time, she didn't look so friendly.

Her eyes darted from me to Francis's door. All remained quiet inside. The lady was obviously interested in why I was hovering outside my neighbour's apartment when my own front door stood ten feet to the left.

"Just delivering some wine," I said, holding the bottles aloft.

The woman nodded a disbelieving acknowledgement, tutted and made for the stairs. Waiting until the main entrance door closed with a bang, I turned my attention back to Francis. All was deathly quiet inside. I knocked lightly.

Nothing.

A few moments passed, and I knocked again. Finally, I heard footsteps on the other side. Light, but definitely coming in my direction. The sound of the lock unlatching and the handle clicking before the door opened with the slightest of cracks. I could just make out Francis's eyes peering from the gloom within.

Has she got all her curtains closed?

"Yes. What is it?"

Taken aback by her hostile response, I held a bottle of wine high enough for her to see.

"Just wondered if you fancied a drink? I've got a bit of a favour to ask too. Need to pick your brains, if you—"

"I'm busy, Matt. It'll have to be another time."

As I attempted to glance over her head, she pushed the door tighter still. Only the tiniest of cracks remained.

"You okay?" I mouthed, barely audible.

She nodded unconvincingly and pushed her door shut with a firm push.

Listening for any further voices within, all remained extremely quiet on the other side. However, as I reluctantly turned away, I heard the male speak again. He had lowered his voice but still spoke loud enough for me to hear.

"Has he gone?"

26

Two weeks would pass by before I saw Francis again.

Intrigued by who had been in her apartment and maybe a little jealous too, I'd remained in my lounge until the early hours waiting for the sound of her door opening. But I heard nobody leave. In fact, I'd fallen asleep. The next thing I knew was Francis messaging me to say she had departed early the following morning to visit her mum. It left me feeling uneasy, but I felt a lot worse when I bumped into our elderly neighbour a couple of days later.

"Is your friend okay now?" she asked, without a 'hello,' or a 'good morning.'

"My friend?"

"Apartment 404. Your neighbour. The door you were standing outside the other day. Pretending to deliver wine."

What's her bloody problem?

Deciding she was just being nosey, plus a little condescending, I attempted to brush her aside with a shrug of my shoulders. She hadn't quite finished.

"You haven't seen her then?"

Why is she pushing this so much?

"No. Not for a few days. Why do you ask?"

The woman appeared offended at my brash response and obviously didn't take kindly to people speaking to her that way.

How ironic.

I could tell she wanted to tell me more. The quintessential nosey neighbour.

"The day after you were hanging around outside her—"

"I wasn't *hanging* around. I was taking her wine."

"Whatever. That's none of my business."

But you sure as hell want it to be.

"Anyway, the following morning, she left very early."

Deliberating whether to inform her I already knew that, she continued before I had the chance to say anything.

"And she left with a man."

Her information momentarily floored me.

He stayed all night?

"Oh, okay."

Feeling disconsolate that Francis could indeed have another man in her life, I turned to unlock my door. My neighbour was obviously more astute than I'd initially given her credit for.

"No, that's not all." She raised her voice slightly, grabbing my attention. "I don't think they are an item, as such."

She smiled to reassure me.

"As when they left, they weren't talking. In fact, they looked furious at each other. Anyway, she was so preoccupied with trying to get away, that she didn't see me standing in my doorway."

Just happened to be there, did you?

"And that's when I noticed it."

She now had my full attention. By the look of the expression etched across her face, she was loving her position of power. If she'd had the nerve, I swear she would have charged me for further information. Realising I had to remain patient, as well as polite, I fixed on a smile and nodded politely for her to continue.

"You'll never guess."

Oh, just fucking tell me.

"I'm useless at guessing. Can you just tell me, please?"

"Well, when she turned around after locking her door…"

Stop dragging it out.

"…she looked like she'd been arguing with that fella."

"What makes you say that?"

"Because that's when I noticed she had a bloody great black eye."

As soon as I escaped from my neighbour who obviously wanted to talk forever about the incident, I tried to call Francis. It went directly to voicemail, as did every subsequent call I made during the following two weeks. Text messages remained undelivered. At one point, I considered calling the police, but I couldn't cope with more questions. Besides, I'd only be digging myself deeper and deeper into affairs that had nothing to do with me. I imagined DCI Small probing me on how well I knew Francis, if we'd had intimate relations, and the inevitable knock-on effect if Amelia found out.

Whilst Francis had been away, I returned to the estate agents with a copy of my curriculum vitae. I'd had a brainwave to give my previous employer as a referee, the company in North London, citing that my ex-wife still worked at Opacy. I'd added we were going through a difficult divorce settlement and it may affect any forthcoming reference. Fortunately, my new boss, John Brookes, had been totally understanding and agreed to my preferred contact. He told me it was just a 'box ticking exercise' anyway. A week later, he called to confirm everything was in order and that I could start whenever I wanted.

It sounded perfect and much better paid than I initially expected. Obviously not what I'd been used to, but it would cover my rent and some of my bills. John had added that if the arrangement worked out, I could do extra hours whenever it suited me. The prospect of not eating into my savings pleased me immensely. All I had to do was log onto their website every few days, and choose which viewings I could cover that week. Just what I needed.

When I met Amelia the following week, I decided not to mention the job. We discussed baby names but came to no conclusion. When she broached the subject, full of enthusiasm, I didn't have the nerve to tell her I'd forgotten all about it. My preoccupation with Francis's black eye, Julia's awful predicament, and starting a new job had been at the forefront of my thoughts. Instead, I made up names on the spot, each of which Amelia quite rightly dismissed as absurd.

"You haven't given it any thought whatsoever, have you?" she asked after I suggested naming our child after me. Even I had the decency to go red at my stupid idea.

"I have, it's just difficult."

"Probably shacked up with another woman, are you?"

Shit.

Fortunately, my face already resembled a ripened tomato, so I could hide my embarrassment behind my previous faux pas.

"I do not know what you're talking about, and I find it quite offensive too."

Amelia smiled.

"Yeah, whatever."

Did she know something? Of course not, it would be impossible. She didn't even know where I lived.

"Be as sarcastic as you like, Amelia, but I have nothing to hide. What about you? Have you met anybody else?"

The question tumbled out of my mouth before I had a chance to stop it. Halfway through, I knew I'd made a mistake. She replied through gritted teeth.

"I'm expecting *our* baby, you idiot. I've been suffering from morning sickness and goodness knows what else. What time do I have for anybody else? Besides…" she sat back, giving herself chance to regain control, "…we're married, Matthew. You may want to remember that because I will never forget."

It came as a surprise just how much her words affected me.

I won't forget, either.

Apologising, I suggested we brought the meeting to an end. It hadn't gone well, and I had to admit it was down to me. We parted with the usual air kiss. Guilt riddled me as she walked away with her head bowed low.

After a full day of showing prospective clients around West London apartments, I finally returned to my own. It was exactly two weeks since I'd heard Francis and her 'friend' on the other side of her door. As I fumbled for the key to my door, Francis's opened. She took one look up and immediately tried to retreat inside. But she stumbled, and I was quick, and I got across before she could shut herself away.

"Leave me alone, Matt," she protested, staring at my foot wedged in the doorway. "I just need to be on my own for a while."

But Francis didn't know me that well and didn't understand all that I'd been through. I'd had enough of the bullshit and being given the runaround. Although I knew it was wrong, I barged my way into her apartment before shutting the door behind us. Francis didn't put up a fight. Instead, she reluctantly lifted her face.

Looking at her eye, I needed to know whether our nosey neighbour had got her facts right.

Although the substantial bruising had subsided, and Francis wore a lot of make-up, I could make out some yellowing underneath the eye socket. It spread an inch along her cheekbone.

"What's that?"

Instinctively, she tried to cover it with her hand, spinning away at the same time.

"It's nothing. And it's none of your business."

"Francis." I grabbed her arm, pulling her hand away. "If somebody has hit you, I want to know."

"I fell," she said. "Tripped and caught my face on the edge of the work surface." She nodded towards the offending corner in her kitchen.

"But I heard a man's voice in here. Two weeks ago. You sounded as though you were arguing."

Francis laughed. A sarcastic laugh. She mellowed, confident in her version of events.

"Quite the Sherlock Holmes, aren't you, Matthew Walker?" she replied sarcastically.

"Who was it, Francis? If you're seeing somebody..."

She took a step towards me.

Involuntarily, I stepped backwards. I'd asked too many questions and annoyed her. The last thing I needed was to be mixed up with a woman in a relationship, especially if he had a tendency towards violence.

"I've told you, I fell. That man you heard is a friend of my mum's. He lives near her. And every time I go to visit, he sticks his nose in and tells me I don't see her often enough. He's been around here a couple of times. Always saying what I should and——"

"I've never seen him."

I did not know whether she was telling the truth. Again, like so many other things in my life, it sounded perfectly feasible, yet somehow flawed.

"Perhaps because you drink too much whisky in the evenings and consequently sleep until lunchtime every day? If I don't have a visitor between noon and five o'clock, you're in constant danger of missing all the fun."

Francis laughed. That same laugh as when I'd first met her. A little too nervous to come across as genuine.

I was no expert on human behaviour, however, I had reached the point where I wouldn't believe the postman had a letter for me until I read the address on the envelope.

27

IT FELT good to be working once more, and the option of choosing when I wanted to suited me fine. However, by the time I'd completed three weeks, we'd reached the middle of July and summer had hit the South East of England with a vengeance. The stifling heat of daytime barely dissipated during the night, and my already sporadic sleep pattern went from bad to worse.

Francis suggested I visited a doctor to be prescribed some sleeping pills. I'd never taken anything to help me sleep or to keep me awake or anything in between. The thought of popping drugs to help with a natural phenomenon felt alien, but after seven months of deprivation, I knew I had to try something.

A few days later, her bruising had subsided, and I didn't mention it again. However, I noticed that her enthusiasm had dwindled towards me, maybe she was purposefully holding herself back? We had made up soon after our altercation, but I didn't push things. It wasn't in my best interests to be involved with anybody. It felt more like a fling, anyway, akin to a holiday romance. Two people in the right place at the right time, or the wrong place at the wrong time, depending on one's outlook on life. Did she feel the same, or had her visitor had an influence?

During a day off work, I knocked on her door and asked if she would like to go for a coffee, or maybe a lunchtime drink. Francis declined without hesitation. She said she needed to visit her mum.

Despite the knockback, I decided I needed some air anyway. Following another restless night, I considered a visit to a pharmacy near the tube station. Maybe try an over-the-counter remedy to help with my sleep. My mum had always said if the medicine was herbal, you weren't pumping yourself full of unnatural chemicals.

Having a purpose for going somewhere made me feel better about venturing out. Without a goal, I inevitably ended up in a pub or drinking copious amounts of caffeine, just for the sake of it. Maybe the combination of both had been the major culprit for my lack of sleep. But deep down, I knew the real reason. It wasn't as though I didn't sleep at all. In fact, some nights I wished I hadn't, given the hideous and lifelike nightmares which accompanied it.

Instead of a chemist, I came across one of those health food stores. The ones I'd seen advertising on TV. 'Buy one, get one free'. 'Vitamin this, vitamin that'. Every letter of the alphabet covered and every other substance that humans were supposed to generate themselves, all available in the form of a pill.

The sales assistant had been delighted to help. Maybe sleep deprivation had been her area of expertise. As soon as I'd mentioned I suffered from insomnia, or sporadic sleep patterns, her face lit up. She pointed out several glass jars, full of all colours of the rainbow. It reminded me of being in a sweet shop as a child, but instead of a sugar overdose, I had to choose something to knock me out.

She leant towards magnesium. So much so, I thought she maybe had a secret stash of it in some underground lock-up. I imagined my mum smiling, knowing I'd be full of doubt and reservation.

The assistant persuaded me with her favourite brand. She said her husband took the same product every night, and he had slept through for the past five years.

Probably just pleased to block out your voice.

With my glass jar of little white pills safely tucked into my pocket, I made for Costa and another shot of caffeine. I could always cut back tomorrow.

Thankfully, there was a table free outside. Grabbing my usual Americano, I settled down to watch the world go by. I still had so much on my mind. Julia hadn't contacted me yet, although I realised Tracy would have removed her mobile phone anyway, the thought of her suffering from psychosis had got to me. How long had she been ill and what would the long-term diagnosis be? More to the point, would she need to be 'looked after' by her sisters and mother for an eternity? Julia would not want that. In fact, I doubt she could think of anything worse. I needed to know how long she would be under their jurisdiction, but how could I find out? Amelia had gone on the defensive and asked why I had so much interest. Appealing to Tracy or Melissa would be a non-starter.

Katrina!

Mobile phone pals.

Quickly, I composed a brief text and hit *Send.* Purposefully, I kept it short, friendly, and to the point. Placing my mobile on the table, I impatiently glanced towards it, imploring Katrina to reply.

Thinking I could be weeks waiting, my luck changed. Within minutes, she responded. But it wasn't what I'd been expecting.

Aunty Julia isn't staying here anymore.

Believing any follow-up questions to Katrina would be futile, I instead tried Julia direct. Not via text, but by calling her. Unsurprisingly, though, Julia didn't pick up. I left a long message, asking how she was and explaining how worried I'd been. I reminded her of the last time I'd heard from her.

"You said you needed to tell me something, and you wanted to meet. Can you please call me back and tell me what you had on your mind?"

Purposefully, I avoided the bit about meeting in the woods. Although she'd said she needed to show me something, I somehow doubted it. She hadn't even told me why she had asked to meet last time. Besides, I never wanted to be shown anything else in that place again. Instead, I suggested meeting in Russell Square once more. Ending the message with another plea for her to call back, I settled back down to finish my now cooling coffee. And then, out of the corner of my eye, I saw Francis. She walked hastily along the road from our apartment block, before turning right at the junction and away from where I sat. She hadn't seen me at all.

Pushing my drink to one side, I collected my phone and followed her.

As expected, she turned left at the next crossroads and headed along Earl's Court Road, a short stroll from the tube station.

How can I follow her on the tube?

Maybe I could get on the next carriage, but how would I know when she disembarked? Where did she say her mum lived again?

As I tried to think of a way to keep her in my sights, she completely threw me by stopping outside the underground station, but instead of turning left to enter, she turned to her right and waited to cross the busy road. I had to dart into a shop doorway to avoid her seeing me.

Waiting until the pelican crossing beeped, I stepped out of my temporary hiding place and zigzagged between stationary vehicles to join Francis on her side of the road. She turned left and then immediately right onto Hogarth Road, a wide street housing a mixture of small shops and elegant houses and hotels.

Where is *she going?*

Fortunately, not once did she look behind. Not until she stopped to cross the road.

Shit.

Darting up some steps towards a huge red door, I halted halfway, crouched down, and peered between the balustrades. Francis appeared to be looking directly at me but soon turned on her heels, crossed the road, and continued with her hasty stride.

Creeping back down the steps, I remained on my side of the road. The street curved slightly to the left, and I had trouble keeping up as she again quickened her pace. And then, out of nowhere, she ran up some steps to her left and disappeared through some sliding doors.

Waiting until I was convinced she was out of sight, I walked along the road until I could see where Francis had gone. The glass doors slid effortlessly open again, and a couple walked out of the hotel arm in arm.

Park Lane Kensington Hotel.

Why on earth would Francis be going into a hotel?

Begrudgingly, I turned to walk home. I couldn't just hang around outside and wait for her. Besides, she could be in there for ages, overnight even.

Once back at my apartment, I unlocked the door and pushed it open. That's when I noticed the note on the floor.

Gone to Mum's for a few days. See you when I get back. Sorry if a bit grumpy earlier. F x.

Later that night, as I sat on my sofa watching some inane cop show on TV, I heard a noise on the landing. At first, I ignored it, but the sound of jangling keys soon followed it, directly outside my door. Muting the television, I stepped quickly and quietly across the room and peeked through my spy hole.

And I made it just in time to see the distorted shape of Francis disappear inside her own apartment.

28

FINALLY, the following Monday morning, I met with Julia. She'd returned my call later the evening I'd left the message, around an hour after Francis had come home from her secret hotel visit.

Before Julia called, I wrestled with my conscience about whether to bother Francis. Although intrigued to find out what was going on, I knew it was none of my business and besides, I would have to admit to following her. But as soon as Julia phoned, I pushed Francis and her mysterious exploits to the back of my mind. Julia's insistence on where we met helped. I argued that there surely had to be a better venue than the woods, but she remained adamant.

The only other time I'd been there was when I followed Katrina. She'd led me to the grave, well almost, before veering off and retrieving the burner phone from underneath some rocks. I'd promised myself that would be the last time I'd ever venture anywhere near that place, but Julia's call had left me with little choice. Her erratic behaviour worried me, and I knew I owed it to her.

Whilst on the call, I mentioned Katrina. It crossed my mind that she would find us in there, given how much she liked to wander around alone. Julia informed me that whilst she'd been *staying* with the family, Katrina hadn't been authorised to go into the woods.

"With Amelia and Tracy at work, only Melissa and Katrina are in the house. Katrina is no longer allowed out whilst on her own with Melissa."

Is that true?

But as I objected, Julia spoke over me. Incoherent words and incomplete sentences. Knowing my protests were futile, I told her to rest up over the weekend and call me if she needed anything.

Psychotic behaviour? It was all becoming overbearing.

We met in the village at the bottom of the hill. Personally, I'd seen nobody venture up into the woods that way. It was a steep climb, too steep for the casual walker, and besides, there were far prettier walks from the village along the river and across the downs. Besides, the dense tree line looked creepy, even to those who did not know what had happened in there, however, many locals knew. You could almost read people's thoughts as they ventured out for a stroll, 'should we climb the forbidding hill to the murder spot or continue along the tranquillity of the stream?'.

Once I spotted Julia, a nervousness crept over me. She meandered, slowly, unnatural, her head bowed at an acute angle. What if she has a 'chemical imbalance', as Amelia had so eloquently described it? Maybe the variance could trigger some kind of episode up in the woods? What would I do with her, up there, alone? Just the two of us.

When she finally reached me, her appearance didn't put my mind at ease. She wore a baggy sweatshirt and ill-fitting jeans. She looked as though she had lost even more weight since I'd last seen her. The clothes hung from her body, matched by her gaunt-looking face. Julia displayed all the attributes of somebody who had gone past caring a long time ago. Unable to avert my eyes, I recalled the night we first met in a London hotel. She'd listened intently to my woes about losing my parents and trying to find some focus in life and she suggested I apply for the job at Opacy. How little did I know of her involvement in the process? We'd spent that night together, even though I've always doubted either of us had craved it. Too much drink and a shoulder to cry on had been the underlying factors, for both parties.

"Ready for the climb?" I asked, as her eyes ignored mine and ventured up the hill instead. She grunted a reply, barely audible and certainly not comprehensible. Before we'd even begun, I regretted agreeing to meet her.

After only a few minutes of the ascent, I noticed her struggle. The gradient was indeed harder than it had initially appeared. My choice of T-shirt and shorts were proving a wise decision, whilst Julia kept wafting the front of her sweatshirt to circulate some air.

Eventually, as we approached the summit — it felt like we'd climbed a mountain — I suddenly realised where we were. More to the point, how close in proximity to the grave of Ryan Palmer, and where Lee Blackmore had received his fateful blow from Graham. Despite the sweat clinging to my back, I involuntarily shivered as the visions cascaded through my mind. Thankfully, after letting her pass, Julia turned slightly to the left, away from where the bodies once lay.

Where is *she going?*

She continued without once looking back.

"This way," she called over her shoulder, breathless and wheezing.

"Need a break?" I asked.

Julia ignored me and instead caught me by surprise as she increased the pace. Soon, she disappeared into dark, dense woodland, so thick with foliage the sun could barely penetrate at all. Feeling extremely exposed, I soon scurried after her. And as soon as I caught up, Julia replied, her words intermittent between deep breaths.

"No. Let's get this over and done with."

Shit.

I'd never ventured into that part of the woods before. I hadn't even realised they extended so far back. The pathway had disappeared from view, but fortunately, the fallen pine needles left the ground relatively flat and free of obstacles. However, we both occasionally tripped, and I continually cursed the tree roots for daring to occupy their own domain.

Without warning, the situation hit me like a sledge-hammer. Here I was, being led alone, deep into an area of the woods I'd never been, by a member of the Reid family. Why hadn't I thought of it before? Julia had always appeared to have my best interests at heart, but after all, she *was* a member of *that* family, and a little unhinged too.

Not 'a little unhinged', Matt. Bloody psychotic.

Stopping abruptly, I took out my phone.

No signal.

At first, Julia didn't appear to notice, but after a few more steps, she turned.

"What's wrong?" she asked, suddenly looking as though she was enjoying her day out. I realised how dark it had gone. Dark enough to struggle to distinguish whether it was night or day outside in the real world.

"Just need a minute," I pretended. "Thought I'd got a message."

At least I'd fulfilled my purpose and put some distance between us. If I had to, I could turn and run. Julia wasn't fit. I could easily lose her, if I knew my way back out, of course.

"There's no phone signal in here," she said, looking as if she was pleased about it. "Come on," she insisted, with a weird jerk of her head.

"Where are we going?" I asked, putting my phone away. "I'm not sure I like——"

"I have to show you, Matthew," she replied, before turning and quickly rediscovering her momentum. With a hasty glance around, I knew I had no choice but to put my trust in her. The path behind looked daunting, dark, forbidding, and full of things that live in the woods. Instead of walking, I ran after Julia.

How the hell does she even know where she's going?

Everything appeared identical to me. Tree after tree, symmetrical distance apart. Same roots, indistinguishable foliage, the ground flat and coated with pine needles, leaves and brambles. I felt lost. My heart pumped and my forehead dripped with sweat.

A noise, a snapping sound. Something scurrying in the distance. A deer? Rabbit? How the hell should I know? I was a city boy and did not know what creatures may lurk in the shadows of an otherwise uninhabited woodland.

"Nearly there," she said, several paces ahead of me.

Did she just laugh?

And then, out of nowhere, something different to focus my attention on. It felt good to focus on something manmade rather than on what nature had intended.

On initial sighting, the wooden shack appeared to be in a state of ill repair. The wood was rotten, especially along the base where it met the damp ground. I doubted that part ever dried out. The combination of mildew and cobwebs made the windows impossible to see through, especially from our distance.

"What is it?" I stupidly asked as I caught up with Julia. She stood with her hands on her hips, watching, listening. At least she didn't reply with the obvious answer.

"It belongs to the family. It's been here for years."

The family.

"Years?" I replied, not daring to move any closer.

"Yes. Years."

Her voice changed, forcing me to look at her. Julia stood motionless, staring off somewhere in the distance.

"You okay?"

Please say you are.

She ignored my question and began to babble. Short, intermittent bursts of information.

"It's got electricity. Illegal I think. Father connected it. No, somebody else did. Must be from their property. They ran a cable one day, all the way up here. Through the woods. Through the trees…"

Her words trailed off. She'd become lost in her own world.

It's just you and her.

Following her eyes, I peered through the trees in what I presumed was the direction of the main house.

"How far away are we?" I asked, suddenly aware we might not be that far. I had to keep Julia focused.

"Not sure. Four hundred? Five hundred yards?"

"Over a quarter of a mile of underground cabling? Jeez, that must have taken some doing."

"We used to play here. As kids…"

Julia trailed off again, reminiscing, her eyes glazed.

Although I hadn't expected to see a cabin in the middle of nowhere, it soon lost my interest. It looked dilapidated, fit to collapse. Surely Julia hadn't dragged me into the woods to see *that*?

A sound somewhere in the distance instantly alerted us. Julia jerked next to me, her hand clutching mine. At least it snapped her from her trance. We scanned the woods, the darkened trees appearing to take shape, moving in tandem, bearing down on us.

Julia walked away.

"I need to show you something else, Matthew. The real reason we are here."

29

Before I could probe any further, Julia had already put some distance between us. Although petrified by what the *real reason* could be, I found it difficult not to stare at her instead. Her jeans hung loosely from her backside, so much so that I feared they might fall to her ankles at any moment. But Julia was oblivious, not just to her attire, but seemingly oblivious to everything.

You need to get out of here.

"It had better be quick," I called after her, "else I'm going back."

Julia turned and smiled. She knew I wouldn't be going anywhere without a chaperone.

Walking deeper still into the relentless woodland, I struggled to keep track of both distance and direction. Apart from the shack, there had been no discernible landmarks. As I became more and more concerned for my safety, out of nowhere, Julia stood perfectly still. Nothing obvious came to light. But what had I been expecting? A pub with an attractive beer garden?

"There," she said.

Quickly, I joined her, desperately needing the whole shitty experience to be over and done with. Following her finger, I spotted exactly what she was pointing at.

"Holy shit." I couldn't help myself. "Not another one."

The neat mound of earth appeared identical to the other grave in the woods, the one that had contained the remains of Ryan Palmer. Same length, same width, same height. As if they had been bought from a shop selling ready-made burial mounds. However, it was the handmade cross protruding at the far end which grabbed my attention.

Just as on Ryan's grave, two twigs crudely wound together with green wool, stood upright out of the soil. Three fresh flowers lay next to it. My mouth opened and closed, unable to form any words. Meanwhile, Julia had turned to look at me. I hadn't noticed until she spoke.

"There's nobody in it, Matthew. It's for Katrina's sake."

In tandem, we slowly walked towards it.

"What, a pretend grave for a teenager? What kind of sick—"

"Father is in there."

"What?"

Spinning to face her, I realised how bloody scared I was. Stuck in the middle of the woods with a psychotic woman talking in riddles about things that would make no sense to anybody else in the outside world. But this wasn't the real world. This was my crazy fucked up world amid a crazy fucked up family. The same family who made an imaginary grave to allow a child to grieve.

"Father left home when Katrina was four or five years old."

Unbelievably, Julia's tone sounded relatively normal.

No more gibberish. I couldn't help but study her as she spoke. She appeared to be enjoying her story, again lost in her own world. She didn't move. Every part of her was as still as a statue, apart from her lips moving and her mouth slowly turning into a smile.

"But she doted on her grandfather. He built her a swing in the garden. She still plays on it today."

Yes, don't I know?

"He used to take her for long walks in the woods. They used to play hide-and-seek. She loves these trees."

That's how she knows them like the back of her hand.

"Then, one day, he disappeared."

Julia snapped her fingers. She'd dropped into some kind of hypnotic state. Talking in a monotone, as if reciting a pre-rehearsed speech for the umpteenth time. It would be futile to interrupt her, so I let Julia continue.

"It happened just before she was due to start school. During a long, hot summer. Things had been bad between Mother and Father. Graham moved in too. I'd only just met him."

Julia paused, contemplating.

"Ha!" she snapped, as if to banish her husband from memory.

"Father couldn't stand him." Julia snorted and finally turned her head to face me. "Funny that. None of you men could stand him, could you?"

I'd been unable to reply. Both her story and her mannerisms mesmerised me.

"Katrina began to have nightmares. Horrible nightmares. Screaming out in the middle of the night. She would wet the bed and refuse to turn her lights out."

I recalled my conversation with Amelia. It had been at the café, the day she'd told me she was pregnant. I'd asked about Katrina, accusing Tracy of drugging her. But Amelia had ridiculed my suggestions.

'Katrina had shown traits of very odd behaviour from an early age, maybe as young as two years old. She'd suffered from disturbing nightmares, often waking in the night screaming, her pyjamas drenched in sweat. On many occasions, she told Ryan and Tracy of seeing someone in her room. Sometimes, this person would carry a knife, threaten her, whilst on other 'visits', he would climb into bed with her, stroke her hair, and sing a quiet lullaby, until she drifted off back to sleep.'

'By the time she reached five, the child psychiatrist had recommended Katrina be homeschooled. He'd tried in vain to understand her behaviour. Some days, she would act normal, hold a decent level of conversation, but she counteracted this with levels of aggression he had never witnessed before. He'd diagnosed her with a dissociative identity disorder. Katrina had multiple distinct identities.'

The bit about the child psychiatrist recommending Katrina be homeschooled tied in with Julia's account, as did the age when he had suggested such a thing. Maybe Katrina had suffered nightmares from the age of two. However, it would be the day her grandfather disappeared that finally tipped her over the edge.

But why had he left? Forced out by the family, Graham, or by his own free will? As far as I could recall, the family had never mentioned him, or had they? Another conversation with Amelia came crashing into my thoughts. It had been on New Year's Day, the exchange as clear as the mock grave which lay before us.

"Hang on, Julia," I said, subconsciously reaching out to stop her from continuing.

Once I had Julia's attention, I explained how Amelia had reacted on the first day of the year, the day we drove to visit our prospective new house in the country. We'd only gone on my suggestion, I'd needed to get away for a few hours, suffocated by the long holiday and being held indoors with *them*.

The car journey had soon descended into an argument. I'd criticised Amelia for buying lavish Christmas presents which she'd bestowed upon the family, using our savings intended for our prospective new house. Amelia had defended her actions, of course she had, citing how grateful we should be towards her mother, and the rest of the family, for allowing us to stay. I'd become bored with her bullshit, knowing whatever I said, Amelia would have a reply, a defence. Everything had been one long excuse, always safeguarding the family.

So, I changed tack and asked about her father.

'Didn't you say he left home when you were four years old?' I'd asked. Amelia hesitated, my question momentarily leaving her flummoxed. She stared out of the passenger window. To begin with, I didn't think she would give me the satisfaction of a reply, but without her family to help, she eventually cracked. Her head fixed forward again, her eyes not leaving the road ahead.

'Yes,' she said. Then she slowly turned to me. 'Why have you asked about that again?'.

Amelia had been right. I had asked about her father once before. I denied it, or more likely, ignored it.

There must be a reason he left. Nobody just gets up and walks away.

'I was only four', Amelia had replied, anger etched in her every word. 'I don't know.'

She thought I'd let the matter drop, but I waited patiently until her breathing returned to normal.

'Perhaps I'll ask your mother then.'

At that point, Amelia lost it. She slammed the dashboard with her fist and warned me not to do any such thing.

'It's none of your damn business!' she'd shouted.

Julia listened intently until I'd finished. Although her attention span was minimal, she'd obviously found my story compelling.

"She was lying, Matthew. Father could never have left home when Amelia was four years old. That's how old Katrina was when he left. Amelia would have been—"

"She's eighteen years older than Katrina," I butted in, now in full flow. "She would have been in her early twenties. Why would she lie about that?"

Julia knowingly nodded her head.

We stood in silence. So many thoughts tripped through my mind. It wasn't until Julia walked away that something clicked. The obvious question hit me. I called after her.

"Why have you brought me here today, Julia?"

After a few more paces, she stopped and turned. The little colour she'd had in her cheeks had dissipated altogether.

"That day we met."

Her smile unnerved me. What did she find so joyous in all of those surroundings?

"In Russell Square? What about it?"

"You mentioned a guy you saw in the pub?"

I'd forgotten all about him.

The handsome stalker.

"What about him?"

"I didn't pay it any attention, at the time."

"What the hell are you talking about, Julia?"

Keep calm.

Fortunately, she remained steady in her response.

"Not until you pointed out his name, at least."

I wracked my brain.

"Patrick?" I asked. "What about his name?"

Julia looked directly into my eyes.

"Patrick is my father's name."

She pointed to the ground behind me.

"Katrina's grandfather. The person who we pretend is buried in that grave."

30

As we slowly trundled back in the reverse direction, my mind became awash with the guy in the pub. Could he really be the same Patrick? Amelia's father? I tried to recollect his appearance, but it all became too hazy. One thing was for certain, though, he had found me, and not by accident.

Passing the cabin, my thoughts still preoccupied, the noise of a branch snapping made me stop dead in my tracks. It hadn't sounded like the normal crack of twigs, a squirrel, or a fox might make, but something bigger. The sound a human foot would make.

"Did you hear that?" I asked, realising Julia hadn't even stopped.

Scampering after her, I soon realised she had disappeared into another world of her own. Although she didn't smile, she had an air of positivity about her. Humming a tune, keeping her spirits up, internally, at least.

Psychotic.

Without looking back, I concentrated on the ground

below. Julia continued along the track only visible to her, meandering in and out of the dense trees. Finally, after what felt like an eternity, I recognised where we were, the main pathway. With a last glance around, it came as an immense relief when we began the final descent down the steep hill.

Once back in the village, I ordered Julia an Uber. She assured me she would go straight home and lock the door behind her. I also made her promise to call if anything untoward happened. She nodded, but somehow I knew she wouldn't.

We sat in silence. My app informed me the taxi would be another ten minutes. Julia stared up the hill.

"They gave some of Ryan's inheritance money to Graham so he could buy our home."

The way she changed subjects reminded me of Katrina. It struck me that she could even be on the same medication now she'd been under Tracy's ministrations. Julia had recently been cared for, or held, in the family house. And Tracy could administer whatever the hell she wanted.

"What?" I asked. "What has that got to do with anything?"

Julia slowly turned her head, her eyes still focused in the distance, but somehow looking at me. She smiled as she spoke.

"You've noticed we have new windows, haven't you?"
What the hell is this?

"They used more of his money on their home too. New carpets."

"Julia. I'm sorry, you're not making—"

"But they need more, Matthew. They always need more."

With that, she stopped smiling and turned her head to

face the woods again. But she hadn't finished talking, although the tone of her voice had changed. Her enthusiasm appeared totally drained.

"I'm done with all this," she declared.

"What do you mean? Done with what?"

But I'd given up trying to appease her or make sense of what she said. Instead, I looked along the street, begging for the taxi to arrive.

"This family, this whole situation. I can't carry on." She turned to me once more, looking particularly fragile, agitated too. "You should get away, Matthew. You have to. For your sake."

Deciding to placate her, whilst at the same time attempting to hide my fears, I replied.

"If I could, I would. But Amelia is having a baby. I have to see my child, see what happens. That's the very least I can do."

I purposefully missed out any mention of having to hang around until after the trial. I couldn't bear to bring up Graham's name again, for my sake or hers.

Julia nodded and stood as the taxi arrived.

"Did you ever see my garden shed?" she said, smiling as she opened the cab door.

What! Your garden shed? Shit, she's losing it.

Once inside, she fastened her seat belt and looked directly ahead. Not once did she acknowledge me as I waved her goodbye.

Waiting until the taxi disappeared from view, I ordered one of my own. The thought of hiking to the train station and waiting around Epsom didn't inspire me. I had an overwhelming desire to return to my apartment, eat some food, and lie low for a while.

Despite Julia speaking in riddles, I tried to decipher exactly what she had been talking about. New windows, carpets, but always wanting more? But that had been down to Graham, hadn't it?

Julia had invariably been on the periphery of the family life, able to duck in and out as she pleased. The Reids, or more likely her husband, had kept her involved in the game, but she'd always worked alone. Sifting through family archives had been her hobby anyway.

The only tangible thing she'd done had been the night in the hotel when she'd informed me of the job at Opacy. Maybe she hadn't even realised what that had meant, what part she had played.

I could easily forgive Julia. It had all been about what Graham was capable of. She had told me he wasn't exactly subtle when instructing her what to do. I shuddered at the thought of what may have happened under the roof of their house.

Realising I could do no more, I silently prayed she would step away from it all.

'I'm done with all this.'

She was poorly, mentally ill, and I was not capable of helping anybody in that capacity. She'd seemed adamant that was it and she wanted no further contact with the family, did that include me? Had she purposefully shown me the imaginary grave as one final favour? The last thing she knew about but realised I didn't? Did I now have the full picture? Or at least the same information that she held? But why? Maybe for my closure?

Despite hoping that Julia walked away, both metaphorically and physically, I wondered if she had anywhere else to go. Even if she did, it would be best if I didn't know where.

And then there was Patrick. Julia hadn't asked for a

description, which implied she knew who he was. But why would he reappear after all these years? If Julia had been correct, he would have left at least a decade before. Why get away and make your escape, only to return years later?

Maybe the same reason that you're not leaving, Matt? And why Ryan never did. Maybe you can't get away.

Should I call him? What use would it be?

As I sat in the back of the taxi, I stared as the crazy world of London's busy streets whizzed by in a blur. The driver hummed along to a tune on the radio, a song I didn't know.

"Not working today?" he asked, watching me from his rear-view mirror. I hadn't noticed he'd stopped singing.

"No. Not today."

He took the hint and once again, I turned to stare out of the window.

Julia's words came back into my thoughts.

'You should get away, Matthew. You have to. For your sake.'

'I can't. Until the child is born, that is. Until then, I can't move on. Perhaps it will all be okay. Maybe Amelia will realise what is for the best too?'.

Catching the taxi driver smiling whilst glancing in the mirror, I blushed, realising I'd been talking out loud.

Once home, I did as I had promised, locked the door and kept myself to myself. I'd decided not to talk to Francis about her secret hotel visit, or mention the raised voices in her flat again. Maybe the two were connected or, as she'd said, the guy was just a friend of her mum's. Although I'd followed her, it really was none of my business. However, deep down, I'd begun to have feelings for Francis, and my male pride had taken a bit of a beating.

The shot of whisky helped me believe everything would be okay after all. Yes, the family were crazy, but was the idea of a makeshift grave for Katrina such a bad thing? If it helped with her mental health problems, did it matter so much?

After ordering a takeaway, I attempted to settle down with a beer and a Netflix movie. Despite an overwhelming desire to relax, I couldn't stop my mind from racing. Remembering the magnesium pills I'd bought from the health food shop, I swallowed a couple with my drink. They soon had their desired effect. Having fallen asleep during the second half of the film, I retired to bed.

And that night, I slept like a baby.

Was the worst over?

Don't kid yourself.

Little did I know what would transpire over the coming weeks.

And it all started with a phone call.

31

After Julia had shown me the makeshift grave in the woods, I considered asking Amelia about it. Initially, I thought I might nonchalantly drop it into conversation during our next catch-up. However, after sleeping on it, I realised what I'd be letting myself in for.

'What were you doing in the woods?' 'How did you find it?' 'Who helped you?' The list of questions would be relentless. Besides, I had no intention of putting Julia under further scrutiny. She had already suspected being followed and had been subjected to Tracy's infamous nursing skills. I hoped she stuck to her word and made herself scarce.

Two days after leaving Julia, I sat alone, disconsolate in my flat. I'd kept to my promise and hadn't ventured out since. My boss called me though and asked if I was available to do any viewings. Feigning a headache after a fitful night's sleep, I politely declined.

It wasn't far from the truth. After taking the pills and subsequent blissful slumber, the second evening rapidly returned to routine. The nightmares recurred, and at four in the morning, I found myself scrunched up on the sofa watching frivolous TV. I did attempt to read a book for the first time in months. Francis had suggested it and lent me one of hers a week before. She said it would help my mind rest, especially if I read directly before turning the lights out. The novel was a mystery, a whodunnit. Nothing scary. Just an innocent Agatha Christie-type story intended to make the reader think. In principle, it sounded like a good plan. In reality, it sucked. Whatever I tried, my brain wouldn't switch off.

The trip to the woods had been a bad idea. I had found it difficult to shake the image of the grave and the memories that came with it. Everything I did seemed to work against me. I'd tried to placate Julia, but I worried as her mental health continued to spiral. To appease Lisa, I'd moved to a new apartment, but now Francis had come onto the scene and she appeared to carry baggage too. She obviously had private issues, but I was in danger of falling for her. My meetings with Amelia had taken a downward turn, bickering over trivial matters despite my ongoing affection towards her. Tracy would never accept me and Katrina's behaviour still scared me.

The imminent case of Graham's trial had lost my interest. Maybe DCI Small would have allowed me to leave the area, as long as I promised to stay in the country. However, I had to be around for the birth of my child, a phenomenon I still found impossible to comprehend. But I struggled with the wait. Time was dragging. Could I hold it together until then?

The phone vibrating on the kitchen table awoke me. I'd dozed off in the armchair, my body eventually giving in to the relative sanctuary of daylight and the perception of security behind locked doors.

Wearily, I stood, stretched, and retrieved my mobile.

Maybe subconsciously, I didn't reach it in time. And the call ended before it cut to voicemail.

Withheld number.

The feeling felt familiar.

Quickly, I scrolled through the handful of missed calls. There, two months previous, *withheld number*. I'd answered it, but nobody spoke.

A low murmur. The rustling of leaves.

As I contemplated who it could be, the phone rang again. The shock almost made me drop it, juggling before it fell to the floor.

Withheld number.

"Hello? Who is this?"

Pressing my ear close, I tried to decipher any background sounds.

"Please. Who is calling?"

My heart thumped.

"Hello, Uncle Matthew."

Katrina!

"I've got something important to ask you."

"Katrina," I replied, with a tremendous sigh of relief. "Is that really you?"

She giggled. Then silence.

"Whose phone are you on?"

I needed to keep the questions simple. The slightest thing would set her off. She could scream, run, or just stand still in total silence.

"My phone, silly."

"But it doesn't say your number. The one I saw you with in the woods?"

"Mother told me how to do it."

Tracy? How on earth did she know Katrina had a phone?

"I thought it was going to be our secret. We were going to be mobile phone friends?"

"We are, silly."

"So, does your mother know you have got a phone or not?"

Katrina giggled.

"Katrina? Does she?"

It made no sense. The child who had been kept away from civilisation. Never been to school. Had no friends outside of the house. Why would Tracy accept Katrina owning a phone, especially if she knew where it came from? The family wouldn't take the risk of Katrina communicating with anybody from the outside world.

Cursing myself for being too abrupt, it came as no surprise when the other end of the line fell silent. Listening intently, I could just make out the occasional crunching sound of dried leaves underfoot.

She's in the woods.

"Where are you, Katrina?"

I heard a sigh before the phone clicked dead.

Bollocks.

What the hell did she call for?

I've got something important to ask you.

Without knowing the number of the burner phone, I realised I couldn't return the call. I would have to wait to see if she called back. Thinking it unlikely anytime soon, I instead tried to focus on something positive.

Checking the time, just after four, I poured myself a generous whisky. I knew I'd have to go to work the next day, show willing. The initial buzz of doing something new, and getting paid for it, had begun to wane. My dad had always laughed, arguing I was a lazy sod and would live off scraps if it meant not having to go to work. Not entirely true, but near to it. The memory made me smile.

Contemplating whether to seek the company of Francis, I soon knocked that notion on the head too. Socialising felt like hard work. Besides, I didn't know what to say to her. The last time we'd spoken at any length, had been weeks ago, and she'd dismissed her black eye with what I considered a pack of lies. Since then, I'd followed her to a hotel after she'd said she was visiting her mum. More lies.

I also knew how close I'd become to Francis, and I needed to put distance between us. I'd involved Lisa in the past and, as a result, she had made herself scarce. But I liked Francis. She was good company. Could I be using her? Not wanting to blame myself for everything, I realised that pain and torment were never far away in my life.

The whisky soothed me. My hands stopped trembling and my stomach became unknotted.

After more drinks – I couldn't honestly say how many I'd had – I stood, purposefully strolled out onto the landing and knocked on Francis's door.

"Matt. Hey. Come in."

Walking directly past her, I continued to her lounge and promptly sat myself down.

"Make yourself at home, why not?" She smiled, following me in.

As I acknowledged her, something clicked, and I realised where I was. Standing too quickly, I instantly felt dizzy and glared at my host with wide-open eyes. I couldn't recall the last few minutes at all. What the hell was happening to me?

"Hey, sorry. I don't know what—"

"Have you been drinking, Matt? You stink of booze."

"What? Yeah, sorry. Only one whisky. Just now. I had a weird phone call. It—"

"Sit down. You need to calm down. I'll make us coffee."

"Coffee." I laughed. "Good idea."

But I didn't take a seat. Instead, I followed Francis into the kitchen.

"Sorry, Francis. I should go. I need to sleep."

"You'll stay until I know you're okay. You sure you've only been drinking whisky?"

Attempting a laugh, it came out as a snort. The room spun.

"Yes. Just one shot. Maybe two. Honest."

Francis looked up and smiled.

A few minutes later, we returned to the lounge and Francis placed two steaming mugs of coffee on the table between us. She opted to sit in the spare chair. I'd been expecting her to sit next to me.

"Thanks," I said, retrieving the mug. The hot drink looked good. I wanted to feel it burn my throat and my chest. A hit of caffeine to alert my senses.

"Remember before, when I suggested maybe you need to see a doctor, Matt? Are you registered with one locally?"

Placing the mug back down, I looked at Francis as if she'd proposed open heart surgery.

"A doctor? Why the hell do you keep saying I need to see a doctor?"

"Just to talk things through. You're going through a lot. Most people would need to talk to someone."

"What makes you say that? I'm going to be a father, that's all. It's not as though almost every damn guy doesn't have to go through that at some point. And if you must know, I picked up some sleeping pills at the health food shop the other day."

Unable to stop myself, I was aware my words were tumbling out in a slur.

"And are they working?"

"Yes. They are actually. Well, they did the first time I—"

Francis placed her drink down and stepped over to sit next to me. She took my hand in both of hers and rested them on her lap.

"Hey, it's okay. I just think you need something stronger than a few herbal pills from that kind of store. A GP would prescribe you proper medication. That's what you need. Regular sleep, away from those nightmares."

Even in my state, I knew it made sense, but I wasn't thinking coherently. Without warning, I stood, knocking my coffee over on the table.

"Bloody hell, Matthew. What the hell is wrong with you?"

"Sorry. I, erm…"

As she dashed to the kitchen, she shouted over her shoulder.

"Maybe it's best if you go. You're not very good company when you act like this."

After glaring at the large puddle forming across her table and slowly dripping onto the laminate floor, fortunately missing the expensive rug, I left without another word.

Returning to my kitchen, I drank a pint of water and refilled the glass.

An hour later, whilst half asleep, my phone rang. Floundering, I noticed my hand shake as I read *withheld number*.

'*I've got something important to ask you.*'

"Uncle Matthew?"

I did not placate her.

"Yes? What is it, Katrina?"

"Why were you and Aunty Julia in the woods the other day?"

32

WHAT THE HELL?

Dumbfounded and hungover, I couldn't form any words. Where had she seen us, near her grandfather's grave? Hadn't Julia said that Katrina was no longer allowed in the woods? My head spun, a combination of confusion and waning alcohol.

"Erm, no. We weren't there, Katrina."

"Liar!" Katrina snapped, sending a chill down my spine such had been the ferocity of her reply.

She laughed, or maybe *cackled* would be a more accurate description.

"Where did you think you saw us?"

"On the footpath, silly. You were both walking quickly. You went past father's grave and down the hill. I watched you."

Father's grave.

Letting out an audible sigh of relief, I prayed that was the only place she'd seen us.

Now needing to get her on my side, I tried a different tack.

"In fact, we were there. We came to see you."

She giggled but offered no reply.

"We wanted to know you are okay."

Nothing.

"*Are* you okay, Katrina?"

Still nothing.

My heart quickened.

"Katrina?"

"I have to go. Mother said I'm not allowed to talk to anyone."

"Is your mother with you then?"

"No, silly."

The line went dead.

Staring at my phone, I stood and paced the room. I believed Katrina. Tracy wouldn't have been with her when she made the call. Katrina could only tell the truth. That was her trait, which I loved and loathed in equal measure. You knew exactly where you stood, but the truth could also hit you like a sledgehammer. Julia must have been mistaken, or had Tracy or Melissa told her a lie?

Should I check for myself? Go to the woods and find Katrina?

Don't be stupid.

I spent the next few days shacked up alone. I'd phoned in sick, ordered groceries online and kept myself indoors. The only person I'd wanted to see had been Francis, to apologise for my behaviour, but the stubbornness inside me implored her to knock on my door instead.

Sleep still eluded me. The pills from the herbal shop were akin to taking sweets. Fortunately, the dreams hadn't been so vivid, maybe due to me not being able to drift into a deep enough slumber. However, my lack of sleep concerned me. The birth wasn't due for two months and I couldn't continue with little or no rest for that amount of time.

'*Maybe you need to see a doctor.*'

Perhaps Francis was right.

On Saturday morning, I finished reading the book. I'd been awake since four in the morning. At least it gave me an ideal opportunity to return it to Francis. So, just before nine o'clock, I walked to the local Costa and bought us both a large Americano and a butter croissant. It felt incredibly cheesy, not my style at all, but still a way of saying sorry.

"Oh. It's you."

Good start.

"Peace offering," I replied, holding out the cardboard tray of drinks and a paper bag containing food. I'd tucked her book under my left armpit. Fortunately, Francis stood to one side and motioned for me to pass.

As I stepped by, Francis grabbed the novel.

"Did you read it or put it away because it had no pictures?"

Thankfully, when I turned, she was smiling, a sarcastic grin etched across her face.

"It was good. Although I guessed whodunnit after only a few chapters."

"Of course you did."

She joined me in the kitchen. Taking one croissant from the bag, she placed it on a plate and grabbed herself a coffee.

"Best keep the lid on yours," she added, as she walked to the lounge. "You might just spill it."

"Yeah. I'm sorry. Hope it didn't stain anything," I said, scuttling after her with the bag and a drink.

"It's taken you days to ask, so I guess you're not that bothered."

We sat in the same two chairs. I wasn't hungry, but the coffee tasted great. As soon as I finished, I contemplated going back to fetch another, such had been the hit. Francis must have noticed.

"You still look like shit. Have you slept at all since I last saw you?"

"Not much."

She sat and listened, whilst eating and drinking, as I told her about my sleepless nights and details of the intermittent nightmares.

"It can't be easy," she added, once I'd finished.

"Perhaps it will all be okay once the baby is born."

"Maybe," she replied, unconvinced. Francis collected her plate and empty cup and returned to the kitchen.

The noise of her coffee machine whirring into action sounded like music to my ears. I'd had the initial kick and now I craved more. Picking up the bag, I tore off half of the sweet croissant and savoured the sugar rush. Still eating, I joined Francis in the kitchen, the prospect of more caffeine too much to resist.

"I've been thinking about your idea, Francis," I said, instantly regretting talking with food in my mouth. Fortunately, Francis didn't appear to be too disgusted.

"Oh yeah?" she asked, turning and passing the first coffee to me. "Which great idea is that?"

"About seeing a doctor. You're right. I have to get on top of my sleep. Perhaps cut down on the booze too."

"Maybe you need to see a shrink instead."

Francis smiled broadly, her dimples exaggerated. Out of nowhere, she leant forward and kissed me.

"What was that for?" I asked, unable to hide my pleasure.

"Because I care for you. I want you to be well. I'm sure everybody does."

Everybody?

Francis turned to make herself a drink, replacing the used coffee pod in the machine.

"Yeah. I do for sure. And I'm certain your wife does too, especially given she's pregnant with your child. You should be more grateful that people do care for your welfare."

"Thanks," I said, disappointed she'd placed herself in the same pigeonhole as Amelia. "Anyway," I continued, "I'm sure I'm still registered with a doctor out Epsom way. I think I'll make an appointment."

Francis turned to face me.

"Epsom? That's bloody miles away. Don't you want to register somewhere closer?"

"Know of a good local shrink do you?"

We both laughed before stepping close again. This time we kissed with more intensity.

The sound of my phone vibrating awoke me. It took several seconds to register where I was. A quick glance over my shoulder told me all I needed to know. Francis slept quietly. She looked comfortable, so peaceful.

Rolling onto my side, I retrieved the phone. I noticed my clothes strewn across her bedroom floor.

The headache kicked in and my mouth felt dry. As I tried to focus on the small screen, I saw I had one new message.

Too late for me x

33

Double checking Francis was still asleep, I slowly manoeuvred my way out of the bed. Pulling on my boxer shorts, I tiptoed towards the kitchen. My head hurt like hell. Had we drunk that much?

With a quick glance at the bedroom door, I clicked my phone and replied to Julia.

What do you mean? What is too late for you?

After staring at a blank screen for several minutes, I realised I had little choice but to find out for myself. It could take days before Julia responded, if ever. But it wasn't the time span which worried me. Something wasn't right. Despite the psychosis, I hadn't expected such a cryptic message. With just four words, she'd raised my anxiety to a whole new level.

Sneaking back into the bedroom, I collected the rest

of my clothes. As quiet as a mouse, I tiptoed towards the door.

"That's not a very nice way to treat a girl the morning after."

Shit.

"Oh. You're awake," I grinned. "Sorry, didn't mean to disturb you."

Francis sat upright, making no attempt to cover herself. Instead, she grabbed the corner of the duvet and peeled it backwards.

"It's nice and warm in here," she said, exaggerating her dimpled smile.

Under any other circumstance, I would have literally run and jumped into bed to rejoin her. The idea of a Sunday morning snuggled up under the covers felt extremely tempting. However, the text message had unnerved me. I knew I had to check on Julia.

"Something's come up. I have to dash. Sorry."

Awkwardly, I dressed in front of Francis. It would have been much easier to carry my clothes into the lounge and put them on in a less intimidating environment.

As I tripped my way out of the bedroom, one leg in my jeans, the other trailing out, I heard Francis clamber out of bed behind me.

"Dash where exactly?" she asked, standing in the doorway, pulling her dressing gown together.

"Well, I forgot I'm working today. Got three viewings. Look at me, I look like crap. I need to shower and get dressed."

Francis brushed past me, the scent of her perfume still lingering sufficiently to remind me of the night before. She continued to the kitchen before calling over her shoulder.

"Just be man enough to say you're leaving, Matt. Don't take me for a fool."

Scurrying after her, I reached the island. Leaning against the worktop, I pulled each shoe on by the heel, pushing and twisting my feet until they squeezed inside.

"It's not like that. I'm just…"

Words failed me. I had no excuses left. Fortunately, Francis appeared to mellow.

"Listen. I know you've been through a lot, and what we have between us, well, you don't need anything to happen too fast, too soon. I understand your situation. Honest, I do. Maybe I shouldn't be acting so fast either."

Nodding my head in appreciation, I could have stepped over and hugged her tight for being so considerate. She hadn't quite finished.

"I like you, Matt. You're kind, funny and we're *pretty* good in there, aren't we?" She nodded in the bedroom's direction. I couldn't help but smile.

"Thank you. And thank you for being so understanding. I like you too, and you're about average in there."

She walked over and kissed me on the lips, lingering long enough for me to taste her.

Get away.

Promising to call later, I pecked her on the cheek and returned to my apartment. My hand trembled slightly as I fumbled with the key in the lock. The alcohol or the testosterone? Maybe both.

Showering quickly, I found clean clothes in my makeshift ironing basket — an old washing-up basin left behind by the previous tenants — and returned to the living room to retrieve my shoes.

A door closing somewhere outside on the landing alerted me. It sounded very close. Francis leaving? Surely not. There's no way she could have got ready as fast as me. Maybe somebody visiting her? But who? Surely she wouldn't have let me stay the night if she'd been expecting a visitor so early in the morning? After all, she'd just tried to beckon me back into bed.

Ignoring it, I slipped on my shoes — I really must get into the habit of undoing the laces and putting them on and off in the conventional method — grabbed my phone and keys, and left the apartment. Hesitating on the landing, I stood outside Francis's door for a few seconds, trying to listen for voices inside. But all appeared silent. Maybe it hadn't been her door closing after all.

Fortunately, the train was only a third full. It was still relatively early on a Sunday morning and even London slept sometimes. I guzzled on the bottle of water I'd bought at the bakery outside Earl's Court tube station. I'd already eaten a hot sausage roll whilst waiting on the platform. At least I felt a little better inside, and the headache had dissipated. The last thing I needed was to feel like crap whilst already emotionally exhausted.

However, once I arrived in Epsom, my spiritual home, a wave of sickness washed over me. Suddenly, something felt very wrong. What the hell was it about that place?

Too late for me

Julia's house wasn't far from the station. A ten-minute walk.

The streets were familiar, I'd travelled them many a time with Amelia whenever we commuted to work on the train. I'd also been to Julia's house before on the day I'd witnessed her hand Tracy an envelope stuffed with family trees and curricula vitae. Subsequently, after Tracy left, I went inside to demand the truth. Before that, I recalled sneaking down the alleyway that led to the back gardens. It split next door's house and Julia's; a joint passageway to the rear of both properties. As I approached, I decided that would be my best route again. The front was too exposed, the door opening directly onto a pathway adjoining the main road. An air of vulnerability washed over me as I crossed the street.

The text message had got under my skin. Something didn't feel right.

Your new sixth sense.

A stiff breeze whistled through the alley, catching me off guard although feeling extremely welcoming at the same time. Before then, I'd barely noticed a breath of wind and the air felt thick. With a quick glance in both directions, I dashed into the passageway and scuttled between the two properties.

The garden was exactly as I remembered, overgrown lawn, borders full of weeds, and neglected pots filled with nettles and dandelions. As on my previous visit, the magnitude of the plot of land which accompanied those small houses amazed me. At least a hundred foot long, narrow, yet private, given the six-foot fences which stretched the entire length on either side. The wooden barrier continued along the rear of the properties too. It presented the occupants with both privacy and protection from prying neighbours.

The windows were new throughout Julia's house, along with a back door complete with two long panes of frosted glass.

'You've noticed we have new windows, haven't you?'.

With another glance over my shoulder, I lightly

tapped on the door. Shielding my eyes, I pushed my face against the glass, desperate to see Julia approach. But all appeared perfectly still.

I knocked again, much firmer, certainly loud enough for anybody inside to hear, whatever room they were in. Again, not a sound from beyond the door.

Remembering my previous visit, and how I'd seen inside, I shuffled along to the kitchen window. The same net curtains still hung, and I knew my vision would be limited. However, it had to be better than the frosted glass of the doorway. Dragging an empty plant pot underneath, I tipped it upside down and used it as a makeshift step. Again, I shielded my eyes to see indoors.

As far as I could tell, the kitchen looked clean and tidy. A mug and a small plate had been washed and allowed to dry on the draining board, but apart from that, everything appeared to be where it should be. No dishes, no food items left out, no mail on the table.

Frustrated, I tried to open the back door instead, wiggling the handle far too many times when once would have been enough. It felt as though I knew she was there, but I couldn't make her hear.

Shit.

Is she okay? Has something happened inside?

'*She had a bottle full of pills in one hand, and a bottle of Scotch in the other.*'

I banged with my fist, even though I knew it was futile.

Where is she?

Deciding to go around the front to look through those windows, I ran for the alleyway. But just as I reached the turn, something caught my eye. At the far end of the garden. There. The shed. A dilapidated wooden structure which looked as though a good storm would put it out of its misery. It was a fair size, large enough to contain a multitude of gardening equipment.

But it wasn't a lawn mower or a shovel which had grabbed my attention. Instead, barely visible through the panes of cracked and mildew-covered glass, the silhouette of a motionless figure made me freeze on the spot.

34

INSTINCTIVELY, my eyes scanned the back of the house, the passageway, next door's windows. What was I looking for? Somebody watching? A camera? Paranoia wrapped its fingers around me. Every move I made carried the burden of being watched or followed. Eventually, subconsciously hoping I'd imagined it, my eyes drifted back to the shed at the end of the garden.

The row of houses, which backed onto Julia's, cast a long shadow, which stretched halfway across the unkempt lawn. As I slowly traipsed along the footpath of broken slabs, the drop in temperature hit me as soon as I stepped into the shade. It somehow felt icy cold, despite what could have only been a degree or two difference.

Closer to the shed.

Again, I stopped and glanced over my shoulder, convinced somebody would step out of the passageway, blocking my only route out.

The old shed looked more forbidding the closer I got. A multitude of cobwebs hung in the windows. The wooden slats along the bottom lay rotten and decayed, a combination of damp and neglect. The felt roof peeled back, exposing the original structure, long rusty nails protruding. I gulped, like some cartoon character facing his recurrent enemy. Finally, I stood adjacent to the rickety door.

Feeling for my phone, I momentarily considered calling for help. Should I call Francis? The police? DCI Small had said I should ring him if anything felt out of place. But they would only do what I knew I had to do myself. Julia had messaged me, nobody else. It was my problem; the situation we had both been party to ever since that fateful night in the hotel. It's how it all began. I had to go in.

Gingerly, I removed the padlock, listening intently for any sudden movement inside.

Wait.

Had the padlock been looped back through the latch? Impossible for anybody inside the shed to have done so themselves, and likewise, impossible to get out once you were in.

It's your imagination. Of course, someone did not loop it through.

I peeked at the passageway. How quickly could I get there? Get through, and to the relative safety of the other side?

As I placed my fingertips between the gap, a breeze caught the door and it slowly opened. Only an inch or two, but enough to suggest somebody inside could have pushed it.

Your bloody imagination. You need to go in.

My heart pounded. Looking around, I noticed a piece of wood on the edge of the lawn. It had been snapped at one end. Upon closer inspection, it looked as though it had originally formed some kind of wooden prop, maybe a support for a large plant or small tree? It was all I could see, and there was no way I was going to open that door without some form of weapon in my hand.

Gathering the damp piece of wood, I stood just far enough away from the shed door so the end of my foot could reach the bottom and pull it open. Tucking my toes underneath, I slowly dragged the rotten panel towards me. Although somewhat gloomier, it only took a second or two for my eyes to acclimatise to what was inside.

Fuck.

A scream, more like a wail, escaped my mouth. Immediately followed by an onrush of bile, which I somehow suppressed in my throat.

It wasn't Julia's rigid body, which swayed from side to side in the makeshift noose, that freaked me out. It was her face, wide-eyed, following me, and with an unbeliev-able hint of a smile.

Backing away, her eyes never left mine and I tripped on the brick verge of the pathway. Falling backwards, I landed against the fence which divided Julia's garden from next door. But even as I lay there, propped up on my elbows, I couldn't take my eyes off her. Gently swaying, her hands by her side, her feet dangling only inches above the ground.

DCI Small and DS Paine sat on the sofa opposite me. It was the following morning. The detectives had arrived early. DS Paine had his notebook poised, but I didn't notice him write anything down. As far as they were concerned, this was a simple suicide case. Her husband expected to be jailed, an empty bank account, a mountain of rising debts and an eviction order. Why hadn't she told me?

"So, she had no money at all?"

Francis reappeared with a tray containing a pot of tea, three mugs, and a tiny jug of milk. I remembered thinking there would never be enough to go around.

"No, erm, Miss…"

"Baker, I mean, Francis. Please call me Francis." She blushed, and busied herself once more.

Ignoring Francis's stalling over her name, I couldn't shake the events of the previous day. Once I had felt for a pulse, something I didn't really know how to do anyway, I'd dialled 999 and waited in the street until the emergency services arrived. As soon as a police constable had checked me over and written my version of discovering Julia, he disappeared to make the necessary calls. Returning several minutes later, he informed me that DCI Small would come and collect me. I'd insisted on making my own way home before we eventually compromised with a lift from two other officers instead. The constable's superior had also agreed to allow me to rest and put off the interview with the DCI until the following morning. I hadn't realised it would be so early.

Francis had run to my aid as soon as I awkwardly clambered out of the back of the police car. She hugged me and whispered something in my ear, something I didn't quite catch.

"No, erm, Francis. We've had Julia Meadows' records checked out. I don't think I'm talking out of place to tell you she owed a lot of money to many people. Mortgage, electric, gas, everybody. Couple that with a husband who is going to be behind bars for a considerable time, it's no wonder it all caught up and tipped her over the edge."

Had Graham withheld the funds? Stopped all the payments? Practically starved Julia out of her own home? Surely she could have told the authorities?

'She's psychotic, Matt. That's the diagnosis.'

I sat in silence. Whatever I thought or said would never convince the police differently, although it was difficult to disagree with their version anyway. And even if I cast a shadow of doubt, who could verify it? The Reids would back up the belief that Julia had taken her own life, and there would be nobody else to turn to.

Francis joined me on the sofa and began to gently rub her hand in a circular motion across my back. The detectives glanced at one another. Although feeling extremely awkward, I knew it would not be in my interests to make a scene.

"Yes," she replied on my behalf again. "It must have been awful for her."

Her comment came across as sarcastic, or certainly with a lack of empathy. Did she wonder why I had been to the house, worry who Julia might be? Had she somehow seen Julia as a threat to our relationship?

Relationship? What are you thinking of, Matt?

"Any news on the Graham trial?" I asked, desperate to move the conversation along and hopefully lead to the detectives leaving.

"There is actually," DS Paine replied, following a brief glimpse towards his DCI. "The dental records have been returned, proving the other body was definitely Ryan Palmer."

DCI Small took over.

"Graham Meadows has now admitted manslaughter to both Ryan Palmer and Lee Blackmore."

"Manslaughter? It's murder, isn't it?"

The chief inspector explained the difference. Neither killing would have been premeditated. Graham had admitted following Ryan Palmer into the woods to 'check where he was going' and had acknowledged 'finding Lee

Blackmore in the woods' where an altercation had taken place.

The DCI didn't take his eyes off mine. Was he expecting me to flinch, to divulge further information? I couldn't help but think both killings had been *premeditated*. But, as with Julia's death, I knew it was pointless to put across a different point of view. It would lead to more questions than answers and maybe yet another statement, followed by another trip to the police station. He put my mind at ease when he reminded me that Graham was also on trial for the murder of my aunt. How could I have forgotten?

Once he had finished, I nodded and offered my thanks for keeping me up to date with the case. As soon as they stood, I instinctively followed their lead and stepped towards the door. With another quick glance at each other, the detectives made their way to the exit.

"Thanks again," I said, opening the door. DCI Small patted me on the shoulder as he left.

"If there's anything else, just call. You've been through a lot, Matthew."

"I will," I replied, imploring them to leave.

He stopped.

Shit. Just go.

"There is one thing, actually."

Of course there is.

"What's that?"

"It's unusual for a suicide case not to leave some kind of note. A way to reach out, maybe explain some of their thinking. You didn't happen to see anything, did you?"

Trying desperately not to colour up, I shuffled on my feet and turned to face Francis.

"No, nothing," I replied, facing the DCI again. I'd hesitated, but it was still my word against his.

"Okay. As long as you're sure."

Perhaps he knew, but I no longer cared about him, his cohort, or the rest of the police. They had done their bit, arrested Graham, and he would now stand trial for the manslaughter of two men and the murder of one elderly woman. He'd be away for the rest of his life, wouldn't he?

But now Julia was dead too, and ultimately I felt responsible that it was down to me, just like Lee Blackmore's death had been my fault.

After closing the door, I rejoined Francis in the living room. She offered me a sympathetic look and patted the empty seat next to her. Smiling, I instead walked towards the kitchen.

"Coffee?" I asked over my shoulder.

Once out of sight, I felt my back pocket to ensure the note was still there.

35

It took two weeks to get an appointment with a doctor. I'd ignored Francis's advice regarding a local practice and instead stuck with the one I was already registered with, the *family* doctor, back in Epsom. The prospect of finding somewhere new, as well as completing all the forms, didn't particularly appeal in my present frame of mind. Also, I didn't know how long I'd be living around Earl's Court, so what would be the point of locating a new doctor, only having to repeat the entire process the next time I moved? My current residence had never been supposed to be permanent, just a place to keep my head down until the dust had settled, and I found my way in life once more.

The weather had taken a turn for the worse, the clear blue skies replaced with ominous thick grey clouds. They threatened much-needed rain, although it hadn't materialised by the time of my appointment.

Surprisingly, following the discovery of Julia's body, my nightmares had temporarily dissipated. But a few days later, they'd returned with a vengeance. That had been the breaking point, and I finally decided to see someone about it.

I'd barely seen Francis since the detectives left my apartment. The next day, she said she needed to see her mum again. I recalled the hotel visit, but with everything else going on, I'd lost the will to pursue the matter. We'd exchanged a few WhatsApp messages, but they fizzled out too. Unsure of what she wanted from me, from *us*, I knew she could ask herself the same question. As far as I was concerned, the idea of committing to any kind of serious relationship was strictly taboo. Whatever happened between me and Amelia, the last thing I desired was a third party involved. I could imagine how that would play into the hands of the Reids. But Francis appeared non-committal too. One day, she seemed keen, whilst the next she put distance between us.

"Just take a seat. The doctor will call you over the intercom when it's your turn."

The receptionist looked about as pleased to be at the surgery as everybody else assembled in the waiting room. At least the patients had the excuse of something being wrong with them.

"Great, thanks," I replied, rather sarcastically. She looked up from her computer screen, but still held the expression of somebody who'd clearly got out of bed on the wrong side that morning.

Taking a seat at the back of the room, I picked up a well-worn travel magazine. The picture on the cover depicted a family running hand in hand along a deserted beach, a deep blue sea behind them. It made me ache with envy. When had been the last time I'd travelled abroad? My honeymoon, in Corfu. Whilst staring at the photograph, I recollected the holiday with fond memories, the beginning of my new life.

The voice of someone checking in at reception made my hair stand on end.

"My name's Melissa Reid. I have an appointment at eleven o'clock with Doctor Pearce."

Shit!

Shuffling to make myself as small as possible, I lifted the magazine to cover my face. The ageing woman in the seat next to me looked at me, dumbfounded.

Who had Melissa said her appointment was with? Doctor Pearce? The same doctor as me. The *family* doctor. I'd never visited the surgery before and didn't know one general practitioner from the other.

'*I have an appointment at eleven o'clock.*'

Ten minutes after me. That must be the next slot. I couldn't let her see me.

"Are you hiding from anybody in particular?" the old lady asked me. She wore a hearing aid, and, as a result, spoke far too loudly. Fortunately, Melissa had taken a seat on the far side of the waiting room, with her back to us. The problem was that she also sat near the exit. I'd have to walk past her on my way out.

"No," I whispered. "I've got a bad back and I find it hard to get comfortable."

I couldn't help but smirk at my quick-witted response. The lady rolled her eyes before focusing on the magazine I held aloft. Had she even heard what I'd said?

Please don't ask me anything else.

But now she'd engaged me in conversation, she wanted more. However, as she opened her mouth to interrogate me further, the *bing bing* sound of the speakers strategically placed around the room cut her off before she could begin.

'Mrs Colington for Doctor Ahmed', came the announcement. It wasn't very clear.

"Who did it say?" the old lady asked, poking my arm. One or two people looked up and smiled.

I wasn't really listening, love.

"Erm, Mrs Colliford, I think it said."

"Colliford?" This time, she shouted. More people looked on, including one or two others who had turned in their seats.

I nodded, imploring her to shut up.

"I'm Mrs Colington. Are you sure he didn't say Colington?"

How the fuck do I know?

A guy opposite intervened.

"Yes. I think he said, Colington. Are you here to see Doctor Ahmed?"

"Yes. Yes, I am. At half past ten. He's already very late."

Mrs bloody Colington raised her voice on every single word. The receptionist stood to see what the commotion was about. By now, half the room appeared to be focused on her, on *us*.

Bing bing.

'Mrs Colington for Doctor Ahmed.'

"Yes," said the guy opposite. "It's your turn. He's just called you again."

Mrs Colington slowly rose, extremely unsteady on her feet. The guy glared at me. I shrugged my shoulders, much to his disgust. I felt like shouting 'I'm not her bloody carer', but thought that would be inappropriate.

As I held my gaze with the guy, I noticed Melissa shuffle in her seat. She had her back to me, but had she been watching?

Bing bing.

'Mr Walker for Doctor Pearce.'

Shit.

Placing the magazine on the table, I slowly stood. My eyes didn't leave the back of Melissa's head. Had she heard the announcement? Surely *'Mr Walker'* would ring alarm bells?

Carefully, I stepped towards the elongated hallway where the doctors' rooms were located. As I approached Melissa's row of seats, I turned sideways on, my head tilted at a ridiculous angle. One or two people smirked, were they laughing at me? Quickly, I dashed out of sight, the laughter following me.

My appointment took much longer than I'd imagined. I'd hoped it would be a quick diagnosis. 'You're suffering from insomnia. I'll prescribe you some pills' and I'd be on my way. No such luck.

Doctor Pearce began by asking when the nightmares had begun and what may have triggered them, as if he didn't know. He soon changed tack and explored the personal route. Any further problems at home? How are you and your wife getting along now?

Just ask me what you really want to know.

Doing my best to assure him it had nothing to do with my personal life, I tried blaming stress at work instead, finding new business and keeping existing clients happy.

He focused his eyes on me as I spoke. It unnerved me. The longer the consultation took, the more agitated I became. He carried an expression that he knew I was talking bullshit, but he couldn't say as much. Once I'd finished, he went back to his screen, tapping the monitor with the tip of his pen. That irritated me too.

"You're married to Amelia Reid," he eventually said. He smiled broadly as he looked up at me.

Here we go.

"Huh, huh. Why? Is that important?"

My abrupt reply made him baulk.

"No, no, Mister Walker. It's not important. I just like to know who my patients are. I've heard everything is back to normal now."

Is he allowed to say that?

"Yes. It's all good, thanks."

He smiled once more.

I felt like such an idiot. Of course, the local doctor would have known what had happened in the local woods. It would have been all over the neighbourhood, maybe national news at one point. I'd purposefully avoided watching or reading anything connected with Graham and what had taken place that day. Why hadn't I listened to Francis and found a local surgery instead?

"That's good," he replied, although he appeared to be speaking to himself rather than addressing me.

The doctor focused on his monitor again, tapping away at the keyboard. Finally, he spoke, the conversation taking a whole new direction.

"And you and Amelia…"

Not again.

"… how are things? How shall we put this? In the bedroom now?"

What?

With my cheeks burning, I rubbed the palms of my hands along my jeans. He studied me, his eyes never appearing to blink.

I may as well have gone and seen a bloody shrink after all.

"Well," I began, my eyes darting from the doctor to the floor. "Well, as you can imagine, it's not been as *regular* as before."

"Hmm, hmm," he nodded, totally relaxed whilst I begged the ground to open up and swallow me whole.

"I can imagine the stress of what you've both been through will have taken its toll."

As he idly replied, it at least allowed me to think on my feet.

"No, no," I corrected him. "It's not what happened to Graham, I mean, her brother-in-law, you know, him…"

"Oh." Doctor Pearce's interest had rekindled. "What is it then, if you don't mind me asking?"

"Because of the pregnancy," I replied, very matter-of-factly.

"Oh, right. Yes. Of course."

The doctor spun in his seat and began tapping away at his keyboard again. I tried to look over his shoulder, but he noticed and turned the monitor an inch or two further away.

"Okay," he finally said, turning back to me with a fixed smile on his face.

"So," I asked awkwardly, "when did she last come and see you?"

He spoke slowly, unruffled. At least his demeanour had some kind of calming effect on me.

"Mister Walker. Even though she is your wife, that is strictly patient confidentiality."

36

AT LEAST I escaped with a prescription. Doctor Pearce had agreed that my lack of sleep and subsequent nightmares were of genuine concern. He'd put it down to an unnatural amount of distress, which had led to over-exhaustion.

As I left the consulting room, I'd completely forgotten about Melissa. My mind was all over the place. And the discussion with the doctor had lasted well over my allocated ten-minute slot. I'm sure I heard one or two people tut their disapproval as I stepped back into the waiting area.

Clutching the instruction for pills in my hand, I ignored the stares and made for the exit.

"Not going to say hello, Matthew?"

Oh shit.

"Oh, hi, Melissa. Didn't see you there. You not well?"

"What on earth are you doing here?" she asked, standing to air-kiss me whilst completely ignoring my question.

Placing a hand behind my back, I pushed my stomach forward and grimaced.

"Problem with my spinal cord. Been playing me up for a while."

"Well, Amelia never mentioned it and she sees you most weeks."

"Oh, you know me, Melissa. I don't like to complain."

She eyed me full of suspicion, but I didn't care. My conversation with Doctor Pearce would be strictly confidential. Even *that* family couldn't infiltrate the privacy between a doctor and his patient.

Bing bing.

'Miss Reid for Doctor Pearce.'

Thank God.

The colour had drained from Melissa's cheeks. It was her turn to look uncomfortable in my presence. The surgery would have been the last place she'd expected to see me. She half-smiled and walked away.

"Oh, Melissa?"

She turned. I'd enjoyed one of the few occasions I held the upper hand over my mother-in-law.

"Yes?"

Nodding towards the consultation rooms, I couldn't help but get in one last jibe.

"Hope it's nothing serious."

I left with a smile.

Calling at the pharmacist, I collected my prescription. I thought more about Doctor Pearce's reaction. Maybe he hadn't seen Amelia at all and the news of the pregnancy had come as a surprise. Amelia had said all along that Tracy was acting as her midwife, so would the doctor need to be involved at all?

.   .   .

Since my visit to Doctor Pearce, the sleeping pills had had their desired effect, albeit accompanied by side effects. The nightmares had abated, but I'd often wake in the morning drenched in sweat. I put it down to the deep sleeps I'd been dropping into, I'd be comatose within seconds of my head hitting the pillow.

I'd also attempted to slow down my drinking. Realising I couldn't go cold turkey, I nonetheless rationed my intake. Francis had lent me one of those drink measurers, the equivalent of a single or a double. Of course, I always opted for the large size, but I noticed the bottle had lasted all week instead of a couple of days.

But the real reason for wanting, no *needing*, to watch my alcohol intake was to stay in control. Apart from Amelia's impending birth – I couldn't go picking up the baby stinking of stale whisky – Julia's suicide had hit me hard. It would have been so easy to spiral further downwards, hit the bottle big time and possibly even give up. Except for losing my parents, death had never played an immediate role in my life before. But Julia's demise had felt so personal, as if I'd lost a small piece of myself.

'I'm done with all this, Matthew.'

And for the first time in my life, I felt alone. Despite being a drifter, I had always needed company. Maybe it's why I had never settled down before meeting Amelia. I was one of those people who sought companionship without commitment. But at that point, I needed togetherness. But who could I turn to?

Sure, Francis listened, but she didn't know the facts. Purposefully, I had handpicked snippets of information whenever I wanted clarification or a fresh set of ears. She was a good listener, but I had no intention of dragging her into the thick of it. I'd done that with Lisa, and she had lost her job and almost her sanity. I hoped she was safe and building a new future for herself. Lisa was a decent person, and so was Francis. I couldn't let the same happen to her. The only other person I could turn to was my ex-wife.

By the end of the week, it was time for my semi-regular get-together with Amelia. Normally, part of me would look forward to it. After all, she *was* carrying my child. But that week, following my visit to the doctor, I'd been dreading it. Melissa would have told her she'd seen me. What should I say? More importantly, it would be the first time we'd met since I'd discovered Julia's body. Amelia had called me afterwards and offered her sympathies, which I felt was a nice touch, but something about discussing it face to face made me feel uneasy.

The weather had remained unpredictable, so I grabbed the table inside and at the back of the café. For a Friday morning, it was relatively quiet.

'Good', I thought aloud, as I entered.

"Sorry?" asked the girl behind the counter.

Blushing, I ordered my usual Americano, and quickly sat down, facing the outside world, waiting for Amelia. She didn't arrive alone.

What the hell?

Amelia stepped into the café, chaperoned by Tracy.

What is she doing here? Is it because I saw their mother at the surgery?

"Hi, Matt," Amelia said, air-kissing me. "Don't mind if Tracy tags along today, do you?"

"Well, actually—"

"Hello, Matt. Don't worry. I didn't want to be here either."

Amelia sat opposite whilst Tracy returned to the counter to order their drinks. She didn't offer me one. Leaning across the table, I spoke through gritted teeth.

"What the fuck is she—"

"Now, now, Matt. It's just the last few times we've met. You have rightly wanted to understand all kinds of things about our baby. Tracy is much better qualified to answer than me. She's the medical expert, you know."

Inevitably, my eyes strayed to Amelia's bump. At least she wore a proper maternity dress, not some ridiculous baggy jumper that she could have borrowed from an overweight uncle. And she'd been right about my questions. As the impending birth approached, I had asked more.

"Didn't you say you were at Epsom hospital though? Surely Tracy can't override—"

Immediately, Amelia shook her head, stopping me mid-sentence. Tracy rejoined us with their coffee.

"I take it you're okay, Matthew?" she asked. I didn't offer a response.

Amelia continued from where I'd broken off.

"You're right. I saw someone right at the beginning. Somebody to clarify I am indeed pregnant. But since then, Tracy has been my acting midwife." She turned to her sister and held her hand. "Haven't you, my angel?"

"Yes. And the perfect expectant mother you've been too."

I'm going to be sick.

Tracy beamed in admiration at her sister. They were like a fucking double act.

"Apart from the morning sickness, of course."

They both laughed.

"So, what about the actual birth?" I intervened. "You delivering that too, Tracy?"

She met my attempt at flippancy with a straight-faced response.

"Of course. Why shouldn't I?"

"Because you're not fucking qualified for a start," I retorted, desperately trying to keep my temper under control.

"What makes you say that, Matthew? There are many things you don't know about me."

Resisting the urge to throw my boiling drink in her face, I instead turned my focus back onto Amelia. She rested one hand on her stomach whilst sipping coffee with the other.

"Can I feel? You know, if it's kicking or whatever?"

The sisters briefly glanced at one another. My sudden brainwave had caught Amelia off guard. Tracy spoke first.

"What, in the middle of a crowded café? I don't think that's appropriate. Do you, Amelia?"

Amelia had never shared the confidence and awareness of her older sister. Tracy reminded me of an old-school headteacher, stern and set in her ways. Far too mature and wise before her time. But Amelia still had an air of youthfulness about her. A vulnerability. No wonder she always needed one of her family by her side. Someone to keep her in check, stop her from saying or doing the wrong thing. Her ever-so-slightly rebellious attitude had been what had attracted me to her. Somebody who plays by the rules but hadn't necessarily always wanted to. I'd often wondered what she would have been like away from that house. What if we had bought the little cottage in the country together? Would she be growing her favourite vegetables in the garden by now, preparing for the life ahead with our baby boy?

She shook her head in response to Tracy's get-out clause, no doubt glad of her sister's quick thinking.

"Maybe outside then." I pushed my luck. "I could walk you back to the office."

Tracy stood, scraping her chair backwards.

"Come on, Amelia. I said it would be trouble if you kept involving him."

"*Involving* me? I'm the bloody father. And I only want to feel my baby kicking. That's all quite normal, Tracy."

Amelia intervened. She didn't want a scene. She beckoned Tracy to sit back down, which she reluctantly agreed to.

"The thing is, Matt," Amelia addressed me calmly. "Once you made it clear you didn't want to return home, both Tracy and Mother suggested we didn't have these meetings. They assumed it would cause me, and my child, stress."

My *child*.

I looked from my wife to her sister, and back again.

"So, why did you?"

"You know why. I've always hoped you would come back. If you saw our child growing inside me, I thought it would make you think. Want to be part of it?"

"I've kept up these meetings, haven't I? If I'd wanted to get away, I could have gone months ago. I'm only here because you *are* pregnant."

Plus, the police have told you not to go anywhere.

"And that's what I keep telling Tracy and Mother," she replied, doing her utmost to raise a smile.

She looked lost. Trapped somewhere between me and her family. I'd seen the same look before, on more than one occasion.

Tracy tutted, rolling her eyes at the same time.

"Move on, sis…" she said.

'Sis'. She's never called her that before.

"Have his baby, and we'll all help raise him."

"And me, Tracy? Do I have a say?"

"You've had your say. You've abandoned us. Just like Ryan couldn't remain loyal to the people who loved him the most. And look what happened to him. And now——"

Amelia reached out and grabbed Tracy's arm.

"And now, who?" I asked, my eyes flicking between them.

"Nobody," Tracy replied. "I meant Graham."

Watching as they left the café, Amelia glanced over her shoulder, her eyes searching for me.

The entire scene had felt so surreal. Why had Tracy really shown up?

And when she said, *'And now.'* And now who?

Amelia had cut her off. Tracy tried to correct herself and mentioned Graham instead. But I knew she hadn't meant her ex-husband at all.

She'd almost let it slip.

'…And now, Julia.'

Graham's wife. Their sister. The woman I'd found hanging in her garden shed.

37

Is that genuinely how Tracy's mind worked?

'You've abandoned us. Just like Ryan did.'

Is that *really* the way they think? Abandoned? And now Julia? Had she deserted you too?

But Amelia had told me Tracy had found Julia with a bottle of pills in her hand. She had let herself in and found Julia slumped in the armchair.

'She could hear her inside. Tracy held the letterbox open. Heard Julia mention Russell Square.'

I'd asked if Julia was okay now.

'She's back home. For now. Until she recovers.'

Home?

'In the family home. The doctors are very happy that Tracy is looking after her.'

But it was impossible to argue. Julia had looked, and acted, peculiarly. That large baggy cardigan, her greasy unkempt hair. Her fidgeting. Her raw and bloody finger-nails. Had she been contemplating taking her life back then, and Tracy had caught her just in time?

It sounded feasible, especially considering she had

indeed taken her own life weeks later. But I couldn't shake the feeling that everything appeared to gravitate around that family. The word *abandoned* played in my mind, like a song I couldn't get out of my head. Is that truly how they felt?

But yet again, Amelia had shown glimpses that she still harboured hopes of us getting back together. Could she be the good guy in all of this? The one member of the family who actually cared for somebody outside their inner circle?

My thoughts drifted to the note that I'd found tucked under the plant pot in Julia's shed. Just a few poignant sentences scribbled down and inserted into an envelope with my name written across it. How did she know I would find it and nobody else?

'Did you ever see my garden shed?'

She hadn't been rambling incoherently after all. It had been a cryptic message, but an indication of what she planned to do. The contents of the letter had both scared and fascinated me. Julia had become overwhelmed with life. Although she had never told me, I'm sure DCI Small had been partially correct and her financial situation was perilous. But instead of mentioning her money troubles, she'd written how everything else had caught up with her. The family, her depression, the medication she had to take and hearing voices, 'many different voices in my head.' Julia didn't mention the word 'psychosis' to me, but the contents of the note matched the definition I'd read on the internet.

However, the last words had ingrained themselves in my brain above all the others, like an itch you couldn't reach.

'Amelia really loves you, Matt. From the bottom of her heart.'

. . .

That night, the pills had their desired effect and I slept until mid-morning. After I'd arrived home from the disastrous meeting with Amelia and Tracy, I knocked on Francis's door. The prospect of a Friday evening alone depressed me. I also needed something to take my mind off things. The birth was imminent and Amelia had told me so. Tracy confirmed she thought it would take place before the due date. That was only four weeks away, anyway.

I'd had a mild panic attack on the tube ride home. Everything was happening far too quickly now.

Francis wasn't home, or at least she didn't answer the door. I only knocked once, respecting her privacy. Instead, I cooked myself a simple stir-fry and tried to concentrate on some frivolous Friday night television. Flicking from channel to channel, it greeted me with flashing lights from quizzes or similar entertainment shows. Nothing held my attention. Turning it off, I instead grabbed the whisky bottle and a glass and piped music through my portable speaker. Even that depressed me.

At eight o'clock, I popped two sleeping pills, necked my Scotch, and crashed out on the bed. Remembering nothing else, I awoke twelve hours later.

After soaking in the shower for far too long, I dressed and made my way to Costa for caffeine and some kind of reheated breakfast roll. The sight of Francis sitting alone on one of the outdoor tables took me by complete surprise. From the look on her face, it shocked her too.

"Oh, hi," she said, lacking any kind of enthusiasm.

"Nice to see you too."

Unsure whether she was going to invite me to join her, I took the initiative and asked if she wanted another drink. Reluctantly, she nodded, and I disappeared inside, surprised by how standoffish she'd been.

Half expecting to find an empty table, I returned with two drinks and a bacon roll. Francis remained stony-faced and stared blankly into the distance. Somewhat foolishly, I decided to ask the question which had been on the tip of my tongue for weeks.

"I saw you going into a hotel. About a month ago."

Trying my utmost not to make a big issue of it, I took a bite of my sandwich and casually looked up and down the street.

She glared at me.

This isn't going to plan.

"You *followed* me?"

"Well, no, not followed," I replied with a mouthful of food. Francis looked disgusted on several counts. I swallowed the contents before continuing.

"I'd just come off the tube, near the Police Box, when I saw you on the other side of the road."

"And then you followed me?"

"No, honest. I couldn't catch you up. You were walking too—"

"I don't believe you, Matt. How dare you?"

It was my turn to go on the defensive. Why did I always feel like the guilty party?

"I heard somebody in your apartment. A man's voice…"

Letting it hang, I waited for her to react. At least it stopped her in her tracks, and she momentarily lost the moral high ground to shout me down. But she didn't reply. Not immediately, anyway.

"And I heard him say, 'Has he gone yet?'."

She spun her coffee cup round and round on the table, finally letting it rest with the hole in the lid facing away from her. It infuriated me.

"I've told you before, he's a friend of Mum's. He won't leave me—"

"Bollocks, Francis. Don't treat me like some kind of idiot. What kind of friend of your Mum stays in a nearby hotel? Is he stalking you or something? If so, we need to go to the police."

The mention of the word 'police' seemed to act as the catalyst for her to come clean; well, at least change her story. Who knew what the truth was anymore? She stopped spinning the bloody cup and leant forward slightly, enabling her to drop her voice. I hadn't expected to hear what she said.

"We need to stop seeing each other, Matt. It isn't safe. For either of us."

Instantly losing my appetite, I pushed the plate away.

"What the hell is that supposed to mean? Not safe? Who the hell are you?"

All kinds of scenarios went through my head. Where we'd first met. The day I'd been to look at my apartment. She had subsequently backed awkwardly out of her door, dragging a suitcase behind her.

'Are you going to be my new neighbour?'

She said she was going to stay with her mum for a few days. Had she lied to me from day one?

Francis continued on the defensive.

"What's that supposed to mean? I'm your neighbour, that's all. But you come with baggage, Matt."

"How do you know what *baggage* I come with?" I air-quoted *baggage*, annoyed she had the audacity to attempt putting everything back onto me.

"This Julia woman committing suicide. You *miraculously* finding her body." This time, Francis air-quoted. "Then the police coming around. And look at your health. Up one minute, down the next. Screaming out in the middle of the bloody night. And now your ex-wife is going to drop your baby any day soon."

She stopped talking far too abruptly.

"How do you know it's *any day now?*"

Francis recovered quickly, or more likely, I'd again put two and two together and made five. She raised her voice as if to assert her control.

"Because you told me it's due in September. It's now the middle of bloody August. Even I can do the maths."

We sat in silence, both contemplating what the hell to say next.

"So, what do we do now?" I asked, my tone more neutral. Shouting at one another would get us nowhere.

Francis composed herself too.

"As I said, we can't see each other anymore."

"You live next door. How is that even—"

"I mean, in the way we have been seeing each other. We can be polite as neighbours, but no more. We're getting too close."

"Too close for what, Francis? I'm completely lost. This is to do with your black eye, isn't it? The visit to the hotel. Are you involved with someone else?"

My frustration risked boiling over. Could she be seeing somebody else on the quiet, and had he found out about us? Could I possibly have found myself in even deeper trouble?

Amelia can't find out, not now, not so close.

"I'm not seeing anybody, and I don't like your accusations either that I'm some kind of tart."

She took another deep breath.

"Listen. Can't you just accept what I'm telling you? We've become too involved. It was never supposed to be this way."

I stared at the traffic crawling by. It was obvious

Francis didn't want to divulge any further information. But what could she possibly mean? There's no way she could have planned me moving in next door, she had played no part in it.

Had she?

38

DURING THE NEXT FEW DAYS, we twice 'bumped' into each other, once on the stairwell and once outside our apartments on the landing. It felt incredibly awkward, neither of us knowing what to say. The second time, I fought the urge to hug her and tell her everything would be okay, but I knew she didn't want that. She'd drawn the line in the sand and I would cross it at my peril. Something was obviously amiss, but however many times I played it through my mind, I couldn't come to a satisfactory conclusion. Nonetheless, ten days after our acrimonious parting from the coffee shop, my 'relationship' with Francis was firmly put on hold.

Tracy had been right. The baby was born earlier than the original due date. Almost three weeks early. Trust her to be so bloody perfect again. I'd secretly been hoping for a late delivery just to wipe the smug grin from her face.

You don't like it. She knows what she's talking about.

My phone buzzed soon after ten o'clock in the morning. I'd returned home from an appointment at work, and had a further two viewings scheduled for that afternoon. The return of the fine summer weather had somehow enabled me to carry on doing the job. My initial enthusiasm had dwindled, as it had with almost every position I'd ever undertaken but once the sun had shown its face again, I went about my job displaying just enough eagerness to please both my boss and clients alike. I'd made a few sales, or at least they had credited me with them following showing prospective buyers around. It all felt a bit of a sham, they either liked the property or not. I didn't feel as though I played any part in making them decide.

"Matthew?"

"Amelia? Is that you?"

I knew it wasn't Amelia, and I'd recognised the voice on the other end. My *games* were becoming as petty as theirs.

"It's Melissa. I'm on Amelia's phone."

She went quiet, and I panicked. Another *game* backfiring.

"Is everything alright? Has something—"

"Everything is fine. In fact, everything is amazing! Amelia has just given birth to a beautiful baby boy. They are both healthy. We are all delighted." She paused. "I thought you would want to know?"

Was that a little dig at the end? Why on earth wouldn't I want to know? Resisting the urge to say something incredibly sarcastic, I instead thanked her for calling.

Once I hung up, I forgot about the mind games and allowed the news to sink in. My heart beat loudly and I suddenly felt overwhelmed. Melissa had asked if I would like to visit after lunch.

What, at your house?

"Yes. Yes. I'd love to," I replied. "Thank you."

As I stepped off the train, the same dreaded feeling welled up inside me. A mixture of nausea and trepidation.

You're going to see your son.

I'd rearranged my afternoon viewings. My boss congratulated me and told me to take a few days off so I could 'enjoy the moment'.

You don't know my family, mate.

It came as no surprise that the first sound I heard was the squeaking of the swing in the garden. It felt like some kind of homecoming call. Katrina's greeting. I heard it before I turned the street corner and the house came into view.

Squeak... squeak...

Although I'd approached silently and kept myself out of sight, Katrina had somehow expected my arrival.

"Hello, Uncle Matthew."

How the...

"Hello, Katrina," I replied, as I turned the corner of the house. "How are you?"

"Are they for me?"

She giggled.

I lifted the bunch of flowers I'd been carrying by my side.

"Do you like them?"

"They're pretty."

She was in a good mood. Her yellowing teeth caught the sun. I noticed her lips were split again, tiny cracks full of dried-up blood.

"Have you seen the baby?"

She giggled again.

"Of course I have, silly. And Mother."

What?

"Yes. Of course. Is he good looking like me?"

That caused Katrina to break out into a laugh. Not the hideous cackle that she often broke into, but a genuine laugh. It shocked me to see some kind of normal reaction from her. Whenever I found myself in Katrina's company, I somehow wished I was a qualified psychiatrist. I'd love to help her. Find out what deep underlying source caused her to behave so erratically.

'She's been diagnosed with dissociative identity disorder.'

Then again, I often thought if I delved too far, the results would scare the living shit out of me.

"Matthew! Matthew! Come inside. You must see Amelia's beautiful baby boy."

Amelia's *beautiful baby boy?*

Ignoring her mother's 'not so subtle' insinuation, I called after her.

"Coming, Melissa."

Turning back to Katrina, it dumbfounded me to see an empty swing swaying of its own accord.

Where the hell is she?

The front door closed, and I thought she must have raced inside ahead of me. But, as I made my way to the porch, I saw her running across the expanse of grass and into the woods.

How could she possibly be there so soon?

"Where are you going?" I called after her.

Within a split second, she stopped deadly still. Slowly, she turned.

The smile on her face stretched from ear to ear. Although she was some distance away, it looked as though some cracks in her lips had split. Little trails of blood ran down her chin. And those teeth. Surely they couldn't have yellowed further in that brief space of time?

It's all in your head.

"I'm going to talk to somebody," she called back. The smile faded, and she turned, breaking into a run once more. So fast, she disappeared into the trees before I'd arrived at the door. Katrina's craziness had reached a whole new level. Maybe it was the excitement of the baby? I had to get inside.

"Come up, come up."

Melissa beamed over the balustrade.

That landing.

"They're in your old bedroom."

The memories of the house came crashing back. I glanced to my right. The living room door was slightly ajar and I could see that nothing had changed. The same chairs, the same small square table at the back of the room; nothing different and all in identical positions. The kitchen lay ahead of me. Katrina's pills. Melissa coming onto me. Graham grabbing me a beer when alcohol was strictly forbidden inside the house. He'd said I'd done well, chopping wood or something from memory, and he would make an exception when I did something good.

Crazy idiot.

Tentatively, I held onto the bannister and began the ascent. The last time I'd been up there was when I'd been held hostage in the spare bedroom.

The spare bedroom! Amelia had asked for extra money from the inheritance to refurbish the place. Add better heating, maybe new windows and mainly, to create a nursery. I could see no evidence of any work that had taken place. The receipt she had shown me.

'Dean's Home Improvements'.

By the looks of it, Dean was either bloody useless or didn't exist. But it wasn't the right time to ask, even though I had to know more.

"Quick, in here," Melissa beamed, standing at our old bedroom door. With a hasty glance along the corridor, I took a deep breath and stepped inside.

Tracy sat on one side of the bed with Melissa's chair empty on the other. My wife sat upright, propped up by several pillows. Cradled in her arms was the tiniest little human being I'd ever seen. His eyes were open, looking directly into Amelia's. Scant tufts of fair hair stuck up at the back of his head. I stared in wonder and suddenly felt incredibly emotional.

Why, Matt? You fool.

Amelia noticed. Maybe Tracy did too.

"Can you give us a moment, please?" Amelia addressed both her sister and mother. They looked at one another, nodded, and agreed to leave.

You're too kind.

Melissa brushed my hand as she passed, accompanied by an all too familiar smile.

"Welcome home," she whispered. I knew nobody else had heard.

Tracy offered me the briefest of glances. A 'don't fuck this up' type of look. I didn't give her the satisfaction of a response. Instead, my full concentration fell onto Amelia and the beautiful baby boy in her arms.

"He's amazing," I said, hovering at the side of the bed. I'd waited for the door to click shut before I spoke. Kissing Amelia on the forehead brought out the broadest smile across her face. She looked remarkably healthy considering she'd given birth only three or four hours earlier.

However, it soon transpired that Melissa had told me a little lie. Amelia hadn't *just* given birth when she called me at ten o'clock that morning. In fact, she'd had the baby at four o'clock in the morning, following 'a difficult four or five hours of labour'.

"Why didn't you call me straight away?" I asked, gently taking the child from Amelia before carefully cradling him in my arms. He had the most gorgeous blue eyes and the tiniest of noses. I couldn't help but keep touching it with the tip of my finger.

"I left it to Mother to call you. You're not angry, are you?"

Amelia's eyes begged me. Had this been the moment she'd waited nine months for? I had to remember the past and try not to succumb to the powerful emotional bond which bounced around the room. Our room. So much had happened since, yet here we were, back in our marital bedroom. Newborn baby, husband and wife.

Mother.

Struggling to contain the intensity of the situation, the added thought of my parents looking down threatened to overwhelm me. I allowed myself a few moments' silence to take it all in.

But, despite the temptation to stare and stare in admiration at the miracle held within my arms, my eyes couldn't help but drift back towards Amelia.

She looked so radiant, beautiful. Almost *too* good.

39

DESPITE TAKING one of my pills, that night proved to be particularly restless. It had been the first occasion when the prescription drug didn't do its job. Earlier, after leaving Amelia and the baby, I'd called into the office and delivered my good news in person. My boss had been true to his word and instructed me to take a couple of weeks off. It would be longer than necessary, but I didn't argue. He added that there could be more hours available once I returned. At least I'd be rested up and hopefully put some kind of longer-term plan into action, whatever that was.

Deliberating whether to share the news with Francis, I hovered outside her apartment. Perhaps I could tell her I would move on soon? It might please her, given our last meeting.

'*We've become too involved. It was never supposed to be this way.*'

However, as soon as I raised my hand to knock on her door, I lost all enthusiasm. It had been a long day, and I felt drained. A takeaway, a celebratory drink, and my bed beckoned.

The sight of seeing the baby had knocked me sideways. The build-up to the all-important day had taken its toll. I knew it was why I'd drunk so much and it explained my constant mood swings. Sometimes I thought I'd imagined all that had gone on and doubted my sanity.

'And look at your health. Up one minute, down the next.'

It had been the sole reason I'd hung around London. But now I'd seen the baby with my own eyes, my confused state had reached an entirely new level.

After retiring to bed, I checked the time almost every hour, on the hour. Eventually, I gave up on any prospect of decent sleep, and instead, clambered out of bed and showered. It was still early, around six in the morning.

After two strong coffees, I paced the room and, in fast-forward mode, played out the events in my mind. And the more I recollected, the more confused and angry I became. Something didn't fit. Had they taken me as a complete fool?

My next move was inevitable.

As I made my way to the train station, I recalled the conversation I'd had with Amelia about the hospital she had visited.

'Everything is fine and Tracy went with me. It's the hospital in Epsom. You've no need to get involved.'

But she later added that she only visited one time.

'I saw somebody right at the beginning. Somebody to clarify I am indeed pregnant, but since then, Tracy has been my acting midwife.'

Had she been at all?

Doctor Pearce tapped the monitor with the tip of his pen.

'Strictly patient confidentiality.'

Perhaps I'd got it all wrong and Amelia's version of events could have been truthful, but I had to find out for myself.

At home, I tapped the search criteria into Google and the top result returned 'Maternity Services | Epsom and St Helier Hospital'. Once I disembarked the train, I launched Google Maps, brought up the address and clicked on 'Directions' – a fifteen-minute walk from where I stood. Tapping 'Start', I followed the blue arrow on the map. My heart rate increased with every step.

Whilst navigating along the busy Dorking Road, I knew the entire trip could easily end up futile, a total red herring. Would a visit be on her records, anyway? What if she had gone private? Does that still show up on your NHS details? And what if she'd lied all along and had never been to the hospital? Where would that leave me? Back to the family. Back to Tracy.

'...*She's a qualified midwife too, is she?*'

Once inside the intimidating building — I hate hospitals — I headed for a large semi-circular reception desk in front of the main entrance. I had to act with purpose. If I allowed further doubt to creep in, I knew I would have walked out and dismissed it all as a crazy notion.

As soon as I asked for directions to the maternity ward, the receptionist broke into a smile, obviously categorising me as a new father. Maybe it had been my dishevelled appearance and obvious lack of sleep which had convinced her.

I'm here to reassure myself I'm not going insane, not necessarily because my wife had a baby.

Following the signs along the extensive corridors, I passed a couple of poor patients being wheeled along by porters in mobile beds, drips fixed to their arms, wheezing and coughing. 'Shit', I thought to myself, 'I wonder if I'll ever be like that?'

"Hello. Can I help?"

Another reception desk. A nurse sat on the far side, fixing on her best smile.

"Hi."

A brief silence ensued, and I could feel my cheeks burn.

"Was there something?"

I looked around the ward, each bed cordoned off from view by a vast, light blue curtain.

"It's a kind of strange request, really."

Stammering and bullshitting, I attempted to regurgitate the story I'd practised en route. It had resonated perfectly in my head, but the words tripped over each other and I realised how stupid I sounded. I'd gone with the estranged wife angle, hoping the receptionist might take pity. Continuing, I explained I'd heard she had given birth to my son, adding I desperately needed to find out whether it was true.

"I'm sorry, sir. That's strict patient confidentiality."

Of course it is.

Reiterating my sob story, this time giving Amelia's full name to plead to her good nature, the nurse showed no sign of compassion, and she repeated her stock reply. She was only doing her job, and it soon became apparent how pointless my trip had become. Reluctantly, I turned to leave.

As I forlornly exited the ward, I glanced over my shoulder. The nurse frantically tapped away at the keyboard. Fortunately, she didn't look up, else she would have seen me frozen to the spot.

Coming to my senses, I quickly reached the exit and crouched down behind the corner. From my position, I could still see the nurse. She continued tapping the keys and intermittently scrolled up and down with the mouse. Her face gave nothing away, but I knew my story had intrigued her.

A buzzer sounded from one of the beds. The nurse stopped what she was doing and looked around. After a few brief moments, I could see her tut her disproval and stand to attend to the patient herself. The buzzer sounded again, hastening her movements. In the rush, she left the monitor on.

Go, Matt, go.

Without allowing myself time to deliberate, I stood up, glanced around, and swiftly made my way to the desk. Following a further look around, I ducked behind the table and knelt in front of the computer.

It only took a few seconds to determine what it displayed. A list of names. Although not in alphabetical order, it had to be a list of patients.

Surname. Forename. Date of birth. Date Admitted.

At first, I followed the *Surname* field.

Reed.

Abraham.

Rogers.

Lots and lots more.

But no Reid. What had the nurse been looking for?

Then I noticed the search field at the top of the screen.

The only option I could see to alter was *Date Admitted*. The nurse had been checking from March onwards. Too late. My hand trembled as I clicked on the magnifying glass icon to repeat the search.

I'd set it to the first of February. Maybe that would be too early, given that Amelia said she'd conceived over Christmas, but I had to start somewhere. Besides, my knowledge of when any expectant mother would initially be admitted and checked over bordered on zero.

As I scrolled through the records, I heard footsteps on the far side of the desk. Crouching even lower, my heart drummed as the sound disappeared off to my left.

Allowing myself a few brief seconds to regulate my breathing, I slowly readjusted my position until I knelt back in front of the monitor.

4th February. Collins.

4th February. Anand.

5th February. Campbell.

Shit, shit, shit. This could take all day.

Still, no 'Reid' and I had reached the beginning of March. When had she said she'd visited? Or had she? I cursed myself for barely paying attention.

Dragging the results back to the start, I increased my scrolling speed, trying to take in as many records as my brain would compute. A myriad of names and dates flashed by. But none stood out to me. Still no 'Amelia Reid', no 'Amelia Walker'.

Would she have used a false name? No. You can't. Not where the NHS is concerned. Surely you'd need proof of ID, or they'd match you against your address or GP surgery, wouldn't they?

The sound of a gruff male voice from behind made me jump out of my skin.

40

"Can I help you?"

Losing balance, I tumbled over onto my backside. The janitor stooped over me. Next to him was a yellow bucket, complete with a mop standing upright in a metal frame. And then I heard further footsteps running in our direction from the far side of the desk. The nurse's ruddy face leant over the counter.

"Hey, you!"

In one movement, I stood and paced as fast as I could towards the exit. The janitor shouted something after me, but following a quick glance over my shoulder, he appeared to be in no mood to give chase.

However, the nurse walked in my direction, breaking into a jog as she approached the corridor. But I ran too, and once she realised I was too far ahead, she gave up. Once I reached the far end of the long passageway, I turned into a relatively busy thoroughfare. Continuing to combine jogging and walking, I soon found myself back at the main entrance. The girl at reception offered me a brief smile. I nodded but didn't look back. It wasn't until I found myself outside the perimeter fence and the relative safety of the Dorking Road that I allowed myself to walk at a normal pace again.

Back inside my apartment, I reverted to habit and poured myself a stiff drink. Necking it in one, I poured another. Completing my familiar routine, I collapsed into my armchair, the bottle by my side.

What kind of crazy fucked up day was that?

So many questions, but nobody to ask. Should I confide in Francis? No. She would think me insane too. Who would contemplate hanging around such an unstable family? Maybe somebody just as crazy as them? Besides, I'd already decided not to involve Francis. Her surprise visitor and subsequent black eye still played on my mind.

'We've become too involved. It was never supposed to be this way.'

Knowing I would visit Amelia and the baby later, I pushed the whisky bottle out of arm's reach.

Maybe there was one other thing I could check?

Whilst my MacBook rebooted, I found a pen and scrap sheet of paper. From memory, I wrote what I assumed were Amelia's online banking details. Instantly, I thought I had one digit wrong. The password was simple, she used it for everything and I doubted she would have changed it, but the five-digit code eluded me.

Having logged onto her account in the past, I scribbled down further combinations, knowing I wasn't far out. Maybe the 'four' goes there, or is it at the end? Realising I would only get three attempts, I had to get it right. I also knew that Amelia could see the last date and time I had accessed her online banking. Would she know where to look? Or even notice? Trying my best to think of a reasonable excuse, I launched the web browser and typed in the bank's name. A couple of clicks later, I found myself on the login page.

Surname. Even typing the name 'Reid' made my hair stand on end. Password. Simple, she never changed a password. Five-digit passcode. Shit. This is it, Matt. Three attempts.

I went with my instinct, the first combination I'd written down.

Yes!

Success. I was straight into the list of transactions. And it didn't take long to find a pattern which caught my attention. Every Friday at four pm. The same amount to the same payee.

What the…?

It threw up even more questions than answers, and I already had enough of those bloody things to deal with.

I checked for further regular payments, but none stood out. The original reason I logged in was to check for any monies paid to 'Dean's Home Improvements'. There were no such listings. However, a one-off transaction to a certain individual made my blood run cold.

It left me with no option. Calling the police would be futile. The family would have covered their tracks. I had to act alone, and I had to act fast.

Knowing it would be pointless doing anything that evening, I decided to wait until the following day. Besides, I had to keep up the pretence and call in on Amelia and the baby. If I missed only my second appointment, she, or they, would suspect something. I just prayed she didn't check her online banking and notice somebody had logged on earlier that day.

I needn't have worried. Once back home following our informal meeting, I felt satisfied that she knew nothing about her banking and also nothing regarding my visit to the hospital. Unless they had followed me, she would have no way of knowing.

In fact, I'd surprised myself by maintaining a normal outward appearance. We'd even laughed about my nappy-changing capabilities. At one point, Melissa rushed into the room to enquire what all the merriment was about. She was as desperate as Amelia for a satisfactory outcome. Now our number had been increased by one, that is. But Tracy had stood in the background, stern-faced and doubting, ruining an otherwise amicable hour together.

The following day, I took the tube to Ealing. Approaching my destination, a wave of melancholy washed over me. Suddenly, I felt lonely, the guy with no real friends, no family, nobody to turn to.

Knowing the pub would be relatively quiet on a Thursday lunchtime, I'd sent Patrick a message the previous evening and arranged to meet him then. I'd found the old beer mat in my kitchen drawer, stuffed away with letters and takeaway menus. It contained his name and mobile number scrawled across it in red ink.

"Hello, sir. Haven't seen you for a while. Thought you'd moved away?"

As ever, the landlord found small talk as easy as reciting the alphabet aloud.

"Yes, yes, I have. I've just been back to collect the last of my things."

Unsure why I lied, I quickly realised I didn't even have a bag with me. Blushing, I tried to make out nobody was in, but the landlord's grin informed me to stop digging.

"Pint of bitter?" he asked, saving me from further embarrassment. Nodding, I took my usual bar stool and scouted the premises.

"After someone?"

Jeez, does this guy miss anything?

"I am actually."

As I paid for the drink, I asked if Patrick had been in yet.

Ironically, before he could even reply, the door opened and Patrick strolled purposefully across the pub. However, as soon as he set eyes on me, the smile disappeared from his face. I stood to greet him.

"Not pleased to see me?" I asked, shaking his hand.

Patrick didn't share my enthusiasm.

"Pleased to see you, yes, but I really hoped I never would."

"That's nice to hear," I added sarcastically. "Can I get you a drink?"

We carried our beer to a small round table tucked away at the back of the pub. Patrick suggested it. The barman appeared pissed off that we were stepping out of earshot.

Patrick cut straight to the chase.

"The reason I hoped I would never see you again is that if you came looking for me, I knew you would want something. Or even that you are in some kind of trouble. Which one is it?"

He remained calm. His voice barely deviated. Monotone, yet captivating. I thought of Patrick as an ideal guy to give a motivational speech. He drew you in, and you couldn't help but listen.

"I'm not sure."

"At least you're honest. I like that."

With time against me, I took a huge gulp of my beer and faced him head-on.

"Did you know Julia? Graham's—"

"Wife. Yes, of course I did. Tragic it is too. And listen," he patted my arm, "I know how hard it must have been for you to have found her like that."

Shit. He knows everything.

"How do you know that?"

Suddenly, I became wary. There would have been ways to find out, but he knew far too much. Every detail.

"A little bird told me," he replied, tapping his nose.

Why the secrecy?

Knowing I had nothing to lose, and I hadn't gone all that way just to buy him a beer, I went for the jugular.

"Are you Melissa's ex-husband?"

For the first time, Patrick flinched. Only for a split second, but at least a temporary glitch in his otherwise resolute exterior.

"I am, yes. Julia told you, did she?"

Although I felt a pang of guilt that I'd used Julia's confidential information for my advantage, I knew she had my best interests at heart. Maybe she'd told me, as she knew one day I may need to contact him again?

We discussed Julia for a short while, how I'd initially met her and how I'd kept in touch following Graham's arrest. Her downfall hadn't surprised Patrick, both in appearance or her financial struggles. He said Graham had always been in charge of the household money, drip feeding her just enough to buy food or maybe treat herself to a new dress if she'd been especially good.

'Especially good' What the hell does that even mean?

The more Graham revealed, the deeper my remorse became. If only I had known before. Could I have saved her? Helped her escape before the situation had got out of control? But she'd repeatedly said she would never have gone anywhere else. A feeling of déjà vu engulfed me.

Maybe the same reason that you didn't leave? And why Ryan never did. Maybe you can't get away.

"So, why did *you* leave the house, the family?"

Again, I'd caught him out. I got the impression he presumed he would ask all the questions.

"Same reason as Ryan, I assume. And you, perhaps?"

Patrick told me of how things changed once Graham arrived on the scene. He explained how he manipulated the family.

"Don't get me wrong, they weren't exactly your *normal* family. I'd tried several times to get Melissa to buy a house with me and give that old place to the kids once they had grown up. But she wouldn't leave her daughters or Katrina. Melissa took it as her duty to help raise her and allow Tracy to go to work and live a semi-normal life. The house was falling to pieces, and we needed as much money as we could get our hands on."

Without asking, Patrick collected my empty glass, walked to the bar and returned moments later with two fresh beers. It was as though we had timed the interlude perfectly, allowing me to take in all he'd said.

As I took my pint, he clinked my glass with his.

"Congratulations," he said, before supping the head off his drink.

Holding my glass in mid-air, I gaped at him.

"Whatever for?"

"On becoming a father, of course."

He really knows everything.

"Thank you," I replied sarcastically. "But please tell me how you know so much about me, about them. What have you got to lose?"

Patrick allowed himself time to deliberate.

"Fair enough. You've come this far, Matt, and maybe you deserve clarity. As long as you promise not to say anything, although I know I can trust you."

More intrigued than scared, I nodded nonchalantly, as if he was going to tell me the name of his favourite author or actor.

"Your wife."

Wishing I hadn't acted so casually, I almost choked on the mouthful of beer I'd taken.

"Amelia?"

"Yes, Amelia. She means well, and she thinks the world of you."

Holy shit! My mind went into overdrive. Amelia had kept in touch with Patrick. But how long for? Had they been communicating whilst I'd lived at the house? Did anybody else know?

So many questions that I didn't know where to start. However, Patrick stopped me before I could even begin.

"That's it, Matt. The last I heard from her was via text to tell me she'd had your baby. I don't see her. It's all via messaging. I have one more confession, though."

Patrick admitted to following me the day I'd visited the offices at Opacy. Amelia had tipped him off, and it had intrigued him to see me.

The tube station entrance, a figure descending the steps...

He also confessed to *watching* me from time to time,

especially around Ealing. He hadn't seen me recently. His interest diminished.

'*Pleased to see you, but I really hoped I never would.*'

After disclosing his secrets, he lifted his glass and congratulated me once more, indicating that would be the end of the subject.

Following a few moments' silence, we made small talk whilst finishing our drinks. I'd found out what I needed to know, and I needed to get away. I had no hard feelings towards Patrick.

As he stood to leave, he casually asked why I had moved to Earl's Court.

"A local estate agent suggested an apartment there. He said it—"

"*Local* estate agent, did you say?"

"Yes. Just along the high—"

"Why would a local estate agent suggest a flat in Earl's Court? It's miles away."

Patrick only asked what I would have done myself.

"The agent, Andy, said he knew of a place via a colleague at another branch…"

The colour drained from Patrick's face.

"Did you say, *Andy*?"

I didn't like where the conversation was heading.

"Yes. Andy Coleman."

"I thought I'd seen that bastard around."

Although I barely knew Patrick, it was the most animated I'd ever seen him.

"What are you talking about? Do you know Andy?"

"I could be wrong, and I don't recognise the surname 'Coleman', but did you know Graham has got a brother?"

"A what?"

This time, the colour drained from my face.

"An older brother."

It felt like car crash television. I didn't want to know anymore, yet I pleaded with Patrick to continue.

"And?"

"And his brother's name is Andy."

41

Leaving the pub in a daze, I bid Patrick farewell and subconsciously wandered towards the high street. The thought of Graham having a brother was bad enough, but could it be the same person who found me my new apartment? Nobody was supposed to know where I'd moved to. My fresh start, away from prying eyes?

Without thinking, I found myself outside the estate agents.

What are you even doing here?

Thankfully, it appeared deserted indoors. No sign of customers and no sign of Andy. All of my actions, all of my thoughts, blurred into one. It felt as though I was on autopilot, meandering from one crisis to the next without resolving any.

An elderly couple stood gawping at the listings in the window, intermittently pointing at the odd property. They didn't look like serious buyers, more likely nosey neighbours trying to work out how much their own place was worth. Ignoring them, I stepped inside.

Only the young girl, Katie, appeared to be in the

building. Disappointed, or relieved, I wondered if Andy had popped out, a viewing or a valuation, perhaps? Maybe he was out the back of the office, making coffee in the kitchen area? Fixing on my best smile and at least trying not to look scared, I reminded Katie who I was. With her photographic memory, she soon recollected.

"You lived at number forty-two. Moved to Earl's Court. Andy said he knew of a flat going there."

The mention of his name made me realise exactly where I was. But I held the upper hand. He wouldn't know what Patrick had just told me, if indeed he was Graham's brother. However, in the time between leaving the pub and finding myself inside the agents, I knew he had to be the same person. It all fitted into place.

"Wow. I'm impressed."

She looked at me as I pretended to view some proper-ties which were for sale along the office walls. Unsure what to say or do, I hummed a tune to myself. Katie stifled a laugh.

"In the market again?" She grinned. Her question carried an air of flippancy. She really was quite astute.

"No. Not me. Just looking."

Katie smiled once more. Sarcastically, yet full of fun.

"So, Andy not around today?" I asked, changing the subject.

"Doesn't work here anymore, thank God."

Katie's reply made me stop glancing at properties and instead focus all of my attention on her.

"He's left?"

The bright-eyed girl went on to explain that Andy had resigned two days earlier. He didn't even work his notice period. She said he left of his own accord and didn't ask for any holiday pay. 'Just pay me what you owe me', he'd allegedly said, during the resignation phone call to their boss.

"He left *two* days ago?"

The day my son was born.

She nodded.

"Do you know where he lives?"

"Nope. Nothing. He never told me anything. Just rode into town around six months ago. Introduced himself as the new sales exec. But like I say, thank God he's gone. He was bloody useless at his job."

"So you don't know whether he had a background in property?"

She laughed. Or more of a 'Ha!'.

"No chance. He didn't know a house from a bunga-low. One day I asked him how long he's been an estate agent and he said, 'only recently', or something. Professed to be more of a security expert. Fitting cameras or that sort of thing. I told you I didn't like him."

Looking around the office, it appeared otherwise deserted, apart from Katie's desk. Again, she read my mind.

"Not considering a job, are you? We're desperate."

"Me? No."

As I attempted to decipher what was going on, my eyes drifted back to the sale boards.

"Can I help you with anything else?"

Despite only doing her job, Katie's questions and enthusiasm grated on me.

"Nah. Just looking for Lisa Ingram's place." I turned to face her. "Number forty-two?"

"Oh, you're out of luck if you're thinking of putting in an offer."

"No. I don't want it, just wondered if it had gone yet."

"It went last week."

I didn't let on that I already knew it had sold. I regularly checked online, and I'd seen the week before the status had changed to, 'Sold — Subject to Contract'. I'd paid it very little attention.

"I mean, it's great news," I stumbled for the right words. "Does Lisa know?"

Katie glared at me as if I'd just asked the most ridiculous question she'd ever heard.

"Of course she knows. She had to accept the offer."

Blushing, I tried to recompose myself.

"She's been in then?"

Her reply came as no surprise.

"No need. We did it all via email. She signed the documents electronically. Think she's staying with her mum or something."

"Oh, right," I replied, matter-of-factly. "Did Lisa leave a forwarding address? I'm having problems contacting her on the phone."

"I'm not allowed to give out that kind of information."

Let me guess. Client confidentiality?

Katie shuffled some property details on her desk, indicating the conversation was over.

Thanking her for her time, I turned to leave.

"Actually," Katie said, "I'm surprised you didn't know that Andy has left."

Intrigued, I closed the door and faced her.

Shit. Is she involved too? Does she know Patrick?

"How would I know that?"

"That woman you were with. The day I turned up when she and Andy were arguing about something."

Inwardly, I sighed with relief.

I recalled Francis quizzing Andy. Wasn't it something

to do with Lisa signing the paperwork and collecting stuff from the house?

"What about her?" I asked. Despite my initial reassurance, a fresh wave of anxiety washed over me.

"She's been in a few times since she came here with you. Always spoke to Andy, mostly out the back."

Katie nodded to the closed door at the rear of the office. My eyes narrowed. Was she winding me up?

"You sure it was Francis?"

"Hundred per cent. Pretty girl, dimples when she smiled."

Could it be innocent? Francis could easily have been house hunting. She didn't have to tell me everything. But then why talk in secret?

"Why did she always need to speak with Andy? And why go out the back?"

Katie shuffled her papers once more, clearly bored with my presence.

"Not really sure. As I say, they always went to the kitchen area. I couldn't hear what they talked about, but I recall that most of the time their voices were raised."

42

FEELING as though I'd done several rounds with a heavyweight boxer, I took the tube ride home. My frustration threatened to boil over as I counted down the stops to Earl's Court. It had been days since I'd last set eyes upon Francis and I needed to pay her a visit.

Following the tradition of turning up unannounced, I called at Costa as a form of bribing my way in. Carrying a cardboard tray with two Americanos, I wearily traipsed to her apartment door.

Please be in.

Knocking gently, I took two steps back, suddenly aware of who might be inside. Footsteps approached from within.

The door opened, but only an inch or so. Francis's eyes stood out against the gloom. Stepping forward and lifting the drinks high enough for her to see, I put on my best smile.

"Peace offering?" I said.

"Go away, Matt," she replied sternly, closing the door.

But I'd been expecting it and, stretching my leg out, I placed my foot into the opening at the bottom. Francis responded and tried to bang it shut, but my shoe remained steadfast in the gap. Realising it futile, she stepped away, allowing the door to swing inwards at the same time.

"Please," I said, following her, "I only need to talk for five minutes. Then I'll be gone."

She studied me as if judging whether she could trust me.

"I promise," I continued. "I'm leaving the area."

Francis's expression changed. She looked confused, hurt even. Thinking she would jump at the opportunity of never seeing me again, it momentarily pleased me she might feel the same way as I did. I'd never intended us to be close, nor had I wanted her to become embroiled in my state of affairs. But it was no longer a question *if* she was involved, more to what extent.

However, things were now different. I could no longer be blamed if she had become entangled in my mess. Her involvement appeared to have been instigated well before I ever set eyes on her.

"Where will you go?"

She gestured for me to put the drinks on the table. I recollected spilling the last one I'd placed on the same spot.

"I'm not sure yet, but there are things I need to sort out before then. Starting with you, Francis."

She went straight onto the defensive.

"I've nothing to say."

"More like nothing you're *allowed* to say."

"What's that supposed to mean?"

Although she tried to keep up the pretence, we both knew it was pointless.

A one-off transaction to a certain individual made my blood run cold.

"Is ten thousand pounds the only payment, or do you get more once your part is complete?"

"I don't know what—"

"Leave it, Francis. I haven't got time."

With her eyes not leaving the floor, she sat in silence as I told her of the money missing from my wife's bank account. It hadn't been until Francis had confirmed her surname to the DCI that I'd known her full name.

'Baker, I mean, Francis. Please call me Francis.'

She'd made a mistake that day. I recalled how embarrassed and flustered she'd become as soon as she let it slip. It had been the only time I'd heard her use her last name. Our mail was posted in a metal box in the foyer and we each had an individual key to open our own. She'd never wanted me to collect her letters. I'd never given it a second thought, but once I'd seen Amelia's bank statement and a one-off payment to Miss F. Baker for ten thousand pounds, I'd been able to put two and two together. At least she had the decency to look me in the eye once I'd finished.

"Okay, so now you know. Your family paid me some money. So what?"

"So what?" I stood and paced the room to compose myself. "So what? I gave my wife thousands of pounds to build a nursery for my child. Instead, I find out most of it went to you. What was it for, Francis? And if you don't come clean, we'll ask DCI Small for his thoughts."

"Go ahead. I've done nothing illegal. All I know is that some guy came around, said he had a new tenant lined up for next door and could I keep my eye on him. At first, I told him where to go, thought it was some kind of scam. But once he explained what I had to do, and then offered me money to do it, well, you know…"

"Shit. Why do you need the money? You seem so, so well off."

"We all need a little extra, shall we say? I told you the truth about my mum needing a hip replacement. We got a quote to get it done privately. She was six or seven grand short. This was ideal, especially as the alternative was for me to move in with her whilst we waited for an appointment on the bloody National Health Service. Shit, I would have gone stir crazy."

Normally, I would have seen the funny side of Francis's story. She'd always maintained how boring her visits were but time was pressing and this was far from *normal*.

"And this guy who came to see you? Andy Coleman was it?"

Her face told me the answer before she spoke.

"Yes. He instructed me——"

"The same Andy Coleman who you regularly visited at the estate agents and consequently ended up arguing with in the back room? And who it was I heard in your apartment that day? A subsequent black eye? What were all the arguments about, Francis?"

Francis gave up seeking to cover her tracks. She realised I knew too much, and besides, as she said, she had done nothing illegal. I wasn't even sure whether she'd have to declare the money.

"That fucking nosey bitch across the landing told him that you and I have been seeing each other."

The nosey neighbour catching me attempting to deliver wine.

"Told him we often stayed over at each other's apartments. You see, they had paid me to keep my eye on you. Make certain you didn't go anywhere, or, ironically, get involved with anybody. Sure, we could talk. He encouraged that from the offset. 'Find out what his plans are', he'd said to me. 'Keep him sweet', and all that bollocks. And then one day, he came around when I wasn't in and that nosey cow told him everything."

The 'nosey cow' didn't interest me. I'd been stupid to get involved with Francis and I couldn't go blaming an elderly neighbour. As with every damn relationship I got entangled with, it always seemed to come back and haunt me.

"And he's staying at the hotel around the corner, isn't he?"

Again, I already knew the answer. Amelia had been paying for Graham's brother to stay there. I'd seen it when I accessed her online banking. Every Friday at four pm, the same amount leaving her account. He'd stayed local. It's why he'd suggested the apartment in Earl's Court and why he'd sent me to view two shit flats beforehand. He knew I would grab the opportunity to move into the smart place. And he knew I would act quickly before anybody else could view it. They had lined everything up. And to top it all, they'd even bribed my new neighbour to keep her eye on me.

Had they tried other apartments or had they struck gold with Francis at the first attempt? People would do anything for money, and she was no different.

It then crossed my mind to wonder whether Julia had been involved again. How she used to find information on families and match them with prospective CVs. Had she *found* Francis?

What kind of fucked up family are they?

And they had somehow got Andy a job at the estate agency. More of my money to bribe them or a fake CV? Perhaps both.

Francis interrupted my thoughts.

"I'm not sure if he's still there."

If he's not at the hotel, then where is he?

Shit.

At the house? The house with the family and with the baby? My baby! What the hell? I hadn't even contemplated that.

Call the police.

"When did you last speak to him, Francis?"

With my voice raised, and the colour apparently drained from my face, she glared at me in shock.

"You're scaring me, Matt. Why is that important?"

"Think, Francis. Think!"

"I'm not sure. He called me."

"And? What did he say?"

"He told me I mustn't see you again. Told me if I did 'bump into you' that I had to be friendly, but also to ensure you knew it was all over between us."

'*We need to stop seeing each other. It isn't safe. For either of us.*'

Andy had threatened her. It was obvious. She'd let him down once, and he had given her a final warning.

"Listen. Can you go to your Mum's for a few days?"

"I guess I could. But will you be safe?"

Her concern appeared genuine. I could have kicked myself for allowing her to get so deeply involved.

Reassuring her I'd be fine, I instructed Francis to pack and leave as soon as possible. With a quick hug, I left her apartment.

I ran all the way to the hotel. It must have been a mile, and I hadn't run that far for a long time. Once outside, I sat on a white wall, attempting to get my breath back. If Andy was there, I needed my wits about me, as well as being able to run like hell should the need arise.

The reception was small, and three members of staff were crowded behind it.

"Yes, sir," two of them said instantaneously.

"I'm looking for an Andy Coleman. He's been staying with you for a while."

The two of them looked at one another.

"Listen, I know it's confidential and all that, but I'm his brother. Something has happened and I urgently need to get hold of him."

One guy in a smart black suit began tapping on his keyboard. My tone had frightened him into action.

"He checked out, sir. Yesterday. He has settled all of his invoices."

"And a forwarding address? Please. It's urgent."

The same guy clicked and tapped away again. After what felt like an age, he looked up.

"Sorry, sir. He hasn't left us any further details."

43

THE PROSPECT of having to visit Amelia made me feel physically sick. With all that had gone on, I'd had to put her off the day before, texting to suggest she rested and I'd be around the following day. Ironically, she thanked me for being so understanding.

As I approached the house, I expected the squeaking sound of the swing, but all remained deathly silent. There wasn't a breath of air and the atmosphere carried an intense humidity. Thunderstorms couldn't be far away. The sky had become interspersed with darkening clouds. They somehow ridiculed me, hovering over the woods, threatening to journey the final hundred yards to the Reid household.

With a glance at the upstairs windows, I cleared my throat and gingerly knocked on the front door. As soon as it opened, Melissa beamed from the other side.

"Matthew. Come in. Please, come in."

Attempting my bravest smile, I joined her indoors.

The coolness of the house felt refreshing. My T-shirt

had stuck to my back, and I gently wafted it to allow some air to circulate. At first, I didn't notice Melissa watching me. She smiled.

Feeling a mixture of embarrassment and anger, I averted my gaze and instead looked up the staircase and onwards towards the landing. Melissa read my mind.

"They're sleeping. They both had a long night. Shall we let them rest a while before you go up?"

Not really.

Without waiting for a response, she wandered into the kitchen. Reluctantly, I followed. I watched as she filled the kettle and carried out the everyday routine of making a cup of tea. Melissa acted as if everything was perfectly normal.

Suddenly, it crossed my mind that the family may be in the dark about the entire situation. Did Melissa know that Graham's brother was local? Could Graham have infiltrated it all from his prison cell?

'I know how much you despise him. We all do now. We only did what we did because he told us to. You were right, Matt. Graham is a bully. He threatened us if we didn't comply. Threatened to have Katrina taken away. We did not know he could have been responsible for the death of Ryan, we just assumed he had disappeared, run away.'

"Tracy at work?" I asked, chit-chatting whilst wanting to be anywhere but in a small room cooped up with my mother-in-law.

"Yeah. And Katrina is out playing somewhere."

Playing? She's approaching adulthood. And didn't Julia say Katrina is no longer allowed out whilst on her own with Melissa?

Everything felt like a lie.

"Nobody else in then? Nobody else near the baby?"

Melissa stopped what she was doing. She glared at me as if I'd suggested she were a child molester.

"What's that supposed to mean? Of course, there's nobody else here."

But had she been too defensive? Immediately, she attempted to appeal to my better side, her voice mellowing.

"I wish you would calm down, Matthew. We've told you all that is in the past. It went away when Graham did. We have all learned our lessons and we *all* need to move on. Why can't you accept that? Please?"

Opening the refrigerator door, she brushed her hand along my bare arm. I'd been in similar situations with her before. I'd often wondered how far she would actually take it.

Knowing I had to play it cool, I offered her a brief smile and a nod of my head.

"Sad about Julia, wasn't it?" I said, attempting to defuse the tension.

Melissa passed me a cup of steaming tea.

"Yes. Yes, it was. But I believe she's at peace now. Poor girl suffered from psychosis. Her mind had been all over the place."

She looked sincere, but it still stank of hypocrisy. Julia was her daughter, and I'd have expected her to be in pieces. She was brushing it aside like the death of a celebrity who we only knew from the gossip columns.

"When did you last see her?"

The sound of footsteps above allowed Melissa to duck the question.

"That's your wife and child. They must have woken up. Hang on. I'll make her a cup of tea too and you can take it up. Have a pleasant chat together. Talk things over."

I'm convinced Melissa genuinely believed everything would be okay and we would soon get back together. Her face said it all. A mixture of hope and faith that sense would prevail.

Carrying a tray of tea and biscuits, I found Amelia propped up in bed. The baby lay sleeping in his basket next to her.

"You're looking well," I said, placing the tray on her lap. I kissed her cheek. The whole charade made me nauseous.

"Feel much better, thank you. How about you? Been up to anything interesting since I last saw you?"

What does she know?

"No. I worked yesterday," I lied, "and that's about it."

Leaning over the basket, I kissed the baby on his forehead. He looked so peaceful, so perfect. I so wished my mum could have seen him.

Keep it together.

"So," I continued, sitting on the edge of the bed. "Are you breastfeeding?"

As had been the intention, my question caught Amelia off guard. She placed her cup onto the tray, and with her hand trembling slightly, she spilt some contents over the side. Nervously, she wrapped her dressing gown around her front.

"What kind of question is that?" she asked, blushing.

"Perfectly normal question. I'm the father and I want to know if you're breastfeeding my child?"

"*Our* child. And if you must know, no, I'm not. I tried the first couple of days, but I couldn't get the hang of it. Tracy said it's quite normal, so I use a breast pump. The milk is in the fridge if you want to check?"

That familiar feeling that something wasn't right.

Why so defensive? Aggressive even? I hadn't finished my interrogation.

"Instead of checking your fridge for milk, can I see the nursery?"

I'm sure I heard footsteps outside the door. No doubt Melissa listening in. It wasn't going to plan.

"It's not ready yet."

"Not ready? You asked for the money in March. It's almost September."

"I've been otherwise engaged, Matthew, if you hadn't noticed. I tried a couple of tradespeople, but they are so busy."

"What if I organise it?"

The door opened and Melissa almost fell in after herself.

"Hi. Can I get you two more tea?"

With a pathetic attempt to conceal it, she shot her daughter a concerned look. Amelia offered the slightest shake of her head in return. A 'please don't interfere' look.

"No, we're good thanks, Mother."

"Well, if you're sure."

Melissa begrudgingly left. Following the lightest click of the door, I listened for footsteps descending the stairs. But I heard nothing. I couldn't help but smile.

"What's funny?"

Before I could reply, the baby stirred in his basket. The question I really wanted to ask became stuck in my throat. I knew it would be a terrible mistake to ask her outright. Besides, her mother was ready to pounce and Tracy would be home from work soon. Goodness knows who else might be around. I'd forgotten Andy could be in the house and I didn't want to take the chance of being held hostage again. My past experience still scared me to death.

I changed tack.

"We need a name," I said, smiling towards the adorable little creature now settled in his basket. A mixture of melancholy and guilt washed over me as I realised what kind of environment he was already being subjected to. How could I get him away from this?

Stay in control.

"It's not as though we can keep calling him 'baby' or 'child'. Have you had any further thoughts?"

The neutral territory temporarily appeased Amelia, and a smile returned to her face.

"Oh, I agree, Matt. We really must sort it out, and I've had a brilliant idea."

Oh shit.

Sipping my now cool tea, I dreaded what might come next. Please don't suggest Graham.

"Matthew."

I almost spat the drink from my mouth.

"Matthew? What, as in me, Matthew?"

Amelia laughed out loud.

A footstep outside, the sound of her daughter's happiness no doubt lifting Melissa's mood.

"Yes, you idiot. As in you, Matthew. It will be a lovely gesture and keep your name going for another generation."

She was attempting to cajole me. I imagined the three of them sitting around and coming up with the idea, no doubt believing it as genius. Another pull at my heartstrings.

"I was thinking, Frank. After my dad."

Another footstep on the landing. I smiled, imagining Melissa's face. It had certainly shocked Amelia. I hadn't even thought about naming him after anybody until that moment, but I enjoyed my little game, nonetheless.

"Hmm, yes. That's a marvellous idea, although, well, I kind of don't like that name. Sorry."

We mused over other possibilities, but I was only passing time. I'd gone around to do what I had to do, and now I needed to leave. Amelia had been disappointed and made me promise to call around again the following day. She said she hoped to be up and about and maybe we could take the baby outdoors in his pram. She spoke like Melissa had earlier in the kitchen, as if everything was normal. How could they keep up such pretence?

As I left, I glanced over to the woods. The memory of Katrina standing there on the very first day I'd visited the Reid household. The long white dress, flowing gently in the breeze. Her wild hair sticking up at all angles.

The sound of footsteps approaching from somewhere afar. Instinctively, I knew it was from around the corner, along the road. Then Tracy came into view, lost in her own world, staring at the ground beneath her. She was the last person I wanted to talk to.

Once satisfied neither Melissa nor Amelia were watching, I doubled back and ran up the gentle hill towards Katrina's swing. It stood motionless in the thick, still air. Continuing around the rear of the house, I found myself at the hut. The place where Graham used to chop wood and store it for winter.

Waiting until Tracy was safely indoors, I unexpectedly became drawn towards the trees. A reminder of the last time I'd been in there with Julia and the make-believe unmarked grave for Patrick.

Without further thought, the psychological pull of the woods overwhelmed me.

A calling.

44

THE SHADE of the trees offered instant satisfaction compared to the rising humidity outside. A rumble of thunder sounded somewhere in the distance. The sky appeared to be darkening, exaggerated by the dense foliage, which only allowed thin slivers of light to break through. The overgrown brambles underfoot confirmed I needed to find the major footpath.

What are you even doing in here?

Stepping deeper into the woods, I had to lift my feet high to avoid lacerating my legs. I'd trodden this way before, and thought I only had to keep in a straight line before reaching the primary thoroughfare. But it felt as though it was taking longer than it should have. I couldn't recognise any landmark, any kind of clue I was heading in the right direction. Despite the relative coolness of the shade, sweat soon built and my T-shirt once again clung to my skin. Should I turn back?

Keep going. There's something here.

Eventually, the footpath came into view. As far as I knew, only Katrina used it regularly. I'd heard Tracy instruct her to stick to the path on many an occasion. Apart from when she placed fresh flowers on the makeshift grave of her father, I doubted she ever strayed far from it.

What about Patrick's make-believe grave?

Julia had said there was nobody underneath, just a focal point for Katrina to 'visit' her grandfather. If Patrick was who he said he was, and I had no reason to doubt him, then Julia had been right.

Turning left, I tried to recollect my previous time there with Julia. We had veered off soon after, to the right. The faintest of tracks existed, lightly flattened against the wild brambles and protruding roots. Walking slower than necessary – maybe I didn't want to reach my target? – my eyes remained peeled to the ground below. It was eerily quiet, much quieter than any other occasion I could recall. Whenever I allowed myself an opportunity to look up, the tops of the trees appeared perfectly lifeless. There wasn't a breath of wind and I couldn't hear a single bird chirping or any other sign of wildlife. There had always been a squirrel scavenging or a rabbit hopping around in search of food. It felt as though I were completely alone, as if the woods belonged to me.

After taking a step or two past the trail, I belatedly spotted it meandering down to my right. It didn't appear any further overgrown since we'd last walked it. Maybe Katrina did still go that way?

Unsure why, given my apparent solitude, I glanced around before taking the track. The creepy sensation threatened to overwhelm me. I had to move on.

Before I knew it, I arrived at the semi-clearing and the mound of earth impersonating a grave. Even though I'd been reassured that no actual body lay beneath, it still felt incredibly disquieting.

However, any previous doubts about whether some-body had trodden the path recently were soon nullified. Katrina had. Fresh flowers lay on the top of the soil, alongside her trademark cross of twigs crudely tied together with green wool. Not traditional flowers from a florist, but a combination of dandelions and buttercups, no doubt picked from the garden next to her swing.

Slowly, I circled the grave. Unsure what I was looking for, I nonetheless couldn't take my eyes from it. It looked so neat, so carefully preserved. No weeds sprang from the soil, and the mound was perfectly spherical. Could Katrina maintain it so well by herself? She had preserved the *real* one containing her father just as skilfully, so I figured there was no reason why not. It just seemed so over the top to go to such lengths. But Katrina wasn't like anybody else I'd met before.

Just like the rest of the family.

Exasperated, I became aware there was no real reason for me to stay.

Is this the real reason you're here?

Doubling back, I soon realised I'd somehow left the poorly marked footpath. With panic setting in, I quick-ened my step. Whichever way I turned, nothing looked familiar.

You're lost.

And then, before me, a clearing. And in the centre of the clearing stood the abandoned shack.

Instantly, my heartbeat increased. The sensation of being alone deserted me. I spun around, searching for any sign of life. But everything remained perfectly quiet. Maybe *too* quiet. The clouds above had gathered further still, and another rumble of thunder echoed through the trees.

What the hell are you doing?

As I gingerly approached the old cabin, my focus was drawn to something above the door. What *is* that?

My pace reduced to nothing more than a crawl, my eyes not leaving the small white object attached to the wall. A camera. It gleamed against the mildewed wood. It looked new. How had I not noticed it before? But Julia and I had moved on quickly. The shack hadn't been the reason she'd brought me into the woods.

Surely the camera didn't work? Wouldn't it need electricity?

'It's got electricity. Illegal I think. Father connected it. No, somebody else did...'

Julia had told me.

Fuck.

Something else made me think of security cameras. Where had I heard them mentioned recently? Yes! My conversation with Katie at the estate agents. She'd been slagging off Andy.

'I asked him how long he's been an estate agent and he said not long. Professed to be more of a security expert. Fitting cameras or something.'

The camera appeared relatively new. Could he have fitted it? But why erect such a device on a dilapidated cabin? To keep their eye on Katrina? That would make sense, given the distance from the main footpath.

Creeping up on the shack, I remained tucked behind the camera. Once up close, memories of the shed in Julia's garden came flooding back. The thought of her body hanging inside sent shivers down my spine.

Clambering around the cabin, I reached a window on the opposite side of the door, farthest from the camera. Attempting to peer inside, I soon realised it was hopeless. The glass was covered in a combination of mildew and a mass of spiders webs, inside and out.

Even with my eyes shielded and my face pressed up tight, it proved futile. Some other cover hung on the interior. It didn't look like ordinary curtains, more like an old sheet.

I jumped back.

Shit.

Was that a noise inside?

It sounded like a scraping sound, a scratching against wood.

It's just an animal.

But what kind of animal could be in there? And how the hell had it got in and survived without food?

As I took a few steps backwards, I could hear my heart thud in my chest. Then, standing perfectly still, I listened. Everything remained deathly silent. I prayed for a breath of wind just to rustle the tops of the trees. A bird to sing or even a clap of thunder. Anything to make it feel normal, natural. The humidity had crept up another notch, and I found it difficult to breathe. Taking in gulps of air, I tried to return my heartbeat to something resembling ordinary.

Continuing to explore the cabin, I discovered there were no windows at all at the back. Just panel after panel of green, rotting wood. The sunlight must never reach that side. It looked damp enough to push my finger straight through.

Finally, I found myself back where I started, directly underneath the camera. It pointed away from me. I noticed a faint track leading to the door. It resembled the footpath in the woods which had led me to the grave. Not especially well marked out, but still smoother than elsewhere.

Once trodden in and covered in pine needles, I guessed it might suppress any growth. However, it still didn't mean somebody was visiting the cabin regularly. That's what I told myself, anyway.

The door itself was no different to the rest of the shack. Worn, wet, wood.

Peering up at the camera, I realised I could reach the door handle without coming into view of the lens.

What makes you think it's in use?

My hand trembled as I stretched forward. My fingers gripped the rusty iron doorknob. It felt especially cold, no doubt enhanced against my hot and sweaty grip.

Slowly, it turned. The handle easily rotated towards me before the mechanism inside clicked to its ultimate stopping point.

Shit.

My whole body shook as I deliberated pushing or letting go.

You've come this far.

Opting to push, the door immediately resisted. I pushed again, rattling the door against its frame. But it was no use. It was obviously locked. Bending down, I peered through the keyhole, again to no avail.

Inside was pitch black, the makeshift window covers not letting any of the already weak light enter.

As I stood upright, something on the ground caught my eye. It stood out against the relentless greens and browns of the forest floor. Although tiny, it sparkled whenever a sliver of light caught it. Carefully, I retrieved it between my fingertips and dropped it into the palm of my spare hand.

There was no mistake. It was a tiny earring. And I knew exactly who it belonged to.

45

WHAT ON EARTH would one of Lisa's earrings be doing in the woods? Especially outside an old shack?

Ignoring the camera above, I rattled the door by its handle with much more force than before. But the old shack was stronger than it appeared. The door wouldn't budge. It felt more akin to steel than rotting wood.

"Lisa," I called, my mouth pushed up to the tiny gap at the edge. I kept my voice low, conscious of where I was, and alone. Twisting my head sideways, I listened for any sound within.

"Lisa," I repeated, a little louder.

A scratch from inside.

Fuck.

"Lisa. Is that you?"

More scratching, followed by an indistinct murmur.

Frantically, I ran to the far side of the cabin. The window was larger than the one adjacent to the door, with the added bonus of being farthest away from the camera. Although just as filthy as all the other glass panels, this one contained a tiny crack, running the entire length from top to bottom. Attempting to see inside, another piece of material thwarted me as it crudely hung from above. I figured the broken pane would be my only way in.

Tapping the glass, it rattled loosely against the frame. Not relishing the prospect of putting my bare fist through, I searched the ground for something to smash it with. I found a tree branch, the largest one I could see lying around. It felt rotten and didn't carry as much weight as I'd first hoped, but the glass hadn't exactly felt secure either. One or the other would have to give.

Returning to the window, I knocked the branch against the glass. Everything rattled. Good. But as I lifted my arm back to repeat the action, I heard another murmur.

"Lisa. Are you in there? It's Matt."

Some kind of stifled squeal from inside.

"Stand away from this window if you can. I'm going to smash it."

"Hmm."

Pulling the damp wood over my shoulder, I plunged it forward to the centre of the pane. Simultaneously, I lost grip, and the branch flew straight through. The glass shattered, leaving an almost perfectly circular hole behind.

Struggling to contain my panic, I found a smaller branch and randomly pushed and scraped the remaining glass from the frame. Soon, I'd removed enough to get my arm inside and reach for the latch. It was stiff, but I put my weight behind it. It gave way with a screech, brass against brass, and I pulled the frame open. The gap was just large enough to climb through. Reaching inside again, I grabbed the hanging sheet and tugged it downwards. It had been nailed or tacked to the inside but easily fell free, allowing what little light there was to pour indoors.

Shit. What's that?

On the far side of the room lay a child's doll. Naked and covered in cobwebs, its neck twisted at an awkward angle so its eyes bore directly into mine. I suppressed the urge to scream and run.

With no time to deliberate, I clambered in. Catching my foot against the hanging latch, I crashed to the floor. The pain hit me instantaneously. Shards of glass stuck into my knees and the palms of my hand.

"Bollocks!" I shouted, turning my wrists to inspect the damage. Blood ran freely, and I picked out the two largest chunks from my right hand.

The murmur from elsewhere made me momentarily forget my distress. Standing upright, I could soon decipher the inner layout. The cabin was wider than I'd imagined from the outside. It had some sort of dividing wooden wall along the centre, creating separate rooms. The door was shut.

Please don't be locked.

It opened into a larger room. The door to the outside world lay on the far side, the one with the camera above. Then the acrid smell hit me. On my left stood a makeshift toilet, the stench making me retch.

To my right was a mattress resting precariously on top of a warped and broken bed frame. A brass headboard somehow remained intact at the far end. And that's when I saw her.

Propped upright in the corner sat Lisa, her eyes gaping as wide as I'd ever seen anybody's eyes stretch before. And in her mouth, a piece of white cloth pulled tight behind her head. Her cheeks were filthy with dirt and tears, fresh ones running from the corner of each eye.

As I approached her, she murmured, louder than before. As fast but as gently as I could, I untied the material and pulled it free from her mouth. The blood from my hands quickly spread across the cloth like blotting paper.

Lisa began breathing insanely rapidly. Huge gulps of air inwards followed by spittle and strands of phlegm on each outward breath. She looked like she might vomit at any moment, and I involuntarily took a step back.

"Are you hurt?" I asked.

She shook her head.

Grabbing my phone, I swiped up and begged for a signal. But I already knew the answer. I'd been in this part of the woods before.

Realising she hadn't moved her hands, I leant towards her, our faces inches apart, and undid the same white cloth which had gagged her mouth. Once free, she immediately wiped her face with the backs of her hands. Her eyes remained wide open. I couldn't recall seeing her blink. She nodded to something behind me. Following her lead, I turned and saw exactly what she meant. An identical small camera to the one outside. It pointed directly at us. And, as if on cue, it made a low whirring sound, its minuscule lens moving slowly forwards and backwards inside. Focusing. On us.

Shit.

"Is it them?" I asked Lisa, needing clarification.

"Water," she replied, via an incredibly dry-sounding mouth and throat.

"I don't have any. I've—"

"There." She lifted her right arm and pointed to the far side of the room. Next to the disgusting portable loo were fresh bottles of water, still wrapped in cellophane packaging. Jumping from the bed, I ripped the plastic apart and brought two bottles back to Lisa. As I undid the first, she literally snatched it from my hands. I watched as she devoured the liquid. Most of the contents ran down her chin. Again, I thought she might be sick.

As she drank, I felt a pain hit me from both hands. I could see I was bleeding badly from one or two of the deeper cuts. Opening the second bottle of water, I poured the contents from one palm to the other. The blood ran freely onto the filthy floor below; a tiny stream of red and brown trickled towards the far wall.

Once she finished, she held out her hand for what remained of the second bottle. After draining that one too, she wiped her mouth and looked me in the eye. Lisa was the epitome of fear. She ignored my original question of who might be responsible. What she asked instead took me by complete surprise.

"How's the baby?"

She clung to my arm, her nails digging in.

"What? Why the hell are you asking that?"

Lisa shook, violently. Pulling her forward, I gripped her tight. She felt so thin, and I could trace her shoulder blades as I attempted to quell her shivering.

"How is he?" she asked again, finding an inner strength and pushing me back by the shoulders. She scared the hell out of me.

"He's fine. Good. No, great. Why, Lisa? Why are you so—?"

"Because he's my fucking baby!"

46

Horrified, I stood, involuntarily taking a step back. I'd become oblivious to the camera on the wall. I could only glare at Lisa. Still, she shook, her upper body rocking back and forth. My eyes rested on her stomach, searching for any kind of clue to what she had just screamed.

"Your baby? No, no, it's not your baby, it can't be, it's..."

Lisa moved, slowly sliding herself forward along the bed. The sheet behind was stained yellow. It was my turn to swallow bile and do my utmost not to throw up.

"Matt. You must listen to me."

Her voice resembled how I'd remembered it. The more she spoke, the more her vocal cords stretched and strained into place. At the same time, I lost my own ability to speak.

"Amelia wasn't pregnant. Amelia can't have children. Didn't she ever tell you?"

Maybe.

Still she shook and stifled sobs. But she appeared determined to talk as fast as she could, spill all the information which had been stored inside for months. She glanced at the camera as she spoke. Time was against us.

All I could do was shake my head.

"That night in Cheshire. The night Graham came to the conference."

My brain tried to absorb what it was hearing. Gradually, word by word, I began to comprehend what she was saying. We'd slept together. But hadn't I bought condoms from the bathroom vending machine? It was all such a blur. That night in the hotel we had drunk so much, and afterwards, we had spent the night together. We awoke in the same bed. And then we did exactly the same the following evening. Shit! The second night, I had no precautions.

Lisa kept talking, unmindful of whether it was sinking in. She told me she'd missed her period at the end of January. I'd been staying at her house. And two weeks later, she took a pregnancy test. I recalled her attitude changing around the same time. Towards life, towards me.

"Is that why you wanted me to leave?"

She shook her head.

"I didn't know what to do. I was pregnant and I was sick. I tried to keep out of your way. But then, out of the blue, the day after I took the test, Amelia and Tracy came to see me. They waited until you had gone out. No doubt on one of your trips to the pub."

Even in the most harrowing of circumstances, I felt a glimmer of hope that Lisa could still find a sarcastic dig towards me. The glimmer didn't last long.

"What the hell did they want with *you?*"

But I already knew.

'Oh. You've shacked up with that slapper, Lisa, haven't you?'

"They told me to make you leave. Told me I was

315

destroying their family. And they threatened me if I didn't comply."

"What kind of threat?"

"You know what kind of threat, Matt?"

Struggling to take it all in, I paced the small room. The camera whirred on the wall. Running back through to the other side, I picked up the discarded piece of wood, returned and smashed the camera as hard as I could.

The camera fared better and soon I only held a small, fractured stick in my hand. The camera bent sideways at an awkward angle. Maybe it still worked, but at least it wasn't pointing directly at us. Eventually, I turned back to Lisa. She was sitting on the edge of the bed, weeping. I ran over, sat next to her and cradled her.

"So, why didn't you tell me you were pregnant? Tell me they had visited you? It doesn't make sense."

Lisa looked up and spoke through stifled sobs.

"I never had the chance. Before they left, Tracy found the pregnancy test."

With so many unanswered questions, I began to randomly reel them off anyway. Lisa interrupted me mid-flow.

"Not now, Matt. We have to get out of here. He'll be on his way."

"He?"

Without waiting for a reply, I knew exactly who she meant. Instead, I helped her to her feet and asked if she was okay to walk. She nodded, although we both appreciated we would have to do more than walk if Andy was on his way.

With the only door in the shack firmly locked, we had to clamber through the broken window. Whilst clearing the glass away with my feet, I couldn't help but notice the doll still staring at me. If I didn't know better, I could have sworn someone had placed it there purposefully. Lisa's impatience got the better of her and she pushed me out of the way. With remarkable agility, she soon found herself outside beckoning me to hurry. A few moments later, we were in the woods.

"This way," I said, grabbing her hand, immediately regretting it as the pain reverberated through the shards of glass. Doing my utmost to ignore it, I tried to recall the way Julia had led me to the cabin. With no obvious footpath, I thought if we kept to a route our pursuers didn't know, at least we might stay one step ahead.

After a few minutes, we were deep in the undergrowth. The narrow track gave me some hope that we were on the right course. Lisa suddenly stopped behind me.

"What is it?" I whispered impatiently.

"The baby. I need my baby."

Pulling her down until we were crouched behind the brambles, I held her tight, still finding it difficult to take in Lisa's version of events, even though she'd only confirmed what I already suspected, already knew.

'I can never have children, Matt.'

Amelia had never 'looked' pregnant, never carried it off as I'd seen other expectant mothers do. I recalled the ridiculous outfits. Baggy jumpers in stifling heat and the unnatural way she held her *bump*. Other mums *rested* their hands on their stomachs, but Amelia always grasped it from underneath. Thinking about it, it was almost as if she were scared of something dropping out.

She'd refused to let me feel the baby kick. The lack of any regular visits to a doctor or maternity classes. She had definitely said she'd visited the hospital in Epsom, but I hadn't been able to find any record of it. Doctor Pearce's face when I'd suggested my wife was expecting and the consequential tapping of his keyboard, no doubt checking if it could be true.

But you knew before then. You always knew.

Tracy had seen to it all. The perfect excuse. How could I question a qualified midwife looking after the mother of my child?

The very reason you've hung around.

But Tracy *had* looked after the mother of my child. Lisa. It had all fallen into place the day they had visited her, told her I had to leave and threatened her. Because after the threats, Tracy found her pregnancy test.

Lisa is expecting! The perfect opportunity.

All the family had to do was pretend it was Amelia's child. They were already halfway there because I was the genuine father. Shit. I could even ask for a DNA test and it would come up positive. And then wait until the baby is born and pray that it's enough for me to return. They could work on me and manipulate the situation. Would I cave? Maybe I would. Deep down, I still had feelings for Amelia. She'd suggested we start again in the small cottage, or somewhere similar, as long as it was near the family home. Melissa's expectant face only hours ago.

'Hang on. I'll make her a cup of tea too and you can take it up. Have a pleasant chat together. Talk things over.'

Shit.

Only Tracy had held any doubts. She didn't trust me. They didn't trust Julia either. Knew she was somehow involved. Somebody had followed her to Russell Square and had been outside her house. Scared the poor woman to death, almost literally.

And then there was Francis. She'd told me the truth. Graham's brother, Andy was staying close by. Whilst Francis kept her eye on me, he kept his eye on her. But then I remembered something. The one thing stopping me from putting the last piece of the jigsaw into place.

"We'll get the baby, Lisa. Don't worry. We'll get the baby."

We remained crouched low, Lisa cradled in my arms. She whimpered, her body hiccupping every few seconds.

"You know the estate agents?" I asked.

She nodded, not moving from the sanctuary of my embrace.

"It was you who suggested them. You gave me Andy Coleman's business card. And the day I came back to your house, I saw him on your doorstep. You had just shown him around."

Lisa lifted her head and slowly shook it from side to side.

"No. That wasn't me. As I said, Tracy had found the pregnancy test. But I didn't know she had it. She didn't say so. Then, two weeks later, they came around again. Amelia and I talked, mostly about you, whilst Tracy made us tea. And that's when she drugged me. The next thing I knew, I was in their house. Tied to a bed. They confessed to finding the test."

"So why didn't you leave? You know, in between the first time they came around and then two weeks later?"

Lisa held a gaze as if she found it all too painful to recollect, but she knew I had to know.

"I had made plans. If you remember, I went out several times."

Lisa was changing, her moods deepening, and even her appearance had spiralled downwards. The only time she made an effort was on the odd occasion that she left the house.

"I was looking at properties, but I couldn't afford anything. I hoped Tracy and Amelia had been bluffing, but at the time, I didn't know they had the pregnancy test.

It wasn't until I woke up in their house that Tracy showed me. I presumed I'd put it in the bin."

"So, if they took you away, how did they get your property on the market? I saw the agent leave your house. Andy. You shook his hand."

"Not me. I must admit that one time when I arrived back home, it felt as though somebody had been in. But I don't know. They didn't tell me anything. After they abducted me, they kept me in their house until the baby was born."

I recalled the note left by Lisa.

I'm putting the house on the market. I need to move on.

But it hadn't been the content of the message that had intrigued me. To begin with, they had written it in eyeliner, or some equivalent make-up. Why wouldn't she use a pen? Because she didn't write it, and they had done it in a hurry. And I'd read it until I could recite it word for word, but I still kept reading. It hadn't been the words written down, it had been the handwriting that held my attention. Not Lisa's. Maybe Tracy's, but certainly not Lisa's. I'd seen hers at work many times before. Fuck. Why hadn't I realised?

"But the estate agent told me you've sold, and you signed all the paperwork."

"It wasn't me, Matt. Why don't you believe me?"

'No need. We did it all via email. She signed the documents that way. Think she's staying with her mum or something.'

It wasn't Lisa at all. It was Amelia or Tracy accessing Lisa's emails.

Shit.

"And when did they put you in that cabin?"

"A few times during the pregnancy."

The times I went to visit them. Amelia had never wanted me to go round. She had always suggested the café.

"Tracy would give me something to make me drowsy and the next thing I knew, I was in there. But she didn't keep me there for long. Not until three days ago, after the baby was born."

"You've been in there for three days?"

Lisa nodded.

I'd seen Katrina two days before. She was heading for the woods.

'I'm going to talk to somebody.'

"The only time she came was with a breast pump. I complied. It was the only way I could feel connected to my child."

Holy shit. They are pure evil. I didn't even want to contemplate what they would do with Lisa once she was no longer required.

"Listen. We need to keep moving. Once we find the footpath, I know the back way to the house. Hopefully, Andy, or whatever his real name is, will still be in the woods looking for us."

My suggestion momentarily lifted Lisa's spirits. She gradually stood, gaining renewed strength from some-where deep inside.

Mother's intuition.

After checking my phone for any kind of signal, we continued in what I hoped was the right direction. Every-thing looked identical. I just had to trust my instinct and pray we were heading to the top of the steep hill above the village.

Trying to recall how long it had taken me and Julia to make the same journey, I remembered how much quicker Julia had been.

Their natural habitat.

A clap of thunder overhead made us both jump. The storm was closing in.

Eventually, the overgrown vegetation gave way to a partial clearing. I immediately recognised it. Turning, I reached out my hand for Lisa to grab it. But she had stopped a few metres behind and her eyes bore straight through me. Staring somewhere into the distance, I turned to follow her gaze and I couldn't believe who she had spotted.

47

"Hello, Uncle Matthew."

Oh, please fuck, no.

"Katrina. What are you doing here?"

She giggled.

"I'm out walking, silly."

Lisa caught up with me. Her hand reached out for mine. Ignoring the pain as she gripped my bloody palm, I squeezed hers in return.

"On your own?" I asked.

Katrina wasn't acting any differently than at any other time. Perhaps she wasn't looking for us. Maybe it was purely circumstantial.

"Of course I'm on my own."

But her amiable demeanour didn't last. Katrina's friendly face dropped to a scowl, and she slowly lifted her arm and pointed at Lisa.

"What's *she* doing with you?"

You've got to keep her sweet.

"Lisa wants to see the baby, Katrina. But we want to

keep it a secret from everybody. Do you want to be part of our secret?"

Unbelievably, her face changed back into the happy-go-lucky persona from moments before.

"I like secrets. Mother doesn't let me have any."

I bet she fucking doesn't.

Lisa stepped forward. Slowly, trying not to frighten Katrina.

"I wonder if you could get the baby and bring him out of the house to us? We can wait near your swing."

Katrina appeared happy with the plan. I continued the ploy.

"And if you do, I'll get you the biggest bar of chocolate you've *ever* seen."

Katrina giggled and clapped her hands. Instantly, I put my finger to my lips.

"But shh, else the others might hear."

Slowly, we stepped out of the overgrown foliage and joined Katrina on the path. Still convinced it could be a plot to get us out into the open, I stared intently around. But I couldn't see a soul, and I couldn't hear a thing. Another clap of thunder overhead. Katrina froze to the spot and stared skywards.

Oh, no. Don't freak out. Not now.

"It's just God telling us to hurry, Katrina."

Lisa's quick thinking made Katrina smile. Her yellow teeth grinned in our direction. My heart hammered inside my chest. The whole situation felt so surreal.

"I know a shortcut," she said and ran off like an Olympic sprinter.

"Slow down, Katrina," I hissed. "You're much too fast for us old people."

I heard a giggle and thankfully, she slowed her pace.

Remarkably, we found ourselves behind the storage shed in no time.

She knows these woods like the back of her hand.

Katrina waited for us to catch up. She wasn't even out of breath.

"Can you see who is inside the house, Katrina?"

Without waiting for any further instructions, she fled. I thought I'd messed up the entire plan. But within moments, she was back.

"Aunty Amelia and Grandmother. They said Mother and uncle Andrew are in the woods."

Uncle Andrew.

"But I didn't see them when I was in there. Aunty Amelia and Grandmother are in Mother's bedroom."

She giggled.

"What's so funny?"

"They're packing a bag. Filling it with milk bottles and nappies."

I'd never heard Katrina divulge so much information in one go. I glanced towards Lisa. We both knew exactly what they were planning.

"And where is the baby?" Lisa's impatience threatened to overwhelm her. I shot her a look. It didn't please her.

"The baby is upstairs, asleep, silly. In his basket."

Lisa whimpered behind me. Katrina gawked at her.

"Listen, Katrina," I said, desperately trying to keep up her level of concentration. "If you talk to Aunty Amelia and Grandmother, I'll get the baby. You must keep them in the bedroom. Then, in exactly five minutes," I held up five fingers, "you come back outside to be with us. Then I'll get you the chocolate."

Katrina giggled once more and ran inside.

Taking out my phone, I sent DCI Small a message. At the same time, I told Lisa my plan.

. . .

"I'm coming with you."

Lisa's response hadn't been part of my proposal. I had no intention of putting her through anything else. If I could get the baby to her, I would face the family alone. The prospect of what may happen didn't bear thinking about, but I had to rescue the child, not only for Lisa's sake but for his welfare too.

"No. It's too dangerous," I replied, but Lisa had already begun to stride towards the house. In a vain attempt, I reached out to grab her, but she was too quick and dodged my advance. Angry, but not surprised, I ran after her.

Pausing outside the back door, we could hear voices from inside. Our only hope was Katrina had been correct, and they were gathered in Tracy's bedroom. Tiptoeing across the room, I paused once I arrived at the far end of the kitchen. Sure enough, the voices drifted from upstairs. I turned to Lisa, thinking she had waited at the back door, but she stood behind me, shadowing my every footstep.

"Stay here," I whispered, through gritted teeth, irritated. "And run like hell if Andy or Tracy come back."

Reluctantly, she agreed. Lisa couldn't be sure what room the baby would be in and time was too precious for her to go searching.

Taking the stairs two steps at a time, the voices from Tracy's bedroom became more distinct. Melissa instructed Katrina to go to her room. "Pack your bag, but only with a few clothes," she said. "It can't be too heavy." The prospect of a new adventure could so easily have distracted Katrina from the original plan. Unbelievably, she replied 'no'. Melissa raised her voice, repeating her order.

As I crouched behind the landing wall, Melissa left Tracy's bedroom, dragging Katrina by her hair. Katrina screamed. Such a high-pitched squeal. Although not going to plan, I realised the distraction could be my best chance. Melissa upsetting Katrina had played right into my hands.

As soon as they disappeared along the corridor, I dashed into Amelia's bedroom and found what I needed in the bedside drawer. She never moved them from there. Next, I grabbed the wicker basket by its handles. The baby was fast asleep, oblivious to the screaming which reverberated around the house.

Please don't stir.

Again, taking the stairs two at a time, I passed the basket to Lisa where she frantically paced from foot to foot in the kitchen doorway. Stifling a sob, she held her hand to her mouth when she saw her child.

"Just go," I whispered as loud as I dared.

And she did. Lisa turned and fled the same way we had entered.

A deafening clap of thunder echoed up the stairwell and along the landing, quickly followed by the first splatters of rain against the window. A streak of lightning illuminated the now dark interior. Katrina screamed.

With an overwhelming sensation to run as fast as I could, I knew I had to face the family.

Reluctantly, I walked into the living room and sat in the chair in the corner. Graham's favourite chair.

48

Melissa saw me first. I thought she might pass out. Placing her hand on the doorframe for support, her mouth opened and closed, but no words would escape. Then, as expected, came another scream from above. This time, it wasn't Katrina.

Melissa took one look at me before turning and ascending the stairs as fast as her legs would carry her. I waited patiently for my wife and her mother to return. As soon as they appeared in the doorway, Amelia yelled. Her voice was deep and gravelly.

"Where. Is. He?"

She propelled herself forward, her hands in a strangulation pose as she flew for my neck. But I was too quick. Ducking underneath, and in one swift movement, I stood, turned, and pinned her to the chair.

"He's safe, Amelia. Believe me, he's safe. We just need to talk."

Talk until the police turn up, that is.

"You bastard!"

Out of the corner of my eye, I saw Melissa running

towards me. Her eyes were red and full of hatred. But she hadn't seen who had followed her.

Screaming in a high-pitched wail, Katrina retrieved a fire poker from a brass stand and raised it above her head.

The thunder clapped so loudly it shook the house. The rain hammered down, and only the lightning offered a brief respite from the desperately darkening skies. It felt like nightfall.

As Melissa reached me, Katrina brought down the poker with such force it spun from her hands. But not until she had made contact with Melissa's skull.

The sound was sickening, and Melissa fell, slow motion-like. First, onto her knees, before collapsing forwards with a smack of her face on the floorboards. Behind her, Katrina smiled broadly. As if on cue, lightning again illuminated the room, exaggerating her yellow teeth and the blood seeping from her cracked lips.

Beneath me, Amelia fought to wriggle free, screaming at the combination of her stricken mother and the prospect of losing *her* child.

Attempting to make myself heard above the din of the rain, I shouted at Katrina.

"Give me the poker and run to the end of the garden." Still, she smiled. "Wait for the policemen. I've asked them to put on their blue flashing lights. Just for you."

She squealed with delight. Amelia tried to speak, but I clasped my hand over her mouth. We watched as Katrina fled.

The next sound we heard, I'd been expecting. The back door crashed open. Amelia flinched. Seconds later, in stomped Andy, Tracy bumping into him when he stopped still. Her attention immediately fell onto the prostrate figure of her mother. Blood trickled from Melissa's head wound.

"Mother," she screamed, leaping to her side and kneeling down to feel her neck. But Tracy didn't scare me. It was the sight of Andy bearing down that put the fear of God into me.

How long will they be?

"Katrina did that. Not me," I yelled, desperately trying to stall him. Amelia wriggled beneath me, her face pinned down to the chair. Andy and Tracy had their backs to the door.

As fast as I could, I let go of one of Amelia's arms and swiped at Andy with the poker. Remarkably, it connected with the side of his head. He dropped much faster than Melissa had.

Tracy appeared to panic, and she ran for the front door. Her footsteps soon fell silent, washed away by the storm. Watching through the window, she sprinted towards the end of the path, head bowed yet directly towards the flashing lights coming in the opposite direction. I knew I only had minutes left.

Still holding on tight to Amelia's arm, I turned to face her. She no longer put up a fight. The sight of the poker raised in my right arm and the sounds of sirens outside told her all she needed to know.

But it wasn't the fear in her face that struck me. It was the look of total despair and anguish. She fell limp, and I knew I could let go. Amelia had given up. The baby had meant everything to her.

She collapsed into the chair, her eyes welling up and never leaving mine. She attempted a smile, that same beautiful smile I'd fallen for the day we first met. Our very first road trip together flashed through my mind, the conference in Harrogate. When we first slept together and realised how much we meant to each other. The same road trip where we'd confessed many things. I'd explained about my parents dying, and of my continual search for happiness ever since. In return, Amelia had admitted she could never have children.

'I have irregular periods and a failure to ovulate as a result. I've been told it would be a miracle if I ever had children, Matt.'

That's why her *pregnancy* had always intrigued me. The day she'd told me at the café she *might* be having a baby.

And then suggesting we give our relationship a whole new start.

'You never know, once we've had one, we'll probably want to adopt a baby sister or brother.'

'Adopt'. Why 'adopt' another child if you've just conceived naturally?

But I'd wondered if she could have been wrong about never having a child. Had the doctors been mistaken? Could miracles actually happen? I'd become so mesmerised by the whole charade that a part of me had actually believed it. I'd asked the family doctor and visited the local maternity hospital. Secretly, I hoped it could be true, maybe even as much as Amelia had. After all, what kind of idiot would hang around *that* family after what they'd put me through? I could have run at any point, fled and started afresh. But no, deep down, I'd desperately wanted it to be true too.

You've never stopped loving Amelia, have you, Matt?

Wiping away the tear that fell from Amelia's eye, I dropped the poker and took her in my arms. We hugged with what inner strength we had left. She sobbed and clung to me. It felt like sheer desperation.

The sirens and flashing lights were now at the end of the driveway with a commotion of noise and raised voices. Through the rain-drenched window, I could just make out the figures of Katrina and Tracy. Police were with them, whilst three more walked towards the house, their heads bowed against the downpour.

Holding out the passport and mobile phone I'd taken from her bedside table, I pleaded for my wife to listen.

"Take these, Amelia, and run."

She looked at me incredulously.

"Now! Go! Out the back. Get away. But never come back. Promise me you'll never come back."

Amelia glanced out of the front window and then back at me.

"I love you, Matthew," she mouthed. "I promise with all my heart."

She turned to go before hesitating at the door.

"And, Matt? Please look after our baby."

49

FOUR MONTHS LATER

Lisa passed me the decorations as I hung them individually onto the Christmas tree. All but one, that is. Instead, Lisa had suspended a particularly shiny red bauble on a mobile above George's cot. He would stare at it for what felt like an eternity as it spun and caught the light, making it ever more sparkly than before.

We'd purposefully planned a quiet Christmas, just the three of us. Not that we could have travelled far anyway, given that the Scottish weather had dumped a fresh load of white, pristine snow upon us. Besides, who would we visit? Who could we invite?

I'd already been outside that morning, and almost froze my fingers solid to build George a snowman. Lisa held him at the window so he could admire from the comfort of indoors. But he hadn't been all that impressed. He just gurgled as Lisa lifted him higher and soon his attention turned to what might lie around on his play mat instead.

Lisa had found it hysterical and even had the audacity to take the piss out of me. Apparently, I'd stuck the carrot on at such an angle it looked more like he had no nose but was smoking a pipe instead.

It hadn't gone unnoticed by me that she had insisted on showing George the snowman from inside. She still hadn't built the confidence to venture out far, even though we were temporarily renting a place in the middle of nowhere.

Lisa's house sale was going through, due for completion in early January. We had already agreed that Scotland wasn't a viable long-term option and we would travel back to southeast England in the new year. There was still four months' rent available at my apartment in Earl's Court, and despite my reluctance to move next door to Francis, it would be crazy not to use it as our base whilst searching for our next home.

Without telling Lisa the history behind it, I'd shown her the cute little cottage that Amelia and I had found all those months ago. It was still on the market and Lisa loved it, albeit from looking online. We had an appointment to view it on the tenth of January.

You have to tell her.

Thankfully, the family were no longer our concern.

Graham's trial had taken place only a week after I'd rescued baby George and returned him to his rightful mother. They had given him a twenty-five-year sentence for the manslaughter of both Ryan Palmer and Lee Blackmore, plus the murder of my aunty Edith Weeks. Graham admitted to all three.

Melissa and Tracy Reid, alongside Andrew Meadows, not Andy Coleman as he'd led me to believe, had been given various sentences of up to twelve years each for false imprisonment, or kidnapping. Melissa had suffered a serious head wound from Katrina's blow, but she made a full recovery after a few nights in hospital. Andy, on the other hand, had come round as soon as the police arrived. Dazed, he allegedly put up a fight but had been overpowered within seconds.

Thankfully, Katrina had been absolved of any crimes and she now lives with foster parents who have years of experience in taking on children with a similar condition. The authorities had informed me she would go to a special school to integrate her into society once and for all. Her new whereabouts had been kept a secret, but social care had promised to give me regular updates. I liked Katrina, and apparently she'd told her carers that I was her favourite uncle. Given the choice, I wasn't sure how much of a compliment it had been.

Lisa had rightly chosen our son's name. I tried Frank again, but she gave it about as much thought as Amelia had, although I obviously didn't tell her that. However, she did like the idea of maintaining a family name, even in a small way, and suggested George, after an uncle of hers. He had played a big part in helping her grow up. To be honest, after his start in life, she could have called my son anything.

As for Amelia, the police have never found her. I often speculated where she went on that night of the storm, and in which direction she had run. The police had since dismantled the shack and dug up the makeshift grave of grandad Patrick, thankfully, with no sign of bones underneath. Julia had been right. They had laid nobody to rest. Even Katrina said she had no recollection of any such thing, despite the fresh flowers and homemade cross. She'd said she had never visited that part of the woods before. The police and carers put it down to selective memory, but I remained unconvinced. With Julia gone, I wondered if I would ever know the whole truth.

My mind would often drift to Julia. How desperate she must have been. I would also consider if she had taken her life of her own free will, or had Tracy somehow manipulated her and driven her to suicide? If it hadn't been for the note she left me, I doubt I would have gone back to the woods the day I found Lisa. Something dragged me there. Although I don't believe in the afterlife, I still wonder if Julia had somehow guided me. She'd shown me the grave. Had she purposefully shown me the cabin, too? I'd deliberate whether she had overheard something whilst under Tracy's care at the house. But why not just tell me? One thing she had put in the message was how much Amelia cared for me. I think Julia always knew the feeling was reciprocal.

I had often asked myself if Katrina had some kind of sixth sense, but maybe they all did.

Why not just plain crazy?

DCI Small had quizzed me twice more about Amelia. He couldn't understand how I'd contained both Melissa and Andy, but not my ex-wife. I'd tried to convince him that Katrina had seen to Melissa whilst Andy took all my efforts. During our altercation, Amelia had somehow escaped. He knew he could never prove otherwise. Four months later, they'd still had no luck in finding her.

My ex-wife's whereabouts had particularly agitated Lisa, even though the DCI informed us he presumed she had fled the country. She may be halfway around the world, he'd suggested to appease Lisa.

Soon after, I had filed for a 'divorce petition', or 'dissolution application' via the authorities. I hadn't been told how long it would take, but again the authorities had assured me it would definitely go ahead, such were the exceptional circumstances.

There was also the case of the money in Amelia's bank account, almost half of my original inheritance from my aunt. Again, it wasn't straightforward, and I would need to go through all the proper procedures once I was ready.

Amelia had used her bank card once, the day after she had vanished. I knew she kept the card in her mobile phone case. It had been one reason I'd made sure she had those alongside her passport. She withdrew two thousand pounds over the counter in a branch in Epsom, fuelling my belief that she must have spent the night in the woods. The amount of money, and her *missing* passport, convinced DCI Small she had gone abroad. Each time he raised the subject of how she had found time to collect those vital items, I just shook my head in response. She must have been pre-prepared for what might happen, I'd suggested. Yes. I guess she must, he replied, without looking at all convinced.

It's why we had chosen Scotland, an extremely remote part of Scotland. Lisa had been prescribed an antidepressant to help with her ongoing anxiety. Apart from the police, nobody knew our whereabouts, and more crucially, nobody locally knew of our background, not that we had any neighbours within a mile of our house anyway. I talked to Lisa several times. Although I would initially reassure her, the demons always reappeared days or weeks later.

I'd promised to look for a job once we settled in the south. We needed money. Every day, a little more went out. And every month, the rent made another dent in the savings.

But the prospect of a future together would help Lisa cope. She needed something to believe in, and a stable environment to raise George.

After everything I'd put her through, it was the very least I could do.

She is, after all, the mother of my child.

Isn't she?

THE FAMILY TRILOGY

Part Three - Available Now

DON'T MISS THE DRAMATIC CONCLUSION!

Tell the truth or be the...

LAST ONE TO LIE

Available in both eBook and Print Versions

NEWSLETTER

Sign up to **Jack Stainton's** FREE **newsletter** to be the first to hear of new releases, promotions and giveaways…

www.jackstainton.com/newsletter/

REVIEWS

Enjoy this book? You can make a big difference

Honest reviews of my books help bring them to the attention of other readers.

If you've enjoyed this novel I would be very grateful if you could spend just a few minutes leaving a review (it can be as short as you like).

Thank you very much.

ABOUT THE AUTHOR

Jack Stainton is an author of psychological thrillers.

His first book, 'A Guest to Die For', received critical acclaim, whilst the first in this trilogy, 'You're Family Now', hit the top of three best seller categories for several months in succession.

Jack lives in Devon, England, and he's finally living a lifetime ambition of writing in his favourite genre.

This is Jack's third novel.

———

Sign up to Jack's newsletter at the link below…

www.jackstainton.com/newsletter

———

facebook.com/jackstaintonbooks

twitter.com/jack_stainton

instagram.com/jackstaintonbooks

A GUEST TO DIE FOR

Jack Stainton's debut Psychological Thriller

Available online in both eBook and Print Versions

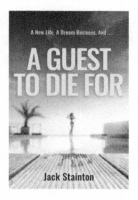

…I bought the book and read it in two sittings. Very good, lots of twists and red herrings.

This does exactly what a thriller should; it keeps you guessing until the end…

Excellent book full of twists and turns. The characters are brilliant… The ending was totally unexpected…

Sucking you in with a dreamy hope of a better start, the fear of what might happen next will keep you turning the pages!

A fantastic, gripping debut!

Made in United States
North Haven, CT
03 April 2024

50822373R00214